To.

Eileen

With my best wishes

Margaret Deckett

# STRAIGHT UP AND DOWN PLEASE

Margaret Duckett

MINERVA PRESS
LONDON
MIAMI DELHI SYDNEY

ISBN  0  75411  206  3




First Published 2000 by
MINERVA PRESS
315–317 Regent Street
London W1R 7YB

Printed in Great Britain for Minerva Press

STRAIGHT UP AND
DOWN PLEASE

*I should like to dedicate this book to some of
my dearest friends, past and present,
Girlie Girl, Patsy and Digger.*

## List of Abbreviations

| | |
|---|---|
| KC | Kennel Club |
| CC | Challenge Certificate |
| CH | Champion (3 CCs) |
| BIS | Best in Show |
| RBIS | Reserve Best in Show |
| BP | Best Puppy |
| BOB | Best of Breed |
| RBOB | Reserve Best of Breed |
| BOS | Best Opposite Sex |

A S FIONA RAN up the stairs she was saying, 'No God, no
please, you can't be so unkind, please, please no.' Reaching
the top of the stairs, she turned into the bathroom. Not
bothering to close the door, she pulled down her tights and
knickers and then, for a moment, stood absolutely still. With a
sigh she sat down on the toilet; thoughts were racing through her
mind and she felt sick with misery.

When the merry-go-round of chaotic thoughts gradually
slowed and finally stopped, Fiona realised that she was freezing
cold. Getting up, she paddled into the bedroom in search of a
towel. Putting it on made it seem so final and a few tears of total
desolation ran down her face. Although the sun was shining
through the window and the day was comparatively warm for
spring, Fiona went to the chest of drawers, pulled out a thick
jumper and pulled it over her head, shivering. She straightened
her shoulder-length brown hair in the dressing-table mirror and,
going downstairs, went into the kitchen, putting the kettle on to
boil. For the first time she did not get that little frisson of pleasure
at the sight of the kitchen's colour and symmetry. They had had a
completely new kitchen installed about a year ago, in preparation
of course. Everything they had done in the past six years had been
in preparation, even every damned thought had been in
preparation, she thought, as she looked around her with eyes that
no longer saw the light reflecting on the honey-coloured pine
doors of the units and the beautiful ceramic floor tiles.

Making a cup of coffee, she took a sip. She had first met
Duncan when he came into the library and had asked for her help
in finding a book. She had been immediately attracted by his

strong, outdoor look, his black hair and blue eyes. He wasn't much taller than she was but he looked athletic. He wanted a book on geology. She had found the appropriate book and stamped it for him.

She took another sip of coffee and settled further into the settee. From that moment it had all been so wonderful – their courtship, their beautiful church wedding and their exciting honeymoon in the south of France. Before they had married, they had discussed the question of a family and had mutually decided to have two children when the time was right. Firstly, they wanted a big house, preferably detached and with a large garden. She had gone on the pill so that they could both continue to work and achieve their ambitions as quickly as possible. Life and love had been idyllic in their first little home, a modern flat, both working full time but racing home to enjoy their evenings and weekends together. Their lovemaking had been so carefree then.

Fiona sighed deeply and drank some more coffee. Oh yes, she thought bitterly, and here it all is, the architect-designed, four-bedroomed, detached house in the large garden, tastefully decorated throughout, the gardens attractively laid out and, of course, conveniently near to schools; and here we are all on our own and now ever likely to be. She burst into tears at the prospect of the dead, bleak years ahead.

Drying her eyes, she looked at her watch and saw that it was nearly twelve noon. I must phone Duncan now and tell him the news. I just couldn't bear to look at his face yet again when he hears it, she thought. How many times had she seen the bitter disappointment in his face, seen it change to a look of sympathy in his eyes and finally heard the cheerful words of encouragement from his mouth? They had both agreed that this would be their last attempt so this time there would be no need for the cheerful, encouraging words – only the disappointment, and she couldn't, wouldn't face that again. By phoning him with the news, he would have the rest of the day to get used to the idea. She picked up the phone and dialled his office number.

The afternoon passed slowly; what a pity that it was Monday, the day that she didn't go to the library at all. Fiona wandered listlessly around the house. I should be tidying up after the weekend and doing some washing, she kept telling herself but the desire, the need was no longer there. What did any of it matter! She wandered up to their bedroom and brushed a wisp of face powder from the dressing table. She smoothed the pretty, white, broderie anglaise bedspread and matching pillows, and sighed deeply.

What had happened to their happy lovemaking? Those warm hours spent cuddling each other, murmuring words of endearment known only to them in that safe haven away from the world – that specialness that was theirs alone. It had all been swept away from them in a storm of questions and samples and examinations. It had de-humanised their rituals. She had felt that they were automatons performing to the dictates of their masters and that their lovemaking, no, coupling, had a mechanical urgency about it now. Everyone concerned had been very kind and had done their best, but would she and Duncan ever be able to get back to the way they used to love?

Fiona again looked at her watch and hurried down to the kitchen. Duncan would be home in an hour and a half and she wanted to have their evening meal absolutely ready. She could rush around and serve it quickly and avoid that look in his eyes. She started to prepare the dinner. She heard his car stop in the drive and quickly put the vegetables into the hot water. His key in the door, she walked into the hall to greet him as she always did.

Shutting the door he turned around, 'Hello Fiona, I'm home.'

Without looking at him she smiled and hurried to kiss him as usual. But it wasn't 'as usual'; she didn't feel 'as usual', she thought, and what a damn silly thing for him to say anyway. She broke away from his kiss, saying, 'Dinner's ready, I'll serve it straight away,' and went back into the kitchen.

The meal was eaten rather quietly. Fiona wasn't sure what her husband was thinking but she knew that her mind was still in a turmoil of misery. She was beginning to feel as if she was in prison serving a life sentence with the future taken away from her. Stop it! Stop it! she thought, and smiling at Duncan she said, 'I'll put the kettle on for the coffee; you turn on the TV. There's that archaeological programme about the pyramids on channel two.'

The evening passed much as usual, but when they went up to

bed and as Fiona pulled the bedspread down she suddenly felt overwhelmed with grief. Duncan, coming into the room quietly, put his arms around her and, turning, she laid her head on his warm, comfortable chest and sobbed deeply. Neither spoke as they got into bed – there just didn't seem to be anything to say. Fiona didn't feel like reading and lay down on her side, facing the window. In a short while, Duncan put his book down and turned out the light.

She lay there in the dark and soon heard his regular breathing, which told her that he was asleep. Anger flared up inside her: how could he sleep! Their whole world had collapsed, their dreams and plans all turned to dust, everything was turned upside down and he was asleep. Again the anger welled up. Had he no feelings at all? Didn't he care? Had he pretended all along?

She took a deep breath and turned on to her back, trying to breathe deeply. It helped and gradually she relaxed and her anger at Duncan subsided. She pushed her hand across the sheet and lightly touched him. This was her Duncan; she knew him so well, they were so compatible. She knew really that he had wanted children. Hadn't he gone along with all that ghastly business three times? Why wasn't he upset, then? Why wasn't he lying awake? Perhaps, her mind turned another corner in its flight, perhaps he was so upset that he wouldn't want her now, would get bored and fed up with her alone and with no hope of a future family.

With a sob, she turned over on to her other side, put her arm gently round his arm and chest, and drew her knees into the bend at the back of his knees. Gradually, the minutes ticked quietly by, his warmth made her drowsy and she slept.

I T WAS ONE of those mornings in early summer when all of nature seemed to be on good terms with one another. As Fiona drove to the library she felt, for the first time in many weeks, a slight lifting of the spirits. As she drove round the back of the building to her allotted parking space, she gave a slight smile to Thelma, who had already parked and was walking into the library. Thelma looked rather surprised for a second and then her returning smile lit up her rather homely features.

Fiona got out of the car and locked it. Have I really been so awful, she thought, as she walked through the library door. As she hung up her jacket and tidied her hair in the mirror, she was thinking about the past few weeks. 'What a grouch you look,' she said to the pale reflection in the mirror. 'For goodness sake, smile.'

It was about three o'clock in the afternoon when a voice suddenly said, 'Hi, Fiona; ages since I've seen you. How are you?' She looked up to see the plump, rosy-faced features of Laura Anderson, a friend for many years. Her fair, curly hair seemed to be rioting over her head and she looked flustered.

'Hello, Laura, how are you? Still busy, I see.'

This remark was engendered by the pushchair beside Laura with the twins in it. They must be at least three now, thought Fiona. Did I send them a birthday card?

'Oh, it never stops; I'm just off now to pick up Tom from school. Thought I'd just have time to dash in and get him books – he so loves us to read him a story at night. Well, must dash, lovely to see you. It's about time that you and Duncan came round for a drink, it's months since you last came.'

'Yes, we'd love that. Bye, then.' Laura was gone in a flurry of books and shopping. Instantly, the smile faded from Fiona's face and her spirits fell once more.

After dinner that evening, when they were drinking coffee, Fiona said, 'I saw Laura today at the library; she was just going to pick up Tom from school. I didn't know that he had started school; it's been so long since we went to see them. She had the twins with her and they must be three now. She wanted to know when we were going round there for a drink one evening.'

Duncan looked up. 'Yes, good idea, haven't seen Michael for ages.'

It was said with such a lack of enthusiasm that Fiona said, 'You don't sound very keen on the idea. We don't have to go if you don't want to.'

'I do – it would make a nice change. I...' he hesitated, '...I just hope that it won't upset you.'

'Upset me? Why should it upset me? I know that Laura's got three children, don't I, and I know that we have none and never will have, don't I. So why should it upset me?'

Duncan looked down again at his paper. 'Alright then, Muppet, give them a ring and arrange an evening.'

Fiona looked at him sharply. He hasn't called me that for months, she thought. She got up. 'I think I'll wash my hair now and then I'll be finished in time to watch *Taggart*.'

In the pale green bathroom she ran the water into the basin and was just bending down to wash her hair when she again caught sight of her face. 'You hardly look like Muppet,' she remarked to the pale face, the dull, green eyes and the too firmly closed mouth in the mirror. Things had not been good between her and Duncan these past weeks. No, that wasn't true, they hadn't had any arguments or anything, but somehow there was a difference in their relationship, a sort of quietness. Their life together seemed to have lost some of its warmth, its excitement, its closeness? Fiona struggled to find the right word. She felt guilty because she knew that she hadn't been especially warm or exciting or close. She just felt let down – cheated by life.

Having washed and dried her hair, Fiona went downstairs, determined to try to snap out of her sorrow and get on with their life together. Sitting down beside Duncan, she said, 'Oh, good. Just in time for *Taggart*. I'm dying to know who the murderer is.'

She rang Laura the next day and arranged to go over on Saturday evening. When Saturday came she got some flowers for Laura and spent some time over her hair and make-up. She was rewarded by the look on Duncan's face.

'You look nice,' he said. 'Have you got the flowers? I've got a rather nice French wine. Should be a good evening.'

'Yes, it should,' she replied, noting that he was putting on a bit of weight round his middle, because his jacket button was a bit strained.

Laura's house was its usual glorious muddle. As Fiona handed her the flowers and kissed her on the cheek she felt a sharp pang at the sight of the twins' small, yellow wellie boots discarded on the floor and the small, brightly coloured anoraks limply hanging on the coat hooks. Michael's tall form appeared from the kitchen door, a bottle of wine in his hand, and the moment of panic passed.

As they went through to the lounge Fiona speculated, not for the first time, on what tall, rugged Michael had seen in small, plain and rather plump Laura. Her thoughts were interrupted by Michael.

'Sit down. I've cleared all the paraphernalia away. Couldn't move in here half an hour ago. Thank heaven for toy boxes and bedtime. Now, what will you have? I've got a lovely drop of Aussie wine, you must try it. What about you, Fiona?'

They were soon all talking and the evening went well. Later, when Laura was bringing in the coffee she said, 'There's something I meant to tell you, though I know that you are going to think us completely mad. Even we think we are, but we've decided to buy a puppy.'

Fiona, who for one awful moment had thought that she was going to say something else said, 'Laura! However will you cope?'

'Oh well, you know me, I'm always rushing round as it is and you know what they say – if you want something done, ask a busy person. No, seriously, both Michael and I grew up with a dog and we want the children to do the same. We think that they are old enough to treat it with respect; I shall see that they do, and then they can all grow up together. We've decided on a Golden Retriever – they make such nice family dogs. Michael's parents have always had one, haven't they Michael, and they say that they have a lovely temperament.'

'Yes, I had some wonderful walks with old Samson when I was a kid,' said Michael.

They finished their coffee and Fiona and Duncan prepared to leave. 'Now, don't leave it so long again. We enjoy having an adult conversation now and again, which doesn't involve Thomas the Tank Engine,' Michael said with a laugh.

'We've had a marvellous evening. Do let us know how you get on with the puppy. We'd love to come and see it,' said Fiona.

With their final goodbyes, they got into the car and drove home in silence, each wrapped in their own thoughts.

'Do you want anything to drink, Duncan?'

'No thanks, I'm fine – just ready for bed.'

Duncan came out of the bathroom as Fiona was sitting at the dressing table, removing her make-up. He stood behind her and put his hands on her shoulders. 'I really enjoyed this evening; it was lovely to see you laughing with Laura.' He slid his hands on to her firm, round breasts. 'I do so love you,' he said as he kissed the top of her head.

They got into bed and he kissed her on the mouth. 'Oh, Fiona, oh Fiona,' he said as he stroked her long slender thighs, pushing her nightie up over her belly.

He lay on top of her and she smiled in the dark. Kissing him, she said, 'I love you too, Duncan.'

It was the first time that they had made love since she had discovered that she wasn't pregnant. Duncan was so gentle and she enjoyed the old familiar sensations again. He was such a handsome man and he felt and smelled so nice; she enjoyed their lovemaking.

She pulled her nightdress down over her legs and turned to Duncan. 'Thank you, that was so nice,' she whispered in his ear before going to the bathroom. Duncan was asleep when she returned but just as she was dozing off, she sleepily wondered if this time she might be pregnant. The thought brought her wide awake.

FIONA WAS BUSY putting returned books back on the shelf. It was a warm day and she was looking forward to getting home and having a long, cool drink in the garden. As she put *The Encyclopaedia of Dogs* back on the shelf she suddenly thought of Laura. I wonder if she's got her puppy yet, she pondered. I'll give her a call this evening.

Duncan phoned to say that he would be slightly delayed because his client had been held up in traffic and would not be able to get to his office until four o'clock at the earliest – it was a contract for a new bridge and he was rather keen to get it. As there was no hurry to get the dinner prepared, Fiona made herself a long, cool drink and took it outside. She sat on one of the chairs on the patio and looked at the garden. It looked lovely; the display of spring flowers was coming to an end but roses would soon be out. Duncan spent a lot of time out there and was rightfully proud of it. The sun was still shining and she closed her eyes and listened to the birds singing. It's company, she thought. You don't feel so lonely when you know that they are sitting in the trees.

She suddenly remembered Laura and the puppy and, getting up, walked into the hall. As she did so, a thought came to her. Why don't I get a puppy? It would be company for me, someone to greet me when I come home. I could come home at lunchtime, too.

It was quite a few minutes before she picked up the phone.

'Hello Laura, it's me, Fiona. How are you and the family? I was wondering if you had got your puppy yet.'

'Oh, hi Fiona. No, we haven't yet, but we've been to see a litter and chosen one. It was so difficult because I wanted all of them! We decided on a bitch puppy and she'll be ready to collect next week. Michael's been busy checking on the garden fences to see that she won't be able to get out. We're so excited, the children ask every morning if we're getting her today. We've been trying to find a name that we all like. It's lovely; we've bought a bed and a blanket for her and a brush and a comb and a bowl – but listen to me rabbiting on. What's your news?'

'Nothing really. We've been wondering where to go for our summer holiday.'

'Well, of course, the puppy will stop us having a holiday this year. By the time she's fully vaccinated it'll be almost time to go back to school. Perhaps we'll manage a long weekend in the caravan at half-term.'

'You sound so knowledgeable, Laura. Have you been reading up on all this dog business?'

'No, not really – haven't had the time – but the woman who bred the puppies was very helpful and answered all our questions. Look, why don't you come over in a fortnight's time. Give me a ring first, just in case.'

'I'll do that. Regards to Michael. Bye.'

Fiona went through to the kitchen and started preparing the vegetables. The more she thought about it the more she liked the idea. She would talk to Duncan tonight. Yes, a dog would be just the thing. It would fill what was, in effect, a gap in their lives now. They could plan lovely walks and holidays with the dog. He would be a companion for them both. She could look through the dog section of the library tomorrow and start reading up on them. She felt quite excited and couldn't wait for Duncan to come home to discuss it.

'Well, I don't know that it is such a good idea, Fiona.'

'But Duncan, it would be wonderful, such a companion.'

'Yes, Fiona, but have you really thought it through? It would also be such a tie.'

'Oh, of course I've thought about it. I could come home in my lunch hour. I could even cut my hours, perhaps. After all, we don't need the money now, do we?'

Duncan was silent for a moment or two and then said, 'I've been thinking too, Fiona, about our future course.'

'You haven't said anything.'

'No, but only because I haven't come up with anything concrete as yet. I've had one or two ideas, though, that I've been floating around in my mind.'

'Well, what are they?'

'They don't include a dog, I must admit.'

There was a pause and Fiona, knowing that Duncan couldn't be hurried, waited for a minute. 'What are they, for goodness' sake, Duncan?'

'Well, one thought was that we might both take up golf. There's that excellent club that Michael belongs to. In fact, it was talking to Michael the other evening that gave me the idea.'

'Golf!'

'Yes, we might both find it very interesting and it's good exercise. We could have a small wager on who gets the best handicap. If we were good enough, in time, there might be the odd tournament or two. There is quite a social life at the nineteenth.'

'What was your other idea?'

'Well, together with the golf I thought that, as we are now footloose and fancy-free, so to speak, we might have more holidays. You know, a couple of package holidays and perhaps something more unusual. I haven't thought it out in any detail.'

'That doesn't stop us having a dog.'

'No, but I don't think that it would be very fair to keep leaving it or putting it in kennels.'

Fiona fell silent as the plain common sense of Duncan's remarks came home to her. She thought for a minute and then said, 'I can't agree. I've always thought that couples who play golf are absolutely boring. All they seem to talk about, morning, noon, and night, is golf. As far as the package holidays etc. are concerned, we could have one each year and put the dog in kennels and then have a holiday somewhere in England and take the dog with us. Lots of hotels make provision for dogs nowadays.'

'True, but it seems obvious that we both need to think more about these proposals. Now, I must go and water those plants that I put in yesterday evening. Shan't be long.'

Fiona went into the kitchen. How was it that Duncan always

seemed to make her feel silly? She always seemed to end up defending her corner. Frowning, she laid the table and went to the door to call Duncan for dinner.

Later in the evening, Duncan was reading the paper and Fiona had a book open on her lap but she wasn't reading. I don't want to spend the rest of my life playing golf, she thought. Nor do I want to go on endless package holidays. She knew people like that and had always privately thought that they were really running away from their own boring existence. What is happening to our lives? We were always so certain of everything. We knew exactly where we were going and what the future held for us. How can Duncan and I have such differing ideas?

One evening, a few weeks later, the phone rang and Fiona answered it.

'Hi, Fiona, it's Laura. Just thought that I'd let you know that we've got our puppy and she is gorgeous.'

'Oh, I'm so glad. What are you going to call her?'

'Now, don't laugh; we are going to call her Delilah – Dee for short. Do you remember that Michael had a dog when he was young, called Samson?'

'Yes, I do, so of course this is Delilah. What do the children think of her?'

'They're over the moon – didn't want to go to bed. Look, you must come over when she has had her vaccinations.'

'Love to. Thanks for ringing, Laura. Bye.'

Fiona went back to the lounge to tell Duncan the news.

'Bit of a fancy name for a dog, isn't it?'

'I suppose it is, but Dee sounds alright.'

'Look, while we're on the subject, you haven't mentioned any more about having a dog ourselves. Thought better of it?'

'No, it's just that you didn't seem too keen so I pushed it to the back of my mind. I would still like one.'

'Right, well then, I agree on one condition, no, two: one, that you join the golf club with me, and two, that you pick a small dog.'

Fiona bent over to kiss him and he pulled her down on to his lap.

'I hope this doesn't mean that I shall now take second place in your affections.'

It was pouring with rain the next morning as Fiona rushed through her household chores in order to get to the library early. Once at work, she went to the dog section and started looking at all the books relating to little dogs. There seemed to be so many small or smallish dogs, most of whom she had never heard of, and she was soon in a total quandary as to which dog she would like. She ended up by taking *The Encyclopaedia of British Dogs* home with her.

That evening, they looked through it, and after about half an hour they had decided that it had to be one of the Terrier breeds. They were shortly down to three, the Cairn, the Wire-haired Fox Terrier and the Cumbrian Terrier.

'These all seem to meet our needs, Fiona, so why don't you have a word with Laura? She seems to be more knowledgeable than we are on the subject.'

By Monday morning Fiona had still not made up her mind as she knocked on Laura's door, the encyclopaedia firmly clutched under her arm. A smiling Laura opened the door with a wriggling mass of golden, silky fur tucked under her arm and two bright eyes peering out.

'Come in, quickly – she's so energetic. I hope you haven't got decent tights on.'

On being placed on the floor, the puppy rushed up to Fiona's shoes and started to undo the laces, chewing them.

'No, Dee, no,' remonstrated Laura, pointing a finger at her. Dee looked up for a brief moment and then went back to chewing the laces. 'See what you're in for,' laughed Laura, scooping the puppy up in her arms. 'Let's go into the kitchen, shall we. Dee can run in and out of the garden and hopefully tiddle out there.'

The puppy continued to be enthralled with Fiona's shoes so she took them off.

'Best thing,' said Laura, 'is to keep all your old jeans, laddered tights and ancient shoes for when you get yours. They are so inquisitive and examine everything, and you can't keep telling them off. I am assured by the breeder that they do grow out of it. Also, do check that all your fences are secure; if there is the tiniest gap, they'll find it. You'll have to watch those lovely plants of Duncan's, too. Dee's had several of ours out already. Now, let's have a look at your book.'

Laura said that she knew someone who had a Wire-haired Fox Terrier. 'She adores it, I know, but she's always talking about keeping the coat tidy.'

'What does that mean?'

'Don't ask me,' said Laura, 'she just says it.'

They pondered over the breed descriptions again and finally Fiona closed the book. 'I like both of these but I have decided on the Cumbrian Terrier. So, what do I do now? Do I order one from a pet shop? I've never seen one, as far as I know. Would they know where to get one?'

'I've a better idea, I'll phone Delilah's breeder. She might know more about them, mightn't she?'

She went into the hall and Fiona could hear her talking and laughing for several minutes.

'I'm sorry I was so long but I was telling her how Dee had got Tom's socks out of the laundry basket and chewed them to bits. Now, to your Cumbrian; she doesn't know a breeder personally, but will find out for us. I'll let you know when she rings me.'

As they walked up the hall, with Dee firmly shut in the kitchen but barking and scratching the door, Laura said, 'Are you sure that you and Duncan really want a puppy?'

They both laughed and, still chuckling, Fiona walked down the path to her car. Driving home, her thoughts were all about the alterations and arrangements they would have to make before the puppy came. She must discuss with Duncan where the puppy would sleep, for instance. They would obviously have to read up about the feeding and training of a puppy, too. She thought that she'd seen a book in the library specifically on this subject. She arrived home feeling quite elated and happier than she had felt for a long time.

It was a few days later when Laura phoned her. 'Hi, Fiona, it's me with some wonderful news. Guess what? My breeder has found a litter of Cumbrian Terrier puppies.'

'Gosh, that's quick. Where are they?'

'Ah now, that's the rub. They're in Cumbria, would you

believe. She said that she had a hard time finding any and finally got on to the Breed Club. Apparently, they're not so popular nowadays and not so many people are breeding them. Trust you to pick something unusual. Anyway, I'll give you the phone number and you can take it from there. Good luck, and let me know what happens.'

Fiona thanked Laura profusely and asked her to thank the Retriever breeder for being so kind.

'Duncan, Duncan, I've got a phone number of a breeder of Cumbrian Terriers and she has a litter now! I'm so excited. Shall I ring her now?'

Duncan looked at her happy, smiling face. Her cheeks were flushed and her green eyes were shining; she looked about twenty-five years old. 'Of course, Muppet; how else are you going to find out about them?'

FIONA DIALLED THE number and a woman's voice answered. 'Hello, I understand that you have a litter of Cumbrian Terrier puppies and I should very much like to buy one. My name is Fiona McCleod.'

'Oh, yes. Have you had a Cumbrian before?'

'No, I've never had a dog before.'

'I see, then may I ask why you want a Cumbrian?'

For a moment or two Fiona was lost for words, she hadn't expected this response. 'Well, we decided to have a dog and looked through the books and finally settled on a Cumbrian Terrier.'

'So I take it that you have, at least, read a book on the breed. Tell me, do you have any children?'

'No, we haven't any children and I haven't actually read a book on the Cumbrian Terrier specifically.'

'Then may I suggest that you get hold of one from your library. It does tell you all about them. Now, do you have a house or a flat and does it have a garden that is fenced?'

'Yes, we have a house with a large garden.'

'Do you work full-time?'

'No, I work from Tuesday to Friday and alternate Saturday mornings. My husband is here, though, on Saturdays and I can go home at lunchtime.'

'I see. Well, I think the next step is that I meet you and that you meet my dogs, don't you? When could you come here?'

'Would next Saturday be alright? In the morning?'

'Yes, that's fine. Come at about ten thirty or eleven. I shall look forward to meeting you.'

Fiona rushed into the garden to find Duncan. 'I've arranged to go and see the puppies on Saturday. Is that alright?'

'Yes, that's okay. Where are they and what's the address?'

'Heavens, I forgot to ask.' Fiona ran back into the house.

A few minutes later she returned with the breeder's name and address.

'That far! We'll have to make an early start. Are we supposed to bring it home with us?'

'No, well, I'm not sure. I don't think so but perhaps we ought to buy a bed and some feeding bowls just in case, but... Oh, I'm so excited that I can't think properly.'

The next day, in her lunch hour, Fiona went to the local pet store. She had never been in this shop and was amazed at the size of it and bewildered by the infinite variety of food in tins, bags and even sacks. There were beds and bedding of many kinds, medicines, tonics, books, cards and the number of toys was overwhelming. In the end she asked an assistant for help. She could have a wooden bed, a plastic one, a wicker bed, or even a bed like a deckchair.

She could have them in various colours or she could even have a beanbag. Looking at her watch, she decided to go for the plastic bed in a blue colour and then quickly bought two metal bowls: one for food and one for water. At least, she thought, as she raced to the car, it's a start.

Over dinner that evening, she regaled Duncan with details of all she had seen in the store and proudly showed him the bed and the bowls. Later, they rearranged the kitchen slightly to accommodate the bed.

'Do we have to put a bed of some kind in it, Fiona?'

'Yes, I shall cut down an old blanket.'

They were up early Saturday morning. It was a lovely day and they enjoyed the journey as they drove towards the Lake District.

As they started to become surrounded by the quiet greenness of the countryside, they recalled the holiday that they had had some years before. They had stayed at a hotel near Keswick and had planned a new walk each day, or a visit to a lake. They had climbed to the top of Skiddaw, hearing the constant sound of rivulets of water running over stones. The gentle sound had delighted Fiona. They had driven to dramatic Wast Water, with its grey screes and deep, dark water, giving it an eerie feeling that made Fiona shiver slightly on a hot day. They saw Dove Cottage, in which Wordsworth had lived with his sister, and laughed together as they recited the poem about daffodils. One day they had climbed Buttermere Fell and looked down on the lake.

The journey passed swiftly as each recalled something from the holiday and before they knew it they were nearing their objective. Following the instructions they had been given, they turned into a quiet country lane and on the left found an old stone cottage. There was a sign outside with a picture of a Cumbrian Terrier on it and a name, 'ARAMINTA'.

Their knock on the door was greeted with a storm of barking. Duncan raised his eyebrows and looked enquiringly at Fiona. 'Be quiet,' a voice was heard to say and then the door was opened by a small, older, plump woman dressed in a T-shirt and jeans. 'Mr and Mrs McCleod? Do come in, but first may I please ask you to remove your shoes. As I have a litter of puppies, I don't wish to bring in any infection.'

The hall they entered was small but the walls were covered in brightly coloured rosettes and photos of Cumbrian Terriers. Some had obviously won at shows and were standing beside large silver cups.

Turning to Fiona, the woman said, 'Oh, you've got trousers on, good – tights and puppies don't mix. Now, are you ready for the onslaught?'

Another door was opened to reveal a large kitchen with a quarry-tiled floor and a large Aga cooker. There was no more time for observation before six dogs enveloped them. Jumping up, they licked their hands and then proceeded to smell their clothes.

'Aren't they delightful?' Fiona said. 'Which is the mother?'

The woman pointed to one of the dogs who had, by then, raced back into the kitchen. 'It's the middle one of those three.' Fiona looked into intelligent brown eyes and it seemed to her as if the dog was weighing her up to see if she was a suitable foster mother.

'All of these dogs have been bred by me. The oldest one is ten

– that's the one sitting by the Aga. This gives you an idea what the puppies will grow into. Now for the puppies. I didn't ask you if you wanted a dog or a bitch. Have you a preference?'

'We thought – Mrs Emsworth, isn't it? – well, we thought that we would like a little girl. Well, that is to say, my wife thought that she would prefer a female.'

They had by now gone upstairs. When the breeder opened a door to a bedroom, four pairs of bright eyes stared at them for just a second, and then four eager little bodies raced up to the edge of the pen. They, as one, put their front paws up on the mesh of the pen and smiled. Well, Fiona thought that they smiled. They were all jumping up and down as if to say, 'Me, me, look at me.'

'Now, if you want a dog you have a choice – there are two dogs – but should you want a bitch then it must be this one.' Bending down she picked up one of the puppies. 'I'm sorry that you can't hold her, but again, it's the risk of infection.'

Fiona looked at the puppy and then at Duncan, who nodded his head slightly and then said, 'Oh, yes please, we should love to have her.'

Mrs Emsworth then went on to explain that the puppy would be ready to go to her new home in twelve days' time, when she would be eight weeks old. 'So, if you are quite sure?'

'Yes, quite sure, I just can't wait,' said Fiona, and with a last lingering look at 'their' puppy, the couple followed Mrs Emsworth down the stairs.

'Would you like a cup of tea?' Mrs Emsworth enquired. 'I will give you a feed chart for the puppy and then we can have a chat and you can ask me any questions that you have.' She disappeared into the kitchen.

Fiona held Duncan's hand and smiled. 'Isn't she just gorgeous?'

'She's certainly a pretty little thing and very appealing. We must be careful not to spoil her.'

Mrs Emsworth came back with a tray of tea, closely followed by a dog. 'I thought that you might like to see the mother on her own.'

Fiona stroked the dog and the three of them chatted and asked questions for about half an hour.

Suddenly, Duncan looked at his watch and said, 'We really must be going, Fiona.'

'I suppose so. Thank you so much; you've been so helpful. We'll see you in a fortnight's time then, on Saturday. Will the same time be alright then?'

'Yes, quite alright. Now, have you got your feed chart and your list of helpful hints? If there is anything that you don't understand just ask. Alright?'

Fiona nodded, Duncan shook Mrs Emsworth's hand and they left. All the way home, Fiona, in a state of excitement, chatted away and didn't notice that Duncan was saying very little.

That evening, after dinner, Fiona was washing up and trying to picture the puppy in the blue plastic bed. She made some coffee and took it into the lounge. 'What are we going to call her?'

'I leave that to you, but I thought that Mrs Emsworth said that she had given her a name.'

'That's just something to do with the Kennel Club. I don't think that we have to call her that.'

'I see. Fiona, this puppy isn't going to affect us, is it?'

'Good heavens, no, why should it?'

'You're not going to get like some silly women who treat their dogs like people, are you?'

Fiona laughed. 'Don't be silly, darling. You won't be playing second fiddle if that's what's worrying you.'

She got up and sat on his lap, put her hands on either side of his face and gave him a long, lingering kiss. They made love that night and it was as warm and as pleasant as it always had been.

Fiona visited the pet shop twice more during her lunch break. Feeling a little more part of the scene now, she bought a dog duvet with a floral cover on one visit, and a blue collar and lead, a squeaky toy shaped like a Wellington boot and a red rubber ring on the other. They invited Laura and Michael over for an evening and all the doggy paraphernalia was brought out for their approval. Most of the evening, in fact, was taken up in discussion about Fiona's puppy and Laura and Michael's Delilah.

It was so very nice, Fiona thought, to be really part of the conversation. Previously, most of their talk had been about pregnancy and babies, to which Fiona and Duncan could add very little. In fact, it was the reason why they had not seen so much of Laura and Michael in the last couple of years. She had felt so envious of Laura and her children and so unknowledgeable about feeds, teething and nappy rash.

On the following Saturday morning Fiona woke early. She lay there, not wanting to wake Duncan but bursting with energy and aching to get up and start the day. After breakfast they again set out for Cumbria, a large cardboard box (recommended by Mrs Emsworth) on the back seat. Arriving at the cottage with its attractive sign swinging in the breeze, they once again walked up the path between the roses, and knocked on the door. Once again they were greeted with a lively doggy chorus.

Mrs Emsworth opened the door and invited them in. 'Your little bitch is all ready for you. She's been wormed and has had her nails trimmed. Have you decided what to call her?'

'Yes, we've decided to call her Sally. Do I have to trim her nails?'

'Well, it is useful if you can manage to do it yourself, but you can have it done at the vet's. Now, before I get the puppy, shall we sort out the paperwork? I have the pedigree here, together with the KC registration form. You will see that she is registered to me as the breeder, so you must fill in this part and send it to the Kennel Club to transfer her ownership to you. I've already given you your feed chart and helpful hints so do you have any questions that you want to ask me?'

'No, but may we phone you if we have a problem?'

'Of course. Now, if we may settle up, I can give you your receipt and then get Sally for you. They're all in the garden in a playpen, as it's such a lovely day.'

When Mrs Emsworth returned with the puppy in her arms, both Fiona and Duncan were surprised at how much she had grown and filled out. Mrs Emsworth put her into Fiona's arms.

'Oh, you're gorgeous; you're so soft and warm.' Fiona felt tears prick her eyelids as she stroked the puppy and buried her face in its hair. The puppy responded by vigorously licking Fiona's face. 'Oh, Mrs Emsworth, I just can't thank you enough.'

'Just look after her and enjoy life together. By the way, don't forget to have her vaccinations and don't take her out until they have been completed. Now, have you brought a cardboard box and some newspaper?'

'Yes, in the car. Thank you once again'.

Fiona got into the back of the car with the puppy so that she could keep an eye on her in the box, and speak to her to reassure her, while Duncan drove home, almost in silence.

THE PUPPY SEEMED to take the motion of the car very well and soon fell asleep. When they arrived home, Fiona carried the box into the kitchen, took the puppy out and placed her on the floor. She stood still for a moment or two surveying her surroundings then, with slightly hesitant steps, started to walk round the kitchen. She sniffed at her bed, sniffed at the bowl and then squatted on her haunches. Before either Fiona or Duncan could move, a steady stream coursed across the floor. The puppy, then feeling much happier, proceeded to inspect everything in the kitchen in more detail and at a much greater rate, finally running into the hall. Fiona and Duncan were galvanised into action.

'Grab her, Fiona, before she goes again on the carpet,' Duncan said urgently as he delicately stepped over the puddle in order to get a cloth and some disinfectant to mop it up.

'Isn't she quick?' Fiona remarked as she re-entered the kitchen with the puppy in her arms. 'It's obvious that we're going to have to be very vigilant in order to train her. Never mind, early days.'

That night, when they went to bed, they were exhausted, having cleared up several more puddles and two poos. They had found Sally in the lounge inspecting the wiring to the television with the idea of chewing it, and later found her shut in one of the kitchen cupboards scratching at the door and crying. So pleased was the puppy to see Fiona, that she licked her face and wriggled in her arms. 'Something else we must remember, Duncan – shut all the cupboard doors!'

Fiona gave Sally a cuddle and a kiss, settled her in her blue bed and went out, shutting the kitchen door. She had arranged to take two weeks' leave from the library, on Laura's advice, so that she could, hopefully, train the puppy to be clean indoors.

Fiona woke early to hear the puppy whining a little. She's missing her brothers and sisters, she thought and, quickly slipping on her towelling dressing gown, last year's Christmas present from Duncan, she ran downstairs to the kitchen. Opening the door, she stood there for a second surveying the floor, which was covered in wet, torn newspaper. The puppy seized the opportunity to rush up to her, run straight through her legs and into the hall. Sally then ran into the lounge with Fiona in hot pursuit.

'Oh, no you don't,' said Fiona, gently picking up the puppy and giving her a kiss. Sally responded by wriggling and then licking her face. Fiona was delighted. She unlocked the back door and put her down on the lawn. Immediately, the puppy stood still, sniffing the air and looking around her with her bright eyes. Fiona stood there for a few minutes but the puppy just continued to look round the garden and made no attempt to squat. She picked her up and took her back into the kitchen. As soon as the puppy's feet touched the floor, she ran a few steps and squatted, not, of course, on the newspaper.

Fiona, having cleared up all the soiled paper and disinfected the floor, made a cup of tea and took one up to Duncan. 'Hello, darling, did you sleep well? I've been busy cleaning the kitchen. I think I'd better buy a mop.'

'Um,' grunted Duncan.

'I think it best if we dress too before we go downstairs to make tea in the morning. She's been chewing my dressing gown and hanging on to it with her teeth.'

Duncan grunted once more and turned over.

Sunday was usually a pleasant, relaxed day for them: Duncan pottering in the garden or reading the Sunday papers, Fiona catching up on bits of housework or ironing. Then, perhaps, going for a drive somewhere and having a leisurely stroll in the country. By the end of this Sunday they were far from relaxed, having cleaned up paper, cleaned the floor and put the puppy in the garden many times, without result.

They had been chasing her around the dining room or the

lounge because they kept forgetting to close the kitchen door quickly enough, and cleaning the lounge carpet when she pooed in there. Feeding her, playing with her, and all the time trying not to tread on her, because she always seemed to want to play with their feet, was an exhausting business.

After dinner, sitting in the lounge with the kitchen door firmly closed, they took stock of life with Sally. 'She'll be up the stairs next,' said Duncan, 'and that I won't have. We'll have to put a gate at the bottom like Laura and Michael had for the children.'

'Good idea; we really need one at the kitchen door, too. Golly, I'm worn out, but isn't it fun. She's just adorable.' Duncan did not reply.

Over the next two weeks, things became less chaotic. Fiona learned to shuffle around to avoid tripping over Sally. She also learned not to wear shoes with laces because they were always being undone, even with double bows. She watched Sally and knew the signs for wanting to puddle or to poo. Duncan raised his eyebrows when Fiona first used this euphemism but as Fiona remarked, 'What else do you want me to call it?'

When Sally nearly ran into the fish pond, Duncan was told to make a mesh frame to cover it. It became increasingly difficult to race Sally out of the kitchen and shut the door, so Duncan was persuaded to also make a small wood and mesh door to place in the doorway, which they could step over. 'This whole house is being turned over to that dog already,' was Duncan's only comment.

Even so, when it was time to go back to work, Fiona was very worried and upset. The last two weeks had been so rewarding and had flown by. Trying to form a bond with Sally had become so important to her, she was surprised at just how much pleasure it had given her.

On her first morning back at work, she was up early to play with Sally in the garden before she got Duncan's breakfast. She then fed Sally and covered the kitchen floor with newspaper for, although Sally was getting quite good at doing her toilet in the garden, she still had the odd mishap indoors. She wondered how Sally would cope with being left until lunchtime. She kept thinking of her during the morning and raced home at midday to be greeted so enthusiastically by Sally, that she felt guilty at having left her.

As the week went by Fiona felt more and more unhappy. When she tried to tell Duncan how she felt, he didn't sympathise. 'Fiona, stop fussing. The dog looks fit and well, doesn't she? We can't let her rule our lives.'

Another week went by and Fiona suggested to Duncan that she might be able to work one day less at the library. 'After all, we aren't desperate for the money,' she explained.

Duncan felt at a loss to explain this behaviour. Fiona was always so level-headed and practical – this was not like her at all. Although he himself hadn't been too keen on having a dog, he had been quite content for her to have one because he felt that she was at least showing an interest in something. He hadn't said much to her, but he had worried about her lethargy and lack of interest in their life together. Certainly, this puppy had cheered her up because she was singing again as she cooked or worked in the house. But giving up another day at the library – that was another matter altogether.

It was true that they did not need the money as such. They had always been careful and with their combined salaries over the years they had even put a tidy amount into a building society account. It had originally been to provide the children with a good education. Duncan smiled wryly to himself; so many things had had to be rethought lately, but as for Fiona working less... His train of thought was interrupted.

'Well, say something, Duncan, don't keep me in suspense.'

'I was thinking.'

'And?'

'And nothing. No, we don't need the money but we do still have a mortgage and so on to pay and I thought that a few more holidays might be rather pleasant. You know, there are some lovely weekend breaks to be had nowadays. Your salary does help, you know.'

'I suppose you're right and it would be lovely to take Sally to different places. We could take her for walks along the cliff tops or along the beach, couldn't we?'

Duncan did not reply and Fiona, taking his silence as

agreement, went out into the garden to play with Sally, leaving Duncan considering this latest development.

By the time that Sally was five months old, apart from some rather tense moments when she had dug a huge hole in Duncan's flower bed or when she had escaped unnoticed and chewed the leg of one of the dining-room chairs or ruined a pair of Fiona's shoes, life was going along fairly smoothly. Sally was a lively, happy young dog and they had both enjoyed some pleasant walks with her. She was absolutely clean in the house and brought lots of life to it. For Fiona, the thought of the rapturous greeting she would receive as she walked into the house after work or shopping made it all worthwhile.

One evening, talking to Laura on the phone, the subject of Christmas came up.

'What are you doing this Christmas, Fiona?'

'We've been wondering about that. As you know, we usually go to Duncan's parents for Christmas Day and Boxing Day and my father comes to us for the New Year. The trouble is that Duncan's mother and father have two Siamese cats so they don't want us to bring Sally. Duncan wants me to put Sally in kennels but I don't want to. I'd rather that they came to us this year.'

'Well, that does seem a reasonable solution. Don't they like the idea?'

'I think that they feel it's a break in tradition. His mother so enjoys Christmas and goes to town on the food. She is a wonderful cook.'

'Yes, but surely you would like to do all that? I know that I look forward to it tremendously – Father Christmas and all that.'

'Exactly,' said Fiona tersely. 'I have never cooked Christmas dinner.'

When the time came, Fiona flatly refused to leave Sally in kennels. They drove to his parents for dinner on Christmas Day and left quite early shortly after tea. They drove home in silence, each wrapped in their own thoughts. While Duncan put the car away in the garage, Fiona rushed into the kitchen to be met by an ecstatic Sally, surrounded by the new toys that she had been given that morning. 'Hello, sweetheart, did you miss us?'

'Don't be silly, Fiona,' Duncan remarked as he came through

the door. 'Dogs aren't as intelligent as cats; as my mother said, if you're not there they just sleep.'

'When did your mother say that?'

'Does it matter when she said it? It's true, isn't it. There was no need to rush back like that. I must get an antacid tablet; too much rushing around after that lovely meal.'

He went upstairs, leaving Fiona feeling very guilty. Here they were on Christmas Day almost rowing about the dog. His parents had been visibly disappointed with their hurried departure and it had been all her fault too because she didn't want to put Sally into kennels. Perhaps his mother had been right and Sally had slept all the time. We'll stay a bit longer tomorrow. 'You'll be alright, won't you, my poppet. You've got all your new toys and I'll leave the radio on for you for company.' As Fiona cuddled her, Sally looked up at her, as if to say, 'I'll tell you a secret though, I'd rather be with you and Duncan here.'

She ran upstairs to Duncan and flung her arms around him. 'I'm so sorry, darling, I've been terribly selfish. I'll write a lovely letter to your mother thanking her – she really is a wonderful cook.'

'DAD; PHONE, DAD.' Simon heard his son's voice shouting on the other side of the kennel door. Putting the dog he was grooming into its kennel, he shouted back that he was coming. He walked down the path and entered the kitchen door. 'Sod,' he muttered as he tripped on the frayed edge of the mat in the kitchen. He went into the living room and picked up the phone, 'Hello, Simon Philips.'

'Hello, Simon, this is Joan Skipton here. Look, Simon, I know it's a bit early to ask but could I possibly beg a lift from you for Crufts? You are going, aren't you?'

Putting his hand over the mouthpiece, Simon yelled at his daughter to turn the television down. Damn the woman, he thought. She'll want to talk all the way to the bloody show and her dogs will be sick or something. She is judging, though, later in the year so I had better say yes.

'Sorry about that, Joan, kids as usual making a noise. Yes I'd be pleased to take you. It'll be a bit of a squeeze because I'm taking my bitch and my young dog. Hoping for that first CC, you know. How many do you want to bring?'

'Only the one – my dog with the two tickets. Thanks Simon, I owe you one.'

Simon started to go back to the shed.

'You're not going back out there again are you?'

Simon looked at his wife, Mary, and sighed. She never seemed to speak nowadays unless it was to moan about something. Without replying he went back to the shed. 'Hello, my gorgeous girl. Now, where were we?'

While he was grooming the bitch his thoughts strayed back to

Mary. How many years was it since they married? Well, Barry was seventeen so it must be eighteen years. He sighed again, remembering how different she had been then.

His parents had lived in a house on the edge of a small town; he and his brother Peter had spent many happy hours in the woods nearby. They had later moved to a large town when his father changed his job. He had met Mary at a friend's party and he had liked her immediately. She was slim and smartly dressed and she seemed to like everything that he did, including the countryside and animals; he only found out later that it was a very distant liking. The first few months after they were married had been fine but she soon became pregnant with Barry. She'd had a bit of life about her until then – it hadn't been all cleaning, knitting and bloody sewing then. How many times had he wished that they had delayed the kids for a bit. He was fond of them, especially Barry, but they had certainly changed Mary in many ways. They used to go out to the pub for a beer and a game of darts but now it was a glass of white wine (or a G and T – more of a lady's drink, she said) and talking to other women about children, clothes or the soaps.

He sighed, 'Ah well, you're done lass. You see, we'll knock 'em in the eye – perhaps,' he smiled to himself.

He let her out into the run with the other two dogs and sat and watched then running around. After he had tidied away the grooming kit, he called them in and closed the kennel for the night. He stood for a few seconds looking at the other half of his semi-detached house. As usual, there was an almighty din coming from their stereo. They, he thought, had the cheek to complain if the dogs barked now and again. He looked at their half of the semi and thought, as he so often had in the last few years, of winning the pools and buying a house in the country with plenty of land and no neighbours. More dogs, more kennels with bigger runs. God, then he would really hit the big time. He might then win CCs at Championship shows. He sighed and walked down the path to the house, knowing that Mary's ambition stretched to a detached house in a 'nice' part of town with a completely fitted kitchen and gold bath taps.

'It's Laura on the phone for you,' Duncan called up the stairs to Fiona.

She picked up the phone in the bedroom, 'Hello Laura.'

'Hi. How would you like to go to Crufts with me next weekend?'

'What a lovely idea. I've never been to Crufts.'

'It's on for several days, apparently, so would Saturday be alright for you? We could go on Sunday if you can't. I'd prefer Saturday because it would give me Sunday to recover.'

'Well, I should be working, but I'm sure that I could switch with someone. Yes, let's make it Saturday. I'm sure that Duncan will look after Sally.'

'That's another consideration. Saturday is better for Michael because it won't interfere with his golf.'

'What time shall I pick you up?'

'Nineish, if that's okay.'

The news was received by Duncan with a grunt.

'I'm so sorry, darling, I didn't ask you if you wanted to come.'

'No, that's alright. You have a girls' day out. I want to get into the garden, anyway.'

The following Friday, Simon quietly shut the door at 5 a.m. and drove over to Joan Skipton's house. It was ablaze with lights when he arrived and Joan was standing on the doorstep waiting for him. Alan, her husband, came out as he reversed into the drive, carrying a travelling cage and a large holdall. 'Thanks for this, Simon, I just couldn't spare the time.'

'That's okay, Alan,' Simon replied as he got out of the car and opened up the tailgate of his estate car. Alan put the cage and the holdall in and Joan put the dog in the cage and her grooming box beside it.

'That's it, Simon,' she said and got into the car.

As he had anticipated, Joan started talking almost straight away. She started off by saying that Alan was a pig for not taking her today. Her car was in the garage for repair and he knew that she would want him to take her to Crufts. He deliberately made an arrangement to go out.

At this point, Simon closed his ears for a while, yawned and then concentrated on his driving. When he next tuned in, she was discussing their relative chances of getting the ticket today, as opposed to the chances of various other exhibitors of their acquaintance, the quality, or lack of it of their dogs, and their chances. By the time she had got on to gossip about the private lives of several of their acquaintances, Simon had once again switched off. When he at last saw the signs for the NEC, he heaved a sigh of relief.

After unloading and carrying everything into the NEC, finding the correct hall and then the Cumbrian Terrier benching and settling his two dogs in their cages on the benches, Simon poured himself a cup of tea from his thermos flask and vowed to avoid Joan for the rest of the day, or at least until they met up in the junior dog class. Until his class, he chatted to various friends and groomed his dog.

He was rather disappointed to only get a fifth place in his class because he had done better than that at two previous Championship shows.

Joan didn't get placed at all. The judge didn't now show dogs himself, being rather elderly. Perhaps, as he came from the North of England, it was only natural that he seemed to favour the dogs from the North and wasn't concerned that Joan was judging later in the year.

He wasn't in the ring again until the Open Bitch class, which would be in the afternoon so, having arranged to have a drink with a couple of fellow exhibitors later on, he took himself off around the many trade stands in the various halls. Standing at the bar at lunchtime with Joe and Derek, jostled by the crowds and shouting above the noise of the crowd, it was mutually agreed that it was time the judge retired. He was too old to see the dogs properly and was definitely putting up northern colleagues. Finishing their pints and agreeing that they were bloody daft to be there, they laughingly returned to their benches.

In the Open Bitch class Simon could see the judge keep looking at his bitch. His pulse raced and his mouth went dry. Could this be the big one? He started to sweat when the judge again came over and looked at his bitch; she moved slightly and cursing under his breath, he straightened her up again. The judge by now was looking at another bitch further down the line. He then briefly looked at Simon's once again, pulled out the other bitch and then another two. He pulled Simon's out fourth. Damn, not even in the write-up, he thought, as only the first three dogs in a class got a critique from the judge, which would appear in the various dog papers.

As he put his bitch back on the bench he saw Joan looming up, so he hurried off to the toilets. He then wandered off in search of a cup of tea. Bloody rotten sport this is, he thought as he drank the tea. Why the hell do I do it? They are all wheeler-dealing and it costs a fortune nowadays to enter the classes. I must be mad.

Deep down he knew why he did it. Nothing else in his life gave him that adrenaline rush now, nothing else gave him this chance of success. As a civil servant with hardly any more chances for promotion, unless someone senior died or retired, with a wife who was boring and disinterested in bed and out of it and with two teenagers who only seemed to want money from him, he needed some escape, some way to be his own man – this was it.

Joan was waiting when he got back to his bench. 'We're allowed to go now and I'm ready to go if you are.'

They joined the crowds of disappointed, tired, home-going exhibitors and wearily made their way out into the cold. Having loaded the dogs and all the gear into the car, Simon set off homewards. Joan was rather tired and after a few caustic comments about the judge and some of the exhibitors, lapsed into silence. When he finally arrived home, he settled the dogs in the kennel and fed them. In the kitchen, Mary put his dinner on a saucepan of water to warm up, complaining as she did so that the dogs had barked twice and the neighbours had banged on the wall, also that the light bulb needed changing in the bathroom.

'I suppose you had a nice day, did you?' she asked sarcastically.

Looking at her and his sullen teenage daughter, he said, 'Yes, not bad; quite interesting really.'

ON SATURDAY MORNING, Fiona was up fairly early. As she ate breakfast, she told Sally where she was going and that she would look for any of her relatives who might be there. She collected her coat and bag, took Duncan a cup of tea, told him what was for lunch and went out to the car. She picked up Laura and drove towards Birmingham.

'I've never been to the NEC. Have you, Laura?'

'No, don't even know what it stands for.'

'I know that, it's the National Exhibition Centre. Crufts used to be at Olympia in London but they've just moved to Birmingham.'

'Well, I suppose it makes a lot of sense traffic-wise, doesn't it?'

The women continued chatting and soon the directions for the NEC started to appear on the motorway signs. The traffic was building up considerably and a lot of cars seemed to be turning off for the NEC. Shortly, they joined a large queue and it was some time before they were able to park.

'I had no idea that it was on such a grand scale. There are so many people going to it,' remarked Laura as they locked the car. 'Where do we go now?'

They watched what everyone else was doing and joined a steady stream of people going towards two coaches on the perimeter of the car park. Once inside a coach, the atmosphere seemed electric; everyone was chatting and laughing and anticipating the day ahead. The vehicle stopped in a line of coaches, all depositing people at the imposing entrance. They joined the long queue to pay to get in. The atmosphere was beginning to infect them and they both felt very excited. Once inside the enormous hall, the lights, the colour and the noise of many people talking and dogs barking stunned them into silence for a moment.

'I had no idea it was like this, Fiona.'

'Me neither – I don't know quite what I expected but this is… spectacular.'

They continued to stand there, bewildered, getting jostled and bumped by people hurrying here and there.

'Well,' said Laura, 'we came here to see the dogs, so let's go and see them. Wait a moment. Everyone seems to be buying those catalogues. Perhaps they'll tell us where everything is.'

They studied the catalogue for a while.

'The retrievers are in hall two, it says. There are loads of them. I can't find any Cumbrian Terriers though, Fiona.'

They passed stall after stall selling so many 'doggy' accoutrements that Fiona felt that her wonderful pet shop paled into insignificance. They then came to rows and rows of wooden benches with metal sections in them. Each section had a dog in it.

'They're all tied up or in cages,' Fiona commented. 'Well, I suppose you'd have to – you wouldn't want them running around in all this.'

'They all seem quite used to it and happy though, don't they? Oh, look Fiona, there's hall two.'

'There are some Golden Retrievers, Laura, but I can't see any Cumbrian Terriers; in fact, I can't see any terriers at all.'

They were passing some dogs that they had not seen before. They asked a woman who was standing by a dog on a bench and was told that they were German Short-haired Pointers. They both agreed that the animals were absolutely beautiful. Moving on, they arrived at the English Pointer benches and agreed that they too were stunning.

'What lovely heads; I wish that I could paint, Laura.'

In a crowd of people Laura saw a woman walking a Golden Retriever. She jostled and pushed her way through and finally caught up with her. 'Excuse me, can you tell me where all the Golden Retrievers are?'

'Yes, dear, follow me, I'm just going back to my bench.'

Waving to Fiona to follow, she set off to the other side of the hall.

'Look, there are the retriever benches. Aren't we learning the jargon?' Laura said laughingly.

They walked up and down the aisles with Laura emitting Ohs and Ahs at some of the dogs. 'Aren't they all gorgeous? I could take them all home. They aren't all golden though, are they, like Dee? Some of them are really creamy, almost white in some cases. How are they Golden Retrievers?'

Just at that moment Laura saw a familiar face. 'Look, there's Mrs Banbridge, Dee's breeder.' They hurried over to her.

'Hello. Mrs Anderson, isn't it? How nice to see you. How is your puppy getting on?'

'Oh, fine, thank you; how nice of you to remember.'

Mrs Banbridge, who was busy grooming a dog all the time that they were speaking, said, 'I'm sorry but I must rush off now. Young Josh here is due in the ring at any moment.'

'May we come and watch?'

'Of course; that is if you can get near enough to the ring to see.' She walked off with the dog and they followed her.

By standing on tiptoe, they managed to get glimpses of the ring through little gaps in the large crowd of people. There were quite a few retrievers in the ring and it seemed a long time before the judge had looked at each dog. She then called five of them into the middle. She made each of the five run round the ring again and then placed them from first to fifth. A man called out their numbers and gave each one a card. Laura was excited because she knew that Mrs Banbridge had been one of the five but hadn't seen where she was placed. When Mrs Banbridge came out of the ring carrying a card, she told them that she had come fourth. Laura was thrilled and congratulated her effusively. When she started to groom another dog they made their excuses and moved away.

By now they were both feeling hot and very thirsty so they made slow but steady progress through the crowds towards a refreshment sign, looking at more dogs and more trade stands on the way.

'Oh, my feet!' said Laura. 'I wish that I'd worn my old shoes.'

'And me; and we've still masses to see. We haven't even found the terriers yet.'

'Excuse me for butting in,' said a man sitting at their table, 'but the terriers were on yesterday.'

'Oh no,' said Fiona, 'we thought that they would all be here.'

'This is your first visit, then. I'm afraid that different groups are on different days and the Terrier group was yesterday.'

'That's a pity. I didn't know that there were groups. What do you say then, Laura, to another hour and then we'll go home?'

They wandered round and saw several more breeds of gun dog. Fiona asked quite a lot of questions about various ones but fell in love with a Cocker Spaniel with appealing eyes. Laura hauled her away, saying that she had enough with Sally. In the car on the way home, they both agreed that they had had a very interesting, though extremely tiring day.

'It's like a world of its own. I mean,' continued Laura, 'it seems to have a language of its own and as for the trade stands, it's an enormous industry built up around showing dogs, isn't it?'

'Yes, I found it all totally fascinating.'

In the evening, after some hastily prepared salad and boiled eggs, Fiona revived somewhat and chattered for some time about the show. Duncan nodded and smiled occasionally and when the flow subsided, remarked, 'Well, Muppet, you've obviously had a good day out.'

Spring was well on the way now, Sally was seven months old and with the lighter evenings they started to take her out. It was very pleasant walking along, holding Duncan's hand with Sally walking beside them.

Although they were not great churchgoers, they did go occasionally and one Sunday the vicar announced that they were organising several money-raising events in the near future. The central heating in the church was failing and a new boiler was needed, amongst other things. A list of events was at the back of the church, and if anyone could help in any way, could they please let him know. On studying the list, Fiona saw that one of the events was an exemption dog show to be held at the church hall. As soon as she got home she phoned Laura to tell her about it and they both agreed that it would be great fun to enter their dogs in it.

Laura and Fiona now met every Monday afternoon to walk the dogs on the heath. On the Monday afternoon before the show they decided to bathe the dogs on the Friday and not take them out before the show. On Saturday, after an early lunch, Fiona and Duncan walked Sally to the church hall where they met Laura and Michael, the children and Delilah. They discovered that the show started at one o'clock and that there were four pedigree classes – 'That's us,' said Laura – and eight novelty classes.

'I like the sound of this one,' said Michael, 'the dog with the waggiest tail – that's Delilah alright.'

'How about the dog most like its owner? Fiona, you and Sally have both got brown hair.'

Fiona looked up from the sheet of paper. 'Let's be serious and make up our minds. We have got to enter and pay by one o'clock. I shall put Sally in the pedigree puppy class and "the dog the judge would most like to take home" class.'

'And I shall put Delilah in the puppy class also and then the waggiest tail one.'

After they had entered, they looked around at other dogs there and were surprised to see that although some were obviously mongrels, dearly loved pets of their owners, others were not only pedigree but also dogs who were shown and very smartly turned out. They even had the different sorts of leads that they had noticed the dogs wearing at Crufts.

'Fancy coming here,' said Laura. 'I thought that only the people from church and a few local pets would come.'

The first class was announced and they took Sally and Delilah into the ring. A woman came up with a small card with a number on it.

'Have you got a pin, Laura?'

'Yes, but they're in my handbag.' She made frantic signs to Michael to bring the handbag to her and they were able to pin their numbers on to their blouses.

The woman then told them to stand their dogs in a line and the judge came to look at them.

There were ten puppies in the class and as her turn came near Fiona got more and more nervous. She so wanted the judge to like Sally. The judge asked Fiona to put Sally on the table in order to look at her. Sally, who had never been on a table before, thought this was a good game, and putting her front paws on the judge's shoulders, licked her face furiously. The judge smiled, gently putting her back on the table and proceeded to feel Sally's wriggling body. Fiona was red-faced with embarrassment by now and when she heard the judge say, 'Would you walk her straight up and down please,' grabbed Sally and hurried up and down the ring, the puppy jumping and leaping beside her.

Laura didn't have to put Delilah on the table and the judge was able to feel her body quite easily except for her wagging tail. When she was asked to walk, Delilah moved beautifully beside Laura. Having looked at all the puppies, the judge picked out four of them and then picked Delilah fifth.

For a moment, Fiona just stood there until she realised that the steward was telling her to leave the ring; she hurriedly did so, feeling embarrassed. Duncan patted her on the shoulder. 'Pity you didn't get a prize,' Fiona looked at him and felt an unexpected but very strong surge of anger at his patronising manner.

Just at that moment, Laura ran out of the ring with a rosette and a bag of dog biscuits, a big smile lighting up her plump face. 'Look what we've won, isn't it marvellous? Weren't you a clever girl?' She bent down and patted Delilah. Fiona found that her face was stiff with anger. She attempted a smile as she briefly congratulated Laura. Both of the twins wanted the rosette and Michael had to calm them down with the promise of an ice cream. They all went over to the stall where Angela Hammond, the vicar's wife, was serving tea, orange juice, cake and ice cream.

In the novelty classes, Delilah's tail wagged furiously and she easily won first prize, receiving a red rosette and a much larger bag of biscuits. Michael and the children were very excited and rushed up to her to congratulate her. Fiona busied herself with stroking Sally to hide her jealousy. She felt miserably ashamed of herself and told herself not to be so idiotic. Her second class was now called and she went into the ring again. There were only five dogs in this one and when Sally was pulled out fifth Fiona just wanted to run out of the ring. Her feelings were so strong that she didn't say anything when they all congratulated her and Sally, but merely gave the rosette to Laura so that all the children could have one.

When it was suggested that they go back to Laura's for tea, Fiona declined, saying that she had a very bad headache.

The atmosphere was a bit strained when they got home and Duncan immediately went out into the garden, while Fiona decided to dust and tidy the already immaculate lounge. It wasn't till after dinner that Duncan said, 'Whatever was the matter with you this afternoon?'

'Nothing; I told you that I had a headache.' She felt that she couldn't tell him the real reason. The events of the afternoon and her feelings were still paramount in her mind. It had shaken her very much to find that she had felt so strongly about it, and it had come as quite a surprise to her that she so wanted Sally to beat Delilah.

'I particularly wanted to have a chat with Michael about us joining the golf club and having some lessons. I've been told that the professional instructor there is very helpful.'

'Give him a ring now; I'm sure that he won't mind.'

He was gone some time and Fiona sat looking out of the window at Sally, who was playing in the garden. I think she's absolutely lovely, she thought.

When Duncan came back into the room to tell her of his conversation she was only half listening. '...so it looks quite hopeful. Should be fun.'

'Yes,' replied Fiona, her mind still on her feelings of the afternoon.

ON THE FOLLOWING Tuesday, Fiona spent the whole of her lunch break playing with Sally and looking through several books she had brought home from the library. In the evening she hurried home and immediately phoned Laura. 'Hello, Laura. Fiona here. Laura, I've had a wonderful idea and I should like your advice on it.'

'Sounds interesting but I don't know that I shall have the answer unless it's about Thomas the Tank Engine.'

'No, it's about dog showing – you know, the real kind. I thought that I might take it up as a hobby. What do you think?'

'You are joking, aren't you? What about Duncan? I thought that you had already arranged to play golf together.'

'We can do both. I don't foresee any problems. Anyway, what I wanted to ask you is, do you know the name of the local dog training club? I've been reading some of the dog books from the library and several suggest that you start by joining the local dog club to have lessons in ringcraft.'

They chattered on for a while about the dogs and various things, and then Fiona made her goodbyes. She quickly dialled Mrs Emsworth's number. 'Hello, Fiona McCleod here; do you remember, Sally's owner? I thought that I would ring you to tell you of her progress.'

After telling her how absolutely wonderful Sally was in every aspect, Fiona got to the point of her phone call. 'I was thinking that I should very much like to show her. Do you think that I could?'

'Well, my dear, of course you can show her but until I see her I couldn't tell you if she was worth showing. Could you possibly send some recent photographs of her, standing up preferably? That would give me some idea, but it would be best if you could bring her up here for me to see. It might save you a lot of expense and disappointment. Is your husband keen to show her as well?'

As soon as Duncan came home, she eagerly told him of her idea, of her phone call to Mrs Emsworth and how she had requested to see Sally. He was thoughtful for a minute or two. He did not relish having to make that journey again, especially this weekend, because he had arranged to go and have a look around the golf course with Michael. He was very keen for himself and Fiona to start playing. He was a little concerned that this new development might interfere with those plans. Also, he had not forgotten how upset she had been at the church fête. This didn't seem like a well-thought-out idea. His reply, therefore, was very lukewarm. He then told her about his plans for Saturday.

Fiona said nothing for a minute and then surprised herself and Duncan by saying that she would go up there on Saturday by herself and this would leave Duncan free to see Michael. Surprised by her sudden independence, Duncan did not object.

She was a good driver, careful and conscientious, but not an enthusiastic one. In the past, she had always been happy for Duncan to do most of the driving – content just to use her car for work, shopping and the odd visit to relatives and friends. This was such a deviation for her that Duncan was lost for words. When he finally spoke, it was just to say that if she was sure that was what she wanted to do, then by all means do it. He secretly thought that she would change her mind before Saturday.

On Friday evening she filled the car with petrol, went to the supermarket and got some groceries, including something for Duncan to have on Saturday. Next morning saw her up early and breakfasted before Duncan got up. Taking him a cup of tea, she kissed him and left the house.

Duncan heard the car start up and leave as he lay in bed drinking his tea. He was a little disturbed by her actions – it was so unlike her. Finishing his tea, he continued to lie there as he thought over the past year. Throughout their married life it seemed that they had talked and planned their family, and yet it was never mentioned now. They had never really discussed their present situation, never expressed their sadness. He had been so bitterly disappointed when their last attempt had failed and he knew Fiona had been too, which was why he had never told her of his own grief and his concern for the years ahead. Perhaps he should have done.

Not that he minded her having a dog. He had been happy to go along with it as long as it didn't interfere with their lives too much. She was a good wife, a quiet and contented, intelligent woman. She seemed quieter than she used to be but she still seemed to be happy in bed. Nothing wrong there, he thought. This little phase will pass and she'll settle down again. Smiling, he got out of bed.

Fiona arrived home in buoyant mood. While she quickly prepared a meal, she told him how much Mrs Emsworth had liked Sally. In fact, she said, she had been most encouraging, telling her what she needed to do and about the preparation of the dog for showing.

Duncan listened to her, noting how very pretty she looked with her green eyes shining and her hair moving as she spoke. He thought that it would be rather pleasant to make love to her tonight. She looked so vivacious. He asked if she had had a good journey and had she been able to find it alright on her own. She laughed and said that she had remembered it all very well and had gone straight there.

Going to bed rather earlier than usual, they made love. When Fiona went to the bathroom, Duncan remembered, just as he turned over to go to sleep, that he hadn't told her how he had got on at the golf club.

In the following weeks Fiona became very busy putting into practice all the things that she had been advised to do. In no time, she was attending the local dog society's ring-training classes on a Wednesday evening, having enrolled both herself and Duncan as members. She ordered one of the weekly dog papers to be delivered every Friday and groomed Sally every evening, followed by a practice of the ring training in the garden. Duncan went with her to the ring-training classes twice. Each time he had felt like a fish out of water and could not understand how Fiona could find it so interesting. The third week he said that he wanted to stay at home to watch a TV programme. Fiona looked a little disappointed but did not protest.

On the Saturday, Fiona went with Duncan to the golf club to receive instruction from the coach. This she continued to do for several Saturdays but, whereas Duncan showed aptitude and keenness for the sport, Fiona had been very poor and not very interested. A pattern now began to emerge in their marriage. Fiona, still finding the 'dog scene' absorbing, went every Wednesday evening on her own and Duncan went every Saturday for either more instruction or for a game with Michael. His conversations with Fiona were often about getting his handicap down and practising his swing, changing his grip and how he would soon give Michael a run for his money. She would listen quietly, not adding much to the conversation but pleased that he too had found a hobby.

Christmas was approaching and the decision had once again to be made about going to Duncan's parents.

'I'm sorry, Duncan, but I have made my mind up. I am not putting Sally into kennels. I think that this year they should come to us. After all, had we had children, they would have had to come to us years ago.'

Duncan was rather irritated at this turn of events. 'There would have been more reason for them to come then, wouldn't there? Look at Laura and Michael when we were over there last week, telling us about the toys they were buying for the children and how excited the children were getting about Father Christmas. Of course, they would want to come here then to be part of all the fun.'

There was so much tension between them by now that Fiona, determined not to give in and leave Sally, couldn't handle it and went upstairs. She tried not to think about babies nowadays, tried not to look back. He had brought all that pain to the surface again. She went into the bathroom and splashed her face with cold water.

'I'm not going to get upset. I'm not,' she told her reflection in the mirror as she dried her face and hands. Calmer now, she went downstairs.

'I'm sorry, Muppet. I didn't mean to upset you.'

'That's alright. I'm not upset but my mind is made up. Whatever happens, I'm having Christmas here with Sally. You and your parents and my father are welcome to come. I know that I can't produce anything like the dishes your mother does but I shall do my best.'

True to her word and in her usual efficient manner, Fiona embarked on her first Christmas at home. From snatches of conversation that she had overheard on the phone between Duncan and his mother, she gathered that his mother had reluctantly agreed.

As the day came closer, she was really excited about it. The pleasure of making the cake and decorating it, of making the table decoration, of choosing the serviettes and candles and planning the meals, was all novel to her. She just couldn't think why she had not insisted on doing it before. Why had she been so complacent, so content to accept everything the way Duncan wanted it? She did diplomatically ask Mrs McCleod if she would make the Christmas pudding because hers were so excellent. Mrs McCleod agreed and said that she would also make some mince pies and petit fours. By Christmas Eve she was really excited.

Duncan, watching her checking over her arrangements and menus, her cheeks flushed and her eyes shining, felt a pain of anguish as he thought how their Christmases might have been if only...

The two days of Christmas were a success for Fiona. Her careful planning provided interesting and varied meals, her choice of presents was well received and Sally behaved beautifully. As they kissed Fiona goodbye, Duncan's mother and father declared that it had been a very pleasant time and so relaxing. Fiona's father had enjoyed the extra company and made his goodbyes, saying that they must do the same next year. Fiona closed the front door and hugged herself. It had all gone well and when Duncan quietly admitted that it had been a pleasant change, she was overjoyed.

New Year's Eve found them at Laura and Michael's house for a party. There were several other couples there that they knew and the evening went with a swing. On the stroke of midnight, Duncan took Fiona in his arms and kissed her. He then said that his New Year Resolution was that they should go to more parties like this and have more holidays.

Fiona responded by saying that her resolutions were to start going to dog shows and to have a litter of puppies. Duncan's arms slackened slightly and looking into her eyes, he said, 'Are you serious?'

'Yes, I've given it a lot of thought and this is what I really want to do.'

Duncan looked at her, frowning slightly and dropped his arms. 'I know that you want to show, Sally, but where did this idea of puppies come from? Surely it's not a prerequisite for showing?'

'No, of course it isn't,' Fiona said, laughing and hugging Duncan. 'It's just something that I would like to do.'

'Um, well, I don't know about you, Muppet, but I'm ready to go home.'

They both thanked Laura and Michael for a lovely party, wished them once again a Happy New Year, and left.

FIONA BEGAN ENTERING Sally for forthcoming shows in the area – her first show was going to be at the end of February – and she got into the habit of changing into an old jumper and trousers after dinner, taking Sally into the shed and practising her grooming and showing techniques.

Duncan intensely disliked this alteration to their established routine and the loss of his potting shed, which was filled by her grooming table and other 'doggy' equipment. It disrupted his organised gardening programme. All of their married life they had spent their evenings together either companionably at home or with friends, or having a quiet drink at their local pub. He liked to see her sitting opposite him, nicely dressed, and was beginning to find this hobby of hers rather intrusive.

One evening she came in from the shed and, after washing her hands and changing, she sat on Duncan's lap. 'Now, you do know that on Saturday week it's my first show with Sally. You are coming with me, aren't you?'

'No, I'm playing golf with Michael.'

'But I'll be so nervous, I need your support.'

'What about all those people you chatter to on a Wednesday evening; can't they go with you?'

'They'll be busy with their own dogs.'

Duncan sighed. This silly hobby was really becoming a nuisance. 'Oh, alright. I'll phone Michael and cancel the golf but don't expect me to come with you all the time. I want you to come with me to play golf.'

Getting out of the car that Saturday morning at the equestrian centre was a revelation to them both. Dogs of all shapes and sizes were emerging from what seemed to be hundreds of cars. People were shouting, talking and laughing as they got dogs on leads or into cages, together with innumerable bags, boxes, towels and coats. They all seemed hell-bent on hurrying into the arena. The dogs on leads were pulling their owners along; dogs being carried or dogs in cages on trolleys barked greetings to all the other dogs. Duncan later described it to Michael as a scene of organised chaos.

As for the people, they ranged from babies in buggies to toddlers, right through to pensioners. Everyone was well wrapped up against the cold, some arguing, some talking, some shouting instructions to each other, but all striving to get their dogs and equipment into the building as quickly as possible.

Having been to Crufts, Fiona was prepared for the noise, which assailed their ears as they walked in, but Duncan stood still, quite amazed at the animated, noisy spectacle. Realising that he was losing sight of Fiona, he hurried after her. The judging was starting in several rings and they wandered round looking at the various dogs. Fiona explained that she was in the Any Variety Terrier class because there weren't any classes especially for Cumbrian Terriers. From the timetable in the catalogue that she had just bought, it looked as if her classes would not be judged until after the breed classes.

'How long will that be then?'

'I don't know, we shall just have to watch.'

It was three hours later when Fiona's class was announced over the loudspeaker and, by then, Duncan had a headache and was feeling rather irritable. They had done nothing but wander round the rings looking at the dogs, except when they went for a cup of tea, and the people, the lights and the noise and the fact that there was nowhere to sit, had really got to him. Fiona, on the other hand, had enjoyed every minute. She had bought a show lead for Sally and a new brush, and had introduced Duncan to a friend from the training classes.

Fiona was excited and nervous and dying to go to the loo as she finally took Sally into the ring and got her number from the steward. There were several Terrier breeds in the ring, she counted eleven dogs there altogether. When it was her turn to be seen she placed Sally on the table and was so flustered, that when the judge, a small, older man, neatly dressed in a sports jacket and trousers, asked her Sally's age, she couldn't remember! When he asked her to walk round the ring she did so oblivious to everything. She was given fifth place. The steward came up and handed her a piece of card with the name of the Dog Society on it and her place in the class. She also received a rosette made of white ribbon. She picked Sally up and hugged her, rushing, jubilant from the ring.

'She got fifth; isn't that wonderful?'

'Is that it now?'

'For us, yes, but the show will go on to the groups when all the dogs have been judged and then the Best in Show is chosen from the group winners.'

Duncan didn't really understand what she was saying but he supposed that she had learnt all this from her training classes. 'Do you mean that we have waited all this time just for that? How much longer have we got to stay here?'

'I don't know. I'll go and ask Tina – she'll know.'

After about fifteen minutes, during which Duncan finally managed to find a chair to sit on, Fiona returned. 'It's about another two hours or so until the end.'

'What! What else have you got to do?'

'Well, I haven't got any more classes. Why don't we go and have a cup of tea and something to eat?'

'What for, if you've finished. Yes, let's have a cup of tea, but in the comfort of our own home.'

Fiona could see that Duncan was really annoyed, so with a sigh and a long look round the rings she looked back at him. 'Perhaps you're right; perhaps we have all had enough.' She picked up Sally and her grooming box and they left the show.

On the way home, Duncan asked how much prize money she had won. When Fiona told him that you did not get any money, only the card and the rosette, he looked even more annoyed.

'Do you mean that all these people go to all this expense and discomfort for a small piece of card? It's senseless.'

Fiona didn't reply but did privately wonder if hitting a little ball round a field made sense.

Fiona continued to go to the training classes and Duncan to his golf. Six weeks later, when it was time for her second show, Duncan asked her to come to the golf club. He felt far more capable now and wanted her to see how much he had progressed. She agreed, providing that he accompanied her the day before to the dog show. She promised that they would not stay on.

It was worse than he had anticipated. It was being held at another equestrian centre, but this one had huge doors to one side, which were open all the time. There was a bitterly cold wind blowing and, although Fiona had brought two canvas garden chairs this time, some sandwiches and a thermos flask of coffee, he was too frozen to sit still for long. He wandered around disconsolately and saw several other men sitting or standing, looking equally miserable, and derived some pleasure in the knowledge that he was not alone in his dislike of this hobby. He had already noticed that most of the people there were women. Some men appeared to be involved in the actual showing of the dogs and they did seem to be rather businesslike and looked as if they were enjoying themselves.

He arrived back to where Fiona and Sally were waiting to go into the ring.

'We've just been called in; I was frightened that you would miss it.'

He sat down to watch. There were several different sorts of dog in the ring. One he recognised as a Scottie from the whisky bottle advert.

Fiona was placed third this time. Her face was alive as she came out of the ring, holding her piece of card and cuddling Sally. He sighed. She was a sensible girl – she would soon see how stupid this was and pack it up. He would just be patient.

The grooming shed was now adorned with two cards, two rosettes and a large photo of Sally. Duncan came into the shed one Friday evening, saying, 'I've written road numbers and directions down for you. Now, are you sure that you'll be able to find this place?'

Fiona had entered for the Cumbrian Terrier Club Show that was being held in a hall in the North of England. Duncan wasn't going with her because he was in a small golf tournament at the club, for which he was truly grateful.

The next morning, she was off very early. Duncan had got up to see her go. He rather admired her for tackling the journey on her own.

Having stayed talking and having a drink with Michael and one or two others, it was early evening when he came home from the tournament. He was rather surprised and a little concerned to find the house empty. After he had showered and changed, he remembered that Fiona had said that she had made a shepherd's pie, which would only need heating. Having put it in the oven, he made himself a cup of tea and, remembering how those other shows had gone on for hours, he sat down to watch television.

He had nodded off when he heard the front door opening and Fiona's voice. Looking at his watch he saw that it was almost eight o'clock. 'Where the devil have you been? I suppose you got lost on the way home?'

'I'm sorry, darling, only I stayed until the end of the show and I met a woman who lives in Reading, would you believe, and she breeds Cumbrians. Isn't that marvellous? I've had a fantastic day. Sally got a fourth in her class and that is against Cumbrians and a breed show! Wasn't she a clever girl?' She picked up Sally. 'We must give you some dinner. Oh, Mrs Emsworth was there and asked to be remembered to you. She thought Sally was very pretty and—'

Duncan, suddenly remembering their dinner, came out into the kitchen. 'Well, hurry up and feed her because I'm starving. Aren't you?' He quickly took the pie out of the oven. 'I've warmed it up.'

'Thank you, Duncan. I'll just feed Sally and then I'll serve it.'

He had just poured himself a whisky when she came back into the room. 'Look, here's her rosette. Isn't it lovely? It was so much more interesting than the other shows. There were seventy-eight Cumbrians entered. They came from all over the country. I'm absolutely hoarse with talking to everyone. They were all so interesting and I—'

'Did you find the hall okay?'

'Oh, yes, and thank you for the route plan. I had no trouble at all.'

All through dinner she remembered little incidents and recounted them to Duncan. During a lull Duncan said, 'I had a good tournament today; my handicap is improving. Everyone was most complimentary.'

'I'm so pleased for you; pity that I couldn't be there to see it. Now, would you like tea or coffee? I'll just pop out and hang my card and rosette in the grooming shed while the kettle boils.'

In the lounge, he poured himself a larger scotch than usual. Like most men, he did not like change in his home and Fiona was certainly changing. He'd be glad when this fad was all over.

She came into the room with the coffee. 'I was thinking on the way home, we haven't had Sheila and John over for ages. Shall I phone them up and arrange an evening?'

Sheila and John were quite recent friends. The women had got to know each other at the fertility clinic, but when Sheila's second attempt had been successful the friendship had waned somewhat. At a loss as to what to say, Duncan remained silent for a few minutes, then said, 'Do you think that they would be able to get a babysitter?'

'Of course they could. I'd like to see Sheila again and I'm sure they would like to see Sally.'

He stared at her. Did she realise what she had just said? For God's sake, did she really see the dog as a substitute family, because he damned well didn't. This situation was getting out of hand. 'If you really want to then do, but why not leave it for a few weeks until the warm, summer evenings?'

'That's a good idea. In fact, if I left it until August or September, Sally might be pregnant.'

He looked up sharply but before he could speak she went on. 'You see Joyce, that's this woman at Reading, has a stud dog and when Sally comes in season next, I thought that I would mate her and have some puppies. She says that the breed lines are compatible. Then Sheila and John could see the puppies. Yes, I'll leave it until then.'

Anger had been slowly building up in him while she had been speaking. He had never liked women who chattered inanely. Fiona had always been a quiet woman who spoke sensibly. What the hell did she think she was doing arranging to have puppies without consulting him first? Their marriage had been built on mutual respect, mutual agreement. 'What in heaven's name are you talking about?'

'Haven't you been listening? I met this woman, Joyce, who has—'

'I heard all that. Why would you think that Sheila and John would want to come all this way with a baby, to see puppies? In fact, I emphatically disagree with the concept of you having puppies at all. It's a ridiculous idea and you should have discussed it with me before you made any such arrangements.'

Some of the euphoria drained out of Fiona. Why did he seem to get so annoyed these days? 'I'm sorry, darling, I didn't think that you would mind. Joyce and I were talking at the show and we just arranged it. Why don't you like the idea?'

'Because it's totally impractical. This is an ordinary house, not a kennel. You neither have the experience nor the facilities. I shouldn't have to tell you this.'

She looked at him in silence and then glanced round the room. Everything in it was good quality and everything was colour co-ordinated right down to the cream carpet. She sighed. It was all so lovely but so still, waiting, waiting for the children that would never come. She knew that she couldn't go on standing still, comfortably passing the time. It suited Duncan but it didn't suit her.

'I'm sorry that I didn't discuss it with you but I still want to do it. Don't you see that it's important to me? I need to do something challenging.'

'For goodness' sake, woman, you have a house to run, an interesting job and that dog to look after. We have a circle of friends; you've got plenty to do.'

'It's not enough; don't you see, it's not enough now.'

That night when he got into bed he put his hand on her breast and kissed the back of her neck. She sighed and turned into his arms. 'I do love you, you know, Muppet. I want you to be happy.'

'Yes, I know, and I love you very much.'

T HE CHURCH HELD its summer fête in July and, because the previous one had been such a success, they included another dog show in the events programme. Laura was thrilled and asked Fiona to enter Sally, so they could all go together again. Fiona refused saying that she preferred Sally to go to bigger shows now and she didn't think it was fair to pet dogs; she would be coming to the fête though and would cheer her and Delilah on. Relating Fiona's remarks to Michael later that day Laura said, 'This showing is really changing Fiona – she would never have made a nasty remark like that before.'

True to her word, Fiona did attend the fête and happily congratulated Laura and Delilah when they got a first prize.

As August approached, Duncan and Fiona, accompanied by Sally, went to the cottage they had rented in Cornwall. It proved to be a delightful place set in a quiet spot and near to the cliffs. Both Duncan and Fiona relaxed completely; they had some delightful walks with Sally and visited several places of interest. They ate out quite a lot, drank some very nice wine and made love more frequently. As they drove home they agreed that it had been a great success and that they both felt much more relaxed than they had done for some time.

At the end of August, just as Duncan was going to work one morning, Fiona announced that Sally had come in season and that she must remember to phone Joyce Brown that evening. Duncan, who was running a bit late that morning, murmured something and left the house.

Fiona was busy in the library stacking books when a colleague told her that her husband was on the phone. Worried because this was so unlike Duncan, she hurried into the office and picked up the phone.

'Is that you, Fiona? Look, I've been thinking, that phone call you said that you were going to make this evening. It wasn't to that dog woman in Reading, was it?'

'Yes, it was. I want to arrange the mating. She told me to tell her as soon as Sally started.'

'I don't think that you've fully thought this through, you know. Look, please don't do anything until we've had a talk this evening.'

'Alright, if that's what you want. See you at the normal time. Bye.'

She tried to speak to him about Sally before dinner but he would not be drawn, saying that he was tired after a busy day and wanted a drink. It wasn't until later in the evening that he brought up the subject.

'Now that you have had the rest of the day to think about the consequences of such an action, have you changed your mind, Muppet?' Before she could reply, he went on, 'This house is not suitable to have a litter of puppies. Have you considered where they would go? What about the actual birth? Do you think that you could deliver them? What is it all going to cost, especially if the vet has to do everything? Do you know how to feed them? Oh, Fiona, the list is endless. Have you really thought this through? I have and I am totally against it and want nothing to do with it.'

Faced with such antagonism from him, Fiona sat looking at her hands for a moment then replied, 'Please give me credit, Duncan, for having given this a lot of thought. You know me well enough, surely, to know that I wouldn't do something like this without sorting all these things out. The bed could be taken down in the small bedroom and—'

'The small bedroom!' interrupted Duncan.

'Yes, it's ideal for Sally to give birth and for a puppy run. I've read an awful lot about it. Laura has said that she would love to come over and help me, and Joyce Brown has also said that if I were at all worried she would drive over and, as you said, there is always the vet. The puppies are ready to leave home at eight weeks. Again, Joyce Brown has said that she would help me to find suitable homes for them. I did think that if there was a nice one, that I would keep it as company for Sally. I told you that I was going to breed at the party; why have you left it until now to say—'

'If I can be permitted to say something. I know you mentioned it but I thought it was such a ludicrous idea that you must have meant it as a joke.'

'It's not a joke. I really want to do this. It would be very fulfilling and rewarding for me.'

'Fulfilling and rewarding; for goodness' sake, Fiona, don't you see that it's just a substitute for a family. You're well educated and intelligent – surely you can find some other hobby more suited to your abilities and our situation? Come on now, Muppet, it sounds a nice idea to you, but you know that it's just not practical, is it?'

He left the room and went into the garden, leaving Fiona almost in tears. How could he speak to her in such a condescending way? What was the matter with him these days? Would he have been like this if they had had a baby? Would he have been jealous of that too? It was certainly beginning to look as though he was jealous of Sally.

At work the next day, Rosemary asked her if everything was alright, as she seemed so preoccupied. Fiona assured her that all was well but inwardly she kept hearing Duncan's words and wondering if he was correct. She wanted to mate Sally because it would be a new experience. It would be exciting and interesting; an achievement. It was the same with the dog showing – she felt alive when she was at a show, she felt young and athletic. Her competitive spirit had surprised her, as indeed had her great affinity with dogs. Surely all these feelings couldn't be a substitute for a family, as Duncan had suggested? Surely it was just another part of her development – a bit more of the maturing process, a discovery of another side of her nature.

That evening, as soon as she opened the front door, she picked up the phone and rang Joyce Brown. During their conversation, it was arranged on which day next week she should take Sally to be mated. She said nothing to Duncan until the day on which she was due to go to Reading.

She phoned him at his office to say that she was going and would leave him a salad in the fridge. She rang off before he could reply. The phone rang before she got out of the door but she ignored it.

As she drove towards Reading she was a little apprehensive, but when she arrived there and watched Sally being introduced to the stud dog her worries vanished. She was, however, a little surprised to find that she felt slightly embarrassed when they were being mated – as if she were a voyeur. Joyce, however, was so businesslike and normal that she soon relaxed. When she was given the mating certificate Joyce told her when to expect the puppies.

As Fiona neared home her bravado began to disappear and she found herself rehearsing speeches to Duncan about why she had so wanted to mate Sally. As she turned into the drive she told herself not to be so stupid. Duncan would understand; they were so close.

Apart from saying, 'Oh, you're back,' Duncan said nothing for the whole evening. This was such an unusual turn of events that Fiona found herself remaining silent too and they went to bed that night with the matter still unresolved between them.

After seven weeks it became obvious from her plump appearance that Sally was definitely pregnant. As the days went by Fiona's excitement grew until it even affected Duncan a little. He helped her dismantle the bed in the small bedroom, laid a large piece of plastic over the entire carpet and brought in a small table. Fiona placed a piece of sheeting on the table on which she laid cotton wool, scissors a bottle of disinfectant and a hot water bottle. The whelping bed had proved to be a problem but one day, when Rosemary had seen her looking at diagrams of whelping beds in various books, they got talking and Rosemary suggested that her husband make one for her because he enjoyed doing that sort of thing.

The only cloud on the horizon was Duncan. The subject of the puppies had never been raised again and it stood between them like a fog; it upset her to think about it.

It worried him as well. The balance of their relationship, well established over the years, was subtly changing. He didn't like it but didn't know what to do about it.

On the morning of the 25th, Fiona got up to find Sally panting and scratching up her bedding. Shouting for Duncan, she grabbed the book she had from the library, which gave a step-by-step graphic account of the progress of labour. Duncan appeared, yawning and putting on his dressing gown.

'She's started labour.'

'What do we do? Shall I call the vet?'

'No, she's alright at the moment; all we have to do is watch to see when she starts straining.'

'Do you need me? Only I have a hectic schedule of work today.'

'No darling, I'm fine. I'll ring the library to say that I shan't be in today. They're expecting it.'

When Duncan had left, she called Joyce, who gave her lots of advice and told her to call if she needed her. Fiona then took Sally out into the garden for a few minutes and gently carried her upstairs to the whelping bed. When Sally had settled she phoned Laura, who rushed over, eager to help. The morning passed with them checking regularly on Sally and it wasn't until they were having a sandwich at lunchtime that they heard a cry from upstairs. They both raced up the stairs to find Sally panting very hard and straining.

'That's it, Fiona, she's pushing, shouldn't be long now.'

Sally strained twice more and then came out of the bed and stood by Fiona's legs. She strained again very hard and gave a cry as a silvery-white bag appeared from her vulva. They both quickly bent down and as Fiona held her still, Laura took the weight of the bag in her hand as the cord and placenta appeared. Sally looked round at the bag but did not seem to know what to do so the two women took the sterilised scissors and, having gently squeezed the cord, cut it at the correct distance from the puppy. The puppy was now wriggling strongly as they broke the bag. They cleaned it down and showed it to Sally but she only sniffed at it.

'I haven't filled the hot water bottle.'

'I'll do it,' said Laura. 'You wrap the puppy in a piece of that old sheet and keep it warm.'

Laura came back just as Sally started straining again. They quickly settled the now mewing puppy on a wrapped-up water bottle and as soon as they started to stroke Sally, she once again came out of the bed to Fiona.

'It looks as if that is her preferred way of having them, Fiona.'

Sally strained several more times and then another bag started to appear. They followed the same procedure, except that this time Sally broke the bag herself and started to clean the puppy. Soon, two puppies were on the hot water bottle.

'Are they boys or girls?'

'I don't know. Let's have a look. Oh, Laura one is a little girl and the other is a boy.'

Sally started to strain again. Two and three quarter hours later, Laura said, 'Well, I don't know about you but I could do with a cup of tea.' She looked at the bitch lying in her whelping box with four puppies all tucked into her belly and suckling. 'She seems alright, doesn't she? I think that we have disinfected her down for the last time, don't you, Fiona?'

'I think so. She seems very relaxed now and contented. I'll get her a drink of warm milk and if we keep popping up and checking that she isn't straining again or distressed, I think we've done it.' She let out a long sigh and, smiling at each other, the women quietly left the room and closed the door.

Downstairs, Fiona put the kettle on and burst into tears. Laura put her arm round her but said nothing. Fiona had never discussed it with her but she knew how much she and Duncan had wanted a family of their own and she had seen how much this little family had meant to her. Her throat was full too and she had to swallow hard as she comforted Fiona.

'I'll finish this cup of tea with you, Fiona, and then I must go to pick up the children from school.'

'Of course. I just can't thank you enough. You've been wonderful.'

'Loved every minute of it. Must dash now. Bye.'

As Duncan let himself in that evening he was swamped by Fiona hugging him, crying and telling him all about the puppies at the same time. He couldn't get his coat off before she was dragging him up the stairs, telling him to be quiet and to take his shoes off before he went in, in case they were dirty.

'I rang about lunchtime but got no reply. Did you go to the vet's?'

'No; I heard the phone but we didn't dare leave Sally.'

She opened the door and they both crept in. Sally raised her head for a second and then went back to her cleaning and feeding duties.

'Aren't they tiny? How many are there?'

'There are four of them: two boys and two girls. Aren't they just adorable? She's a wonderful mother,' Fiona whispered as she gently pulled Duncan from the room and closed the door. She felt very tired, but warm, warm from the inside, warm and whole.

A WEEK LATER, looking out of the window at the pouring rain, Fiona admitted to herself that looking after Sally, had entailed more work than she had anticipated, but she had adored every minute of it. She was up very early each morning and to bed late so that she could see to Sally and check that all was well. She even got up in the night sometimes if she heard the slightest noise from the small bedroom, but Sally was well and the puppies thrived. She tried not to think about the next week when she would have to return to the library. Laura had been most helpful and had offered to pop over in the morning from Tuesday to Friday to feed Sally and let her out, and to see that the puppies were alright. Duncan would do the same on Saturday morning.

All the same, she was very concerned when she left the little family on Tuesday morning. She had been up very early to change the bedding and to clean the box, to check on each puppy and to feed Sally. She raced home in her lunch break to find a little note from Laura telling her that all was well. Sally was pleased to see her and was obviously undisturbed by the new routine.

That evening and every evening for the next couple of weeks, Duncan found that his meal was not ready for him when he arrived home. Very apologetic, Fiona would rush round preparing the meal and, at the same time, regale him with all the new things the puppies were doing. He too found the little furry bundles a constant source of interest. At the beginning of the third week, they all had their eyes open and began, in slow and stately fashion, to explore their surroundings.

Fiona opened the front door one lunchtime to hear Sally barking. Her heart racing, she hurried upstairs to the little bedroom where she found that one of the puppies had fallen out of the whelping box and had crawled across the floor. Sally was very agitated and the other three puppies were huddled together, frightened of the noise. The adventurous puppy was crying in the corner of the pen. Fiona quickly picked him up; he was a little cool but otherwise none the worse for his journey. With all puppies safely in the fold once more, Sally set about a thorough cleaning of them all. Fiona phoned Joyce Brown, who assured her that this was quite normal and would happen more and more, and that as long as they could not get out of the pen and didn't get cold, all would be fine. She made herself a cup of tea and decided not to go back to the library that afternoon, in case it happened again.

During the course of the next week it did happen more frequently, until it became the norm. It was nearing the time for the pups to be weaned and Sally was tiring of her maternal duties and wanting to be with Fiona downstairs. Once weaned, the pups would need feeding five times a day. This, by necessity, would mean an awful lot of cleaning up as well.

From now on, life for Fiona became frenetic. The pups would not lap milk or anything else – they wanted Sally's milk. Many despairing phone calls took place to Joyce and to Mrs Emsworth, until slowly Fiona got them to eat and weaned them. She could manage the feeding quite well. First feed was as soon as she got up, second feed at lunchtime. No time for anything for herself, Laura did the third in the afternoon, which left the fourth when she got home and the fifth before she went to bed.

Her greatest problems, however, were finding the time to prepare the five meals a day for the puppies and trying to keep them clean! With four puppies having five feeds per day it seemed impossible to keep them always clean and dry. By the time she got home in the evening, the newspaper in their run would be soaked through and torn up, and as for the rest of it! It was on their feet and smeared over their bodies where they had run, played and skidded through it; it was all over their clean bedding from their feet. Fiona had to change her clothes as soon as she got home and set to work cleaning and disinfecting; she was constantly helped by four inquisitive puppies eager to assist by chewing her shoes, her trousers, her hair, and trying to grab the cloth and hang on to it with their new teeth, which were needle sharp.

In spite of everything, she loved every minute of it and would often still be playing with them when she heard Duncan's car in the drive. She would hurry downstairs, guiltily offering to go to the Chinese takeaway or the Indian restaurant, or to the fish and chip shop. Not used to this sort of treatment, Duncan did not take to it kindly, frequently complaining that the food gave him indigestion. His interest in the puppies waned and he began to feel that they were an unnecessary intrusion into their life and couldn't wait for them to go.

'When do you intend selling these puppies?' Duncan enquired one morning, having had to get his breakfast yet again.

'Good thing you mentioned it. I'm supposed to phone Joyce and arrange for her to see them. I'll do it today.'

'Well, don't forget, will you? Why has she got to see them?'

'Because they are from her dog. She wants to see how good they are.'

It was arranged for Joyce to see the puppies the following Monday afternoon. Fiona felt a surge of pride when she opened the door of the bedroom and the puppies all scampered out of their bed to greet them.

'What a lovely litter. You have made a good job of this. Now, let's have a good look at you all.'

After a detailed look at each puppy and then a period of watching each one running round with its siblings, Joyce said, 'Well, you've been very lucky – you have a dog and a bitch who have definite show potential. You are going to keep one at least, I presume?'

Not wishing to go into the problems with Duncan, Fiona said that she had thought of keeping the bitch puppy as company for Sally.

'Yes, but you would want to show it as well, wouldn't you?'

'Oh, yes.'

'Right, well, in that case, in my opinion, you should keep this one. Mind you, with all this space, you should run both of the bitches on for a few months just to see that the adult teeth come

72

in correctly and then pick the best one.'

When Joyce had bustled off in her old estate car, having told her that she would be giving her phone number to a couple who were looking for a Cumbrian puppy, but not to let it go until after Christmas, Fiona went back indoors. For heaven's sake, Christmas! She just hadn't given it a thought.

The puppies would be eight weeks old in Christmas week. Joyce had said that reputable breeders did not sell puppies then in case they were looked upon as a toy, easy to ignore once the novelty had worn off. It was also a difficult time to try to settle a puppy into a new home with all the other activities associated with Christmas. Fiona sighed; she had been sitting up in the bedroom with the puppies, watching them play until it was quite dark. Sighing again, she went downstairs. Dinner had better be a good one tonight, because Duncan was not going to be too happy.

'It's nice to come home and smell something good coming from the kitchen. Had a good day?'

'Yes, dinner won't be long. Joyce Brown came over this afternoon.'

'Oh, yes, and what did she have to say?'

'She was very complimentary, said that two of them had show potential, and that I had made a good job of rearing them.'

'I should think so too, the amount of time you spend on them.'

After dinner Fiona brought the coffee in. 'Duncan, there is one small problem with the puppies. Joyce said that reputable breeders don't sell puppies at Christmas. You know those stickers that you see in car windows, "A dog is for life not for Christmas." She thinks that I should keep them until they are nine weeks old.'

'Out of the question.'

'Why?'

'Why? Because we have had them long enough. Sell them to people without children.'

'I can't. I want to make sure that the people are going to love them and treat them as real living beings.'

'This is getting ridiculous. I thought you said that that woman was going to help you sell them.'

'She is; someone is supposed to phone me shortly.'

'Good. Well, that will be one less. Only three to go.'

'No, I'm keeping the little girl that Joyce said was good. She'll be company for Sally.'

Duncan finished his coffee and put the cup down. 'Two things. What if I don't agree to having another dog in the house, and what do we do with them at Christmas? It's all organised with my mother and I'm sure that she has got everything ordered by now.'

'When was this arranged? You didn't say anything to me.'

'It's been obvious for weeks that, left to you, we wouldn't be having anything for Christmas. Have you made any arrangements?'

'No, I'm sorry about Christmas, I should have realised before but I've been so busy.'

'Yes, that's been the trouble. Too busy for anything but the puppies.'

Fiona felt that he had said that because, apart from the meals, she had often been too tired to make love to him in the past few weeks. How small-minded, she thought. 'I am genuinely sorry that I didn't realise that Christmas was so close and I'm sorry that your mother has made preparations, but the fact remains that they will be here over Christmas and I will have to look after them. Anyway, you don't object to me keeping one, do you?'

Duncan did not reply to her question but told her that he wanted nothing more to do with it. Furthermore, she must sort it out with his mother by explaining the situation with regard to the puppies, and seeing if a satisfactory compromise could be reached.

A difficult conversation followed with Duncan's mother. It became obvious that Duncan had agreed that they would go for the whole of Christmas Day and return on Boxing Day to spend that day with them as well. It was finally decided that they would go for dinner and tea on Christmas Day only. When Fiona put the phone down, she felt that she had been selfish and thoughtless, making everyone fit their Christmas around her and her puppies. Duncan received the news in silence, which made Fiona cringe inside again with guilt. I wonder, she thought, if things would have been like this if I had had a baby and not a litter.

In the event, Fiona did let the people have the puppy that

Joyce had put on to her. They were a retired couple and this was his retirement present from his wife. As they left the house with the puppy wrapped in a small blanket, Fiona felt so happy that she had been able to give such pleasure to someone.

That evening someone else phoned about the puppies.

'Hello, Fiona McCleod speaking.'

'Hello, Simon Philips here. I understand from Joyce Brown that you have a couple of dog puppies for sale and I am interested in buying one. Would it be possible for me to come over and see them?'

'Well, yes, although I only have one now. I have just sold the other one.'

'I understood from Joyce that she thought that one of the dogs was quite promising. Is that the one you've sold?'

'No, he's still here. Are you interested in showing him then?'

'Possibly, if he turns out okay.'

'Oh, I see.'

'Well, could I come round and see him? How would this evening suit you?'

'This evening – well I don't know...' – she saw Duncan nodding his head at her – 'I suppose it's alright; I'll give you our address.'

Although Simon Philips wanted to buy the puppy, he did not wish to take it until the Saturday after Christmas, and Fiona agreed. Duncan was very annoyed.

'Good heavens, Fiona, this means that we shall still have three puppies for Christmas!'

In consequence, they were very late in arriving for dinner on Christmas Day, as Fiona had insisted that the puppies had to have their dinner before they left. Duncan had been very annoyed and when she wanted to leave the moment they had had tea, he accused her of being extremely selfish and thoughtless in front of his parents, much to her embarrassment. It was agreed that he would go over to his parents on his own on Boxing Day for dinner. She felt a little let down about this arrangement but did not disagree with it, feeling that perhaps it was all her fault.

S IMON STOOD WATCHING the water as it flowed underneath
the bridge. It was four months now and he still missed him
like hell, he thought. If only they had not gone on that
blasted holiday. He could still remember how he had felt
when they arrived home, pleased beyond measure that the holiday
was over, pleased to be with his dogs again. Then he had seen
Peter's face. His brother had been staying at their house to look
after the dogs while they were away, and from the look on his face
something was wrong.

'I'm so very sorry, Simon, he was so fast. I just couldn't stop
him. I didn't realise that the side gate wasn't firmly shut. I did stop
the others but, honestly, one minute he was playing and the next
he was gone. I heard the screech of brakes and – well I'm just so
sorry.'

Simon had looked at his brother in disbelief. All he could say
was, 'Which one?'

'Harry.'

'Harry! No!' Simon had then kept his mouth firmly closed
because if he started he knew that he wouldn't be able to stop and
he knew deep down inside himself that it was not Peter's fault.
These things could happen in a matter of seconds. His brother
had tried to put a hand on his arm but he had shrugged it off. 'I'm
going for a walk,' he had said.

'That's right, go off and leave me to sort everything out,'
shouted Mary to his retreating back.

He hadn't even wanted to go on the bloody trip but Mary and
Sharon had kept on and on about a package holiday in Spain.
Everybody they knew had been to Spain but them, everybody said

it was a wonderful place with lots of sunshine and sangria. Simon shook his head. Sangria: it was like drinking spray polish! Mary and Sharon had spent nearly all their holiday covering themselves in suntan oil and frying on the beach so that they could show off their tan when they got home, and Barry had moaned that he missed his mates. What a bloody waste of money it had all been and then to come home to that.

Simon shivered and shrugged his shoulders. God, even when he had gone back home, Mary had been so unsympathetic. She had been loading the washing machine with some of their holiday clothes. 'Did you have to go off like that? Peter was upset enough. It's only just over a year, you know, since Ann died. He was doing us a favour, you know.' Simon had stood watching her as she started up the machine. Typical of her to start the bloody washing the moment she got home. Can't relax and enjoy herself and do nothing. Without a word he had gone into the kennel and shut the door. He started to groom the two remaining dogs. This always calmed him and he had brushed them both with the tears running down his face. Barry came into the kennel and in an embarrassed way had said how sorry he was and that he knew that Harry had been special. Simon had only nodded, unable to speak, and Barry had gone back into the house.

He had phoned his brother later that evening and apologised for going off. He told him that he knew that he wasn't really to blame. His brother, as always, had understood, and they had agreed to meet for a drink some time. He remembered that Barry had gone out to see his mates and Mary and Sharon had gone next door to tell them about the holiday. He had poured himself a bitter and had sat looking at some photographs of Harry. He had had such high hopes for Harry.

Decidedly cold now, Simon left the bridge and started to walk to his car. He had meant to look for Christmas presents when he came out, so he made his way to the town. As he wandered round the stores he was thinking of the New Year and what he would show without Harry. Meg was past her best now and she had never been as good as young Harry. If only Mary hadn't always been so against having a litter from Meg, he could have had a couple of hopefuls now. He had tried to explain all this to her but it had always ended with her absolutely refusing to have anything to do with the dogs. He had said that he would do everything if only she would feed them during the day, but she had still refused. Without her co-operation he knew that it was impossible. When he had asked her why she wouldn't even feed the puppies, the answer was always the same: that she had too much to do. The conversation then followed a predictable pattern, with Mary complaining that if he earned more money and if they had a better house she would have more time to do other things.

'Can I help you?' A young assistant was smiling at him and he found that he was staring at bottles of perfume. He bought a bottle of Mary's favourite scent and some jewellery for Sharon, and left the store. 'To hell with it,' he murmured as he walked to the car, 'it's my bloody Christmas, too.'

At home he phoned Joyce Brown – her stud dog was of similar breeding to Harry. He may have been used recently. Perhaps she would know of a dog puppy. As he replaced the receiver he turned to find Mary standing behind him.

'What's all that about then? You're not thinking of buying a puppy?'

'I'm only asking if there are any about.'

'Good, because if there is any spare money about, I could do with a new vacuum cleaner. That old one isn't picking up properly and I could do with some more money for presents. You spend enough on those dogs as it is.'

He was too tired for an argument so he told her that there were no puppies around anyway. Actually, Joyce had told him that some woman, new to showing, had had a litter from her stud dog. He really became interested when she said that the woman's bitch had been bred from the Emsworth lines. Joyce had told him that she was hoping to go and see them the next day and that if there were a promising dog, she would let him know or he could phone Fiona McCleod himself. He said that he would wait for her call. A tiny spark of enthusiasm was beginning to burn deep inside him. They might be rubbish and then he'd be disappointed, no, best leave it to Joyce, he could rely on her judgement.

Joyce phoned him a couple of days later. She had been to see the litter and told him that they were all nice puppies and that two of them definitely had some show potential. 'They are well worth a look anyway, Simon. See what you think, I'll give you her number.'

He phoned this Mrs McCleod straight away. She seemed a bit uncertain on the phone but did agree that he could go over to see them that evening. As soon as he had had his dinner, he told Mary that he was off to have a drink with Peter. Driving over, he felt excited; he knew that this was going to be a good one. This one would be even better than Harry.

Bit of money here, he thought, as he entered the drive of a big, modern detached house in an obviously 'nice' part of the town. Doesn't look like the usual 'doggy' premises. He rang the doorbell and it was quickly opened by an attractive woman. She was slim, medium height and had fairish hair down to her shoulders. Nice breasts under that jumper, too, he thought, as he held out his hand. 'Hello, Mrs McCleod, I'm Simon Philips, we spoke earlier on the phone.'

He was introduced to her husband and then he followed them upstairs to a bedroom. Three pairs of small brown eyes peered at him from a run.

'The other little boy went this morning.'

'Yes, do you mind if I pick them up. My hands are clean.'

'No, that's fine. Joyce phoned me to say that she had told you about them. I understand that you already show Cumbrians and want him for showing?'

'Yes, as I said, if he turns out to be good enough.' He proceeded to pick up each puppy and stand it on the table. Fiona noticed how very gentle his hands were and how the puppies responded to him.

After looking at the puppy for quite some time he said, 'Well, Mrs McCleod, I quite like this dog. What are you asking for him, and are you prepared to let me have him?'

She looked at Duncan, who nodded at her immediately. She herself had liked the man as soon as she had seen him in the light of the porch. Taller and slimmer than Duncan, he had a sensitive mouth and kind, brown eyes.

'Yes, Mr Philips, we'd be delighted to let you have Bracken. That's what I called him. When would you want to take him?'

'Would early Saturday morning be alright? It'll give me some time to sort out some food, etc.'

He arrived at nine o'clock on the Saturday, much to Fiona's surprise, but she quickly composed herself and invited him in. Duncan had just left to play golf. She gave him the Kennel Club registration papers and the pedigree, and asked if he would like a cup of coffee. At first he refused because he was so eager to get the puppy, but then decided to accept. Over coffee he talked about showing and about his other dogs. Fiona told him that she had shown a little but hoped to do more next year as she was keeping one of the bitch puppies. His enthusiasm was infectious and she found that she was really enjoying her conversation with him and didn't feel worried about Bracken's future. She felt that he would be in very safe hands.

'Could I see the puppy now?'

'Oh, of course, I'm so sorry. I was so interested in all your showing stories, I quite forgot.' She hurried upstairs and collected the puppy.

Simon was in the kennel, talking to the puppy as he stroked it. He wanted to spend as much time as possible with it to gain its confidence and to bond with it. 'It's almost New Year, young'un; soon have more time to play with you when the evenings draw out.' He put the puppy down and went indoors.

Ever since the unexpected arrival of the puppy and the ensuing row, his relationship with Mary and the general atmosphere in the house had been icy. Sharon had, as usual, sided with her mother and was not speaking to him either. He looked at the heavily decorated Christmas tree. Some New Year's Eve this is going to be, he thought. 'Do you fancy a coffee, Barry?' he shouted.

'Yes, okay, Dad,' Barry replied, never looking up from the TV screen.

Simon went out to the kitchen where Mary was making a cake. 'I'm making a cup of coffee; do you want one, Mary?' She ignored the question so he put the kettle on and got out two mugs. 'What's for dinner tonight, I'm starving.'

'You know that we're going next door to their party. You can eat there.'

Roll on next year, he thought. As he was drinking his coffee he suddenly saw a mental picture of Fiona McCleod as she spoke to him about the puppies. Her green eyes had lit up when she had smiled and really she wasn't bad looking. Nice curves too, though a bit strait-laced perhaps.

On impulse he went to the phone and dialled her number. 'Hello, Mrs McCleod, this is Simon Philips here. Just to let you know that the pup is fine and settling in okay.'

'Oh, thank you so much for letting me know. I've been wondering how he's getting on. Do your other two dogs like him?'

'Yes, no problems, and he didn't turn a hair when he saw them.'

'I've sold the other one now, but she isn't going until after the New Year holiday.'

'Very wise. Well, Happy New Year, Mrs McCleod.'

'And a Happy New Year to you, Mr Philips. Bye.'

He stood there for a moment, looking at the phone. I'd have a better New Year there than I'm going to have here, he thought.

Fiona was thinking about what a warm, deep voice he had. She could still see him quite clearly, handling the puppies and talking to her about his other dogs. He had very expressive, artistic hands with long, slender fingers, which he used repeatedly to explain a point. He seemed to understand her feelings about the dogs far better than Duncan and also obviously enjoyed the competition of showing very much. She sighed. This will not do, she thought; we are supposed to be at Laura and Michael's party later this evening. I really must get ready.

FIONA WATCHED HEATHER, the puppy, develop with intense pleasure. Having delivered her and having seen her every single day of her life was, to her, a gift of immense value. Opening her eyes, her first steps, her first bark – all of these things were a wonder. Any thoughts it brought of how much more wonderful it would have been if it were her baby were quickly dismissed from her mind. She did entertain strong doubts though now as to whether she should have agreed with Duncan that they wouldn't adopt a baby, but it was all too late to speculate on that now. Duncan only tolerated this new addition to the household and after a few rejected overtures, the puppy learnt not to bother him.

As winter turned to spring, Fiona was able to see that Joyce had been right in her choice. She felt that she was 'getting her eye in' as the established breeders said. It meant that she was beginning to distinguish between a good show dog and a not-so-good one.

She was impatient for May to arrive, when Heather would be six months old and could be shown. She was going to be so proud to take her into the ring. She had had two phone calls from Simon Philips to let her know how Bracken was progressing. He was apparently very pleased with his progress and was also keen to show him. She was still attending the training classes with Sally and Heather and felt far more confident in her handling of Heather than she had with Sally. There was, however, still a problem with Duncan. She wondered if it had been because of the trouble over Christmas, or because she had gone against his wishes, but he still steadfastly refused to accept Heather. She had been a good puppy too; her only real crime had been to bite neatly all the heads off Duncan's daffodils. Fiona just couldn't understand why he was being so unreasonable – the pup didn't really affect their life together.

She had entered both Sally and Heather for Heather's first show. She got up very early because she knew that it was going to take her longer to get two dogs ready and into the car in their travelling cages. She had bought herself a grooming table with the money her father had given her for Christmas presents.

She felt quite professional as she set off. Duncan had refused to come. It was forty miles to this show's venue. It was an outdoor one and part of an agricultural show. She had entered it because it had classes for Cumbrians.

As she approached the dog show area, she saw Simon Philips already near the show ring, getting his dogs prepared. She could see that he had Bracken with him and started to walk across to him.

He looked up. 'Hello, nice to see you. I didn't know you were coming to this show. What do you think of him?'

'He looks gorgeous.' She quickly put up her table and started grooming her dogs. When it was time for the puppy class both she and Simon walked into the ring. There were five puppies altogether in the class and Fiona was delighted when Bracken was pulled out first and got the red rosette. Heather came third.

'Congratulations,' she said to Simon as they walked out of the ring.

'No, the congratulations are yours. You bred both the first and the third.' He smiled. 'You wait, this is only the beginning. Come on, I'll buy you a cuppa to celebrate.'

As she sat drinking the tea, she studied his face. He was so alive. Was he older or younger than her? She hadn't noticed that his hair was dark brown. He had nice teeth, too.

'So shall we do that then?' he concluded.

'Oh, I'm sorry, I didn't quite hear what you said.'

'Shall we both enter Windsor Championship Show? It's no good our entering Open shows – we shall be competing against each other in the puppy classes. At the Champ shows we shall be in separate classes, won't we. I reckon they'll both be in with a chance by July.'

'Windsor Championship Show! I've never been to one. I'm not ready for one yet, and neither is Heather.'

'Of course, you are. They're no different from Open shows – just bigger and a hell of a lot more expensive. Just do what you did today. Okay then, that's settled.'

'But do you think Heather is good enough?'

'Yes I do, okay, but you'll have to be quick and get a schedule because entries are closing soon.'

As Fiona drove home with the dogs, she reflected on how her life was changing. She drove more, she knew more people, and there was now so much to do and to plan ahead for. She didn't feel quite such a failure now. As she turned into the drive she remembered that she had not made any arrangements for dinner that morning. Perhaps Duncan would have thought of it.

Duncan hadn't, and when she asked him to get some fish and chips he went off in a very sullen mood. Her happiness of the day evaporated in a cloud of guilt.

At two more Open shows where there were Cumbrian classes, Heather got a first in Puppy and Best Puppy in Breed at one show and second at the other. Fiona began to think that Simon Philips had been right in saying that Heather was good. She hadn't seen him again and Windsor was fast approaching. She wondered whether she should contact him and tell him that she had entered for Windsor and then thought better of it – for him it was just another show.

The weekend before the show, he did ring, much to her relief.

'Hello, Simon Philips here. Remember me? Did you manage to enter for Windsor?'

'Yes, I did.'

'Well, how about I pick you up and we share petrol expenses? It'll save a bit, won't it?'

'Oh, I… um, I suppose so. Yes, that would be a great help.'

'If I pick you up about 6.30 a.m., will that be alright? How many dogs will you be bringing?'

'I've only entered Heather – you know, the puppy.'

'That's fine. Plenty of room for the cage. Okay, see you about 6.30 a.m.'

She stood looking at the phone for a few minutes. She hadn't really thought about the expense of showing before. The Championship-show entries were, without doubt, much more expensive than the Open show. She presumed that he had a wife and family so money was very likely a bit tight. She hadn't thought of that before.

Waiting in the hall with Heather, her table, bag and cages, she was tense with excitement. Her first Championship show and, she had to admit, she was looking forward to going with Simon Philips. She heard a car turn into the drive and called up to Duncan, 'I'm off now, Duncan, see you this evening. Enjoy your golf.' There was no reply; he had been very against her going out for the whole day, and in Simon Philips's car. She had explained about the monetary side of it, but he hadn't seemed very impressed. She closed the door quietly and Simon helped her put everything in the back of his rather old Volvo estate.

Fiona found that the journey to Windsor sped by, with Simon telling her about some of the ups and downs of dog showing. She discovered that he had been showing dogs for ten years and had a wife, Mary, and two teenage children.

There were ten puppies in Simon's class and Fiona clapped enthusiastically when the judge pulled him out for first place. He came out of the ring and straight up to Fiona, giving her a quick hug. 'How about that then? We've got a good'un here.'

He released her and smiled. She was so shaken at her response to his touch that she could only smile weakly. Having congratulated him, she hurried away to her bench and poured herself a cup of coffee. What is happening to me, she thought. Heavens, I hardly know the man. He's married and I'm a happily married woman. Don't be ridiculous, she thought, there was nothing in it – just the excitement of the moment – but she could still feel the warmth of his arm around her and the closeness of his body.

She tried to avoid him for the rest of the day. Heather's class had seventeen entries so when she was pulled out in fifth place she was overjoyed. Simon came over to her. 'Hard luck. Never mind, she was looking good. You'll do better next time.'

The return journey was quieter. Both of them were tired.

Simon talked a bit about some of the other dogs that had been there. He suggested a couple of other Championship shows that it might be to their advantage to attend and said that if she were happy about it, he could pick her up again, because it certainly helped with the expenses. I was right, she thought, this is for the expenses.

As they were nearing her house, he asked her if she had a job and if she had a family. She answered very briefly and said that she would let him know about the shows.

During that summer he did take her to two more Championship shows. He was polite and friendly, but never attempted to hug her again. She did notice, though, that other people, mostly women, did congratulate winners in this way, so it was obviously the thing to do. She loved the spectacle of these big summer shows with their massive white marquees. She liked to feel that she was part of it as they drove into the entrance to the show with their car sticker on the windscreen.

She learnt a lot more about showing, too, from Simon, and felt that she was far more competent and confident now. He told her not to let other exhibitors upstage her in the line-up by standing their dogs more in front so as to partially obscure her dog from the judge. He taught her not to let other exhibitors walk their dog close up behind her dog in the ring, thereby upsetting the movement of her dog. She was beginning to see that not everyone's advice was genuine – some of it was bad. She was now able to see that in dog showing some people thought that anything was fair in order to win. She just hadn't seen it before but it did harden her resolve to do better.

She and Duncan had hired a cottage on the Isle of Anglesey for their summer holiday. Duncan had wanted to hire a villa in Portugal but Fiona had refused to kennel the dogs and it had ended with this compromise and a long sulk from Duncan. The holiday was not, understandably, a great success. The weather was rather wet and the dogs kept getting muddy. Fiona, once again, felt that it was all her fault for being so selfish. Duncan reminded her several times that they could have been enjoying the sun and the wine of Portugal. I suppose it is all my fault, she thought, I'm the one causing all the upsets. We got on so well before I had the dogs. Perhaps I shouldn't show them any more. Perhaps I should put them in kennels. It isn't being fair to Duncan.

While she was thinking these thoughts and cooking a meal, Duncan was walking along the beach. The rain had stopped, Fiona was cooking, and he was at a loose end. It's because we didn't have a baby, he thought. She was fine until then, perfectly agreeable. Those damned dogs have changed her out of all recognition, all those damned classes and shows and I don't like her going with that Simon Philips either. We used to have decent evenings but now she's always out grooming. If we go out with friends, all she talks about are the damned dogs and as for the fiasco of last Christmas and the damned puppies. He kicked another pebble along the sand and turned back towards the cottage.

They were both pleased to be home again, although neither admitted it. Gone was the warm, easy friendship they had had – even the lovemaking was dutiful on her part, which again gave her feelings of guilt. He privately felt pleased to see how the garden was progressing and to play golf on the Sunday morning. She, in turn, was eager to check the dog magazines for forthcoming shows. There were quite a few messages for her on the answering machine from doggy acquaintances and her recent feelings of guilt began to fade a little. She had been there for him ever since they had been married, cooking, cleaning, decorating, obedient to his every whim. Now, for the first time, she had something of her own and he was sulking. Well, she thought, I think that I've earned something just for me; after all, I don't sulk about his golf.

The rest of the year continued much the same. The more she learned about the dog show game, even the dirty side, the more she wanted to know. One early morning in December, Simon picked her and the dogs up to travel north for the LKA Championship show. It was a bitterly cold day and they said very little as they drove to Birmingham. Simon seemed tense and Fiona wondered if something was wrong.

He still seemed tense when he went into the ring and Fiona watched as the judge went over Bracken. She knew the judge slightly, having been introduced to him by Simon some time back. The two men were quite good friends, both having started in showing at about the same time. He gave Bracken a first in his class.

After the Open dog class, Simon went into the ring again with Bracken to challenge the other first-prize winners for the CC. The winner of the Open class was given the CC, but then Simon and Bracken won the Res. CC! She knew that Simon was pleased as he walked round the ring for the lap of honour. He hurried up to her, his face alight with success. He put his arm round her and kissed her. All sound, all sight disappeared and her whole being seemed focused on his lips. They stood and looked at each other for a second, quite oblivious of their surroundings.

Simon was the first to move. 'Hey, how's that then? Crufts, here I come. Didn't I tell you he was a good'un? Reserve CC at a year old.'

They moved apart as a man came up to them and slapped Simon on the back. 'Well done, sir.' He looked at Fiona. 'Is this your lovely wife?'

'Heavens no, this is Fiona McCleod. She bred the dog.'

'Hello Fiona, I'm Paul Aston, nice to meet you. I'm sure to see you around now that I know you.'

Fiona looked up as she shook his hand. Paul Aston was tall and well built – you could imagine him on a rugby pitch. Red hair, twinkling blue eyes and freckles completed the picture. 'Hello Paul, it's nice to meet you.'

Fiona got a fourth in her class with Heather and when the time came for them to leave the show, it was almost dark and still very cold. Simon was still on a high and suggested that they stop somewhere for a celebratory drink and a meal. 'Got to celebrate my first Res. CC. Got to mark the occasion.'

At the pub they decided that they ought to phone home to say that they would be a little late back. Mary couldn't be bothered to come to the phone when Simon called and told Barry to say that she hadn't bothered with a dinner for him anyway. Duncan was very angry when Fiona explained the situation and complained that, once again, he was going to have to get a takeaway. He just doesn't appreciate what a big moment this is, she thought, as she walked back to the lounge bar.

After the meal and a couple of whiskies they were both feeling a bit jaded but her heart nearly stopped when Simon suddenly said, 'Look, Fiona, I'm suddenly feeling shattered. What say we stay the night here – separate rooms, of course. This isn't a try-on, honestly.'

Fiona hesitated. She had never been in a situation like this. Did he mean what he said? What about Duncan? He'd be furious. 'Well, I don't know, I mean don't you think that you could drive?'

'I think that I'd like a couple of hours' sleep first. So we might as well have a good night's sleep in comfort and set off early tomorrow.

'Could I drive the car for you?'

'No, 'fraid not. You're not covered on my insurance and you've had a couple of whiskies, too.'

'Oh, dear, well, I'd better phone Duncan again. He won't be too pleased.' She was relieved to get the answerphone. In her room she had a shower, rinsed out her pants and tights and prepared for bed. Without a nightie the sheets felt rather cold at first, but she soon warmed up and, yawning, turned out the light and fell asleep almost immediately.

The knocking on the door awoke her. 'Fiona, Fiona, it's me, Simon.'

'Is something the matter? Are the dogs alright?'

'Yes, I checked on them before I went to bed. Could I come in for a minute? I want to tell you something.'

She wrapped the bedspread round her and opened the door. He came in and just stood looking at her. He was wrapped in a large bath towel. Embarrassed, she sat on the bed.

'Fiona, I woke up and I…' he stopped speaking and just stood there for a moment. 'Fiona, finding you and that puppy was the best thing that's happened to me in years and I just…' He stopped and came forward and, taking her up in his arms, kissed her.

As their lips touched an all-consuming fire was lit in Fiona. Between passionate kisses he held her at arm's length and removed the bedspread, at the same time dropping his towel. His eyes roamed over her body. 'My God, Fee, you're beautiful.'

Panting and trembling like a leaf, she could not reply. He then laid her gently on the bed and turned her over. For a second, Fiona feebly protested, but he started to kiss and caress her feet and slowly worked his way up her long, slim legs and back, ending with her neck. He then turned her over and started to kiss and caress her toes. Fiona was beyond speech or movement; every bit of her body was bursting with passion. He moved to her nipples, caressing his way down her belly with his lips while still stroking her nipples. As he kissed her between her parted legs, she arched her back and shouted at him, clawing at his back, pulling his hair, lost to everything but the overwhelming demands of her body. Their union was instant bliss for her.

She lay in the now dark room, Simon's lovely, hard body beside her. Her thoughts were a racing jumble of amazement, delight and guilt. She had never experienced anything like that wonderful seduction, that explosion of sensual pleasure. Her thoughts strayed back to those glorious, last moments of fulfilment and, sighing deeply, she turned over and slipped into a dreamless sleep. She was awakened by Simon's tongue licking her hard nipples. She groaned and stretched, opening her legs and arching her back.

After a very hurried breakfast, they were both quiet as they drove home the next morning. Every now and again he turned his head and smiled at her, and once he told her that she had made him happier than he had thought possible. As the car ate up the miles, she relived the happenings of the night and his words of that morning. He couldn't know what those words meant to her. Duncan had always said that she was beautiful, but had never enjoyed her whole body as Simon had and had never awakened the passion in her that Simon had. She suddenly realised that she had felt ugly ever since those attempts to have a baby had failed.

Sitting in the car she relived how womanly, attractive and alluring she had felt, such alien feelings. She looked across at Simon. Heavens, she was an adulteress, she had been unfaithful to Duncan. So why didn't she feel guilty? Sensing her gaze, he looked at her and smiled, and she sighed and smiled back.

TRYING DESPERATELY TO look normal as she put her key in the door and called to Duncan, Fiona let out a huge sigh of relief when he didn't reply. Of course, she thought, it's Sunday – he was going with Michael to watch a golf tournament. She was rather disappointed to see that he had not left her a note, as he usually did. She quickly saw to the dogs' meal and then let them out into the garden. Now, she thought, I must have a long, hot bath and wash my hair.

As she ran her soapy hands over her body she thought of Simon's long slender fingers and how they had caressed her in ways that Duncan had never done, how his mouth... She gasped. Here she was in Duncan's house in his bath, his wife, thinking... Quickly she got up and started to dry herself vigorously. What had she been thinking of, what had she done! She must cook Duncan a lovely dinner and clean the house from top to bottom.

She stuck to her plan, although the sheer wonder of last night kept coming back into her mind. When Duncan did come home she was able to say with all honesty how tired she was. He too was rather quiet and did not cross-examine her, much to her relief.

On the whole, the next couple of months were both exciting and worrying for Fiona. The week after she had got back from the show had been very difficult, not that there had been an argument. Duncan had merely listened to her explanation of Simon's tiredness and had then maintained a sulky silence for the rest of the week. Things had been very cool between them and they had not made love, much to her relief. In herself she felt as if she had had a weight lifted from her shoulders. She felt younger, vibrant and more aware of her surroundings.

However, she also felt very guilty with regard to Duncan. She had betrayed his trust and he didn't deserve that; he was and always had been a kind and loving man. She had changed, there was no other explanation for how she now felt. With all these conflicting emotions constantly occupying her mind, she felt a need to talk to someone. On one of their walks together she had, without mentioning Simon, tried to explain her new outlook on life to Laura, but soon realised that Laura was so busy with her children and the ordinary necessities of life that she was not really listening to what she was saying.

She was relieved when Duncan said that his mother had suggested that they just go over for dinner and tea on Christmas Day. Duncan's parents came over to them on New Year's Day, and so did her father.

Remembering Simon's advice, she took care at the next couple of Open shows that she attended to see that no one upstaged her dog in any way. With her new-found confidence, she began to see that it was not always the best dog who won the classes. She began to win with Heather and twice got BOB. Some of the exhibitors who had always been so helpful and friendly in the past now almost ignored her. She began to see for herself that this game was fiercely competitive and often taken extremely seriously by most exhibitors. Yes, she thought, some of them want to win by fair means or foul. I'm learning.

Looking in the mirror one morning, she decided that she needed a change of hairstyle. She had had her hair shoulder length ever since she had met Duncan, but it didn't suit her lifestyle any more. Making an appointment for the following day, she had it cut short in a modern, easy-to-manage style.

Duncan was most upset when he arrived home that evening. 'Good God, what have you done to your hair? It looks awful.'

'I had it cut short because it's easier to manage at shows.'

'Well, it doesn't suit you.'

She was in a turmoil of indecision. It was Crufts Show in a week's time. Simon wanted her to go with him. He had asked her twice now but she had hesitated because she knew that if she went, she would want to make love to him again. Did he want to make love to her again, though? Had she been an easy one-night stand? The whole thing was decided for her when she went down with a bad bout of flu. Duncan commented that she had brought it upon herself with that silly haircut. Simon had rung when he got home from the show but Duncan had answered the phone. He asked Duncan to tell Fiona that Bracken had done well and got a first, but had not gone further.

Her next Championship show was in April. Simon had begged her to enter this one and she had not been able to refuse. Waiting for him to pick her up, she was flushed with excitement. Duncan, looking at her, remarked that he thought that she was getting another cold and perhaps she would be wise not to go. Yes, she thought, I would be wise not to go, but I've been wise for over forty years and now I want to do this. She assured him that she felt well and when Simon rang the doorbell she hurriedly collected the dog and her showing equipment.

Out of sight of the house Simon stopped the car and kissed her. 'God, you've no idea how much I wanted to do that.'

On the journey she told him about her new observations at the Open shows.

'Good Lord, you've only just begun to scratch the surface. What about the phone calls to judges before a show, promising them small gifts and, at the same time, telling them how well a particular dog has been doing.'

'No, are you serious?'

'Of course I am; I was even phoned up the night before I last judged at an Open show and offered two tickets to a football match.'

'What did you do?'

'Ah, that's for me to know and for you to find out. By the way, you do realise that it's Paul Aston judging today?'

'Yes, I did know,' she replied, at the same time suddenly aware of the rather tight and revealing jumper she had decided to put on that morning.

Simon again got a first in his class but did not get anywhere in the challenge. Fiona too came first in her class and was delighted – her very first first at Championship-show level. She did not go any further either, though.

'Couldn't expect it,' said Simon.

'Why?'

'Well, he's currently having a fling with the woman who got the bitch CC and the reserve CC went to a woman who let him have a promising bitch for nothing.'

'But that's unfair.'

'Unfair or not, my sweet, that's how the dog game operates. We've done okay today. How's about we leave now and stop off for a meal somewhere?'

Her heart lurched. She had been so afraid that he wouldn't suggest it. She packed her show gear and went to the Ladies. There were two northern, Cumbrian exhibitors in there. They looked at her and smiled. 'Hello, you had a good day today. You off now, luv?'

'Yes, I did thank you, and yes, I'm just leaving.'

'With Simon, no doubt. Did he give you a lift again?' They looked at each other and smiled knowingly.

Fiona smiled and rushed out of the door. She was appalled. How did they know?

When she recounted the conversation to Simon, he laughed. 'You may feel that you have learned all about the show scene, but let me tell you that gossip is a sub-culture; everyone tries to find out everything they can about other exhibitors. They'll even make up things.'

'But why?'

'You never know when a juicy bit of gossip could be used to do someone down. That way you may go up a bit. After all, it's not much different from the rest of life, is it?' As he said this, he drove into a motel. 'Now, tell me if I've got it all wrong, but I thought that we could take a room and leave at about ten. What do you say?'

Fiona could only look at him and nod her head. They had a quick, light meal and immediately went to their room. He took her in his arms as soon as he shut the door and put the lights on. 'My God, if you only knew, woman, how I have waited for this.' He kissed her urgently and started to undress her; taking off her jumper and bra he cupped her breasts in his hands, kissing her nipples until they were hard. With his mouth sucking on one nipple, he started to remove her trousers.

She was trembling and gasping for breath as she shakily undid the buttons on his shirt. Their lovemaking was urgent and fast the first time, but when his hands and lips began to explore her body again he urged her to do the same to him. Shyly at first, she stroked his flesh with her fingertips but as her passion rose, her hands became more demanding, opening up feelings that she did not know existed. Their passion was intense and satisfying.

Lying in his arms, exhausted, she felt more beautiful than she had ever felt in her life. She giggled.

'What are you laughing at?'

'Just me,' she murmured. 'Just me, I feel so wonderful that I'm laughing for me.'

'You're crazy.'

They grinned at each other, kissed, and then ruefully got up and gathered their scattered clothes from the floor.

When she arrived home she apologised for her late arrival and said that they had stopped for a meal. As was often the case nowadays, Duncan said very little. He poured himself a whisky and said that he had gone to a Chinese restaurant for a meal because there wasn't much in the house, and returned to watch the television. He did not reply when she said that she had left a meal all ready in the fridge, which only needed putting in the microwave.

The following month she decided to mate Sally again to Joyce Brown's dog, and made the arrangements. With her new self-assurance she ordered a small purpose-built kennel to hold six dogs. They had a big garden, as did their neighbours, so she didn't think that it would be a problem. Duncan, she already knew, would not have any more dogs in the house, and if she wanted to keep any of the puppies – and she did – they would have to be reared in the kennel. It was only after she had arranged for a builder to come on the following Monday to lay the concrete floor that she told Duncan.

'No, absolutely not,' he shouted at her, his face going red with fury. 'How dare you do this without my permission? I will not allow you to build a kennel in my garden. You can cancel it now.'

'I'm sorry, but I have already paid for it. After all, I did it because you won't have any more dogs in the house.'

'Paid for or not, you will phone now and cancel it. What do you mean, more dogs?'

'Well, I'm mating Sally again and—'

'What! Over my dead body,' Duncan shouted.

'I told you that I was mating Sally again and this time, if they are any good, I should like to keep a dog as well as a bitch, so that I can have a stud dog.'

'Have you gone stark raving mad, Fiona? Two more dogs; a stud dog. I suppose all this was decided when you had your cosy little dinners with Simon Philips.'

'No, actually I haven't spoken to him about it. This is my hobby and I make up my own mind what to do.'

'It may be your hobby, my girl, but may I remind you that I also live here and that I own half of this house and garden.'

'Yes, that's true, you do; and may I ask you what this house is for if we don't live in it; we merely exist in it. At least the dogs bring it to life. It doesn't look like some damned show house on a new estate now.' For a second she thought that Duncan would slap her face but, after one long, angry look, he went into the hall and a few seconds later she heard the car start up.

It being Sunday, she had some housework to catch up on so, sighing, she went upstairs to change the sheets and towels and so on and put them in the wash. Then, still feeling rather angry herself and, she had to admit, somewhat guilty and unfair, she embarked on a thorough clean of the house.

Later, she suddenly realised that Duncan had been out for six hours. His golf bag was in the hall so he wasn't at the club. Perhaps he was with Michael and Laura. She dialled their number but only got the answerphone. She then dialled his parents' number.

'Hello, Helen McCleod speaking.'

'Hello, it's Fiona here. Is Duncan with you?'

There was a slight pause before she said, 'Yes, as a matter of fact he is. He has had Sunday dinner with us as I gather from him that there is very little to eat in your house. You have apparently been too busy lately to keep the larder stocked. Really, Fiona.'

Fiona was furious. How could Duncan go running to his mother like that and say that there was nothing to eat? He had never done anything like that before. 'Actually, Helen, I was just preparing dinner and was wondering when to expect Duncan home. Now I shan't have to bother.'

She replaced the receiver, went into the kitchen, sat down and burst into tears. The two dogs immediately came over to her and she fondled their heads. 'What a mess, what an awful mess.'

Casting her mind back over the past couple of years, she tried to see what had gone wrong. After that awful business over the failure of the IVF programme, they had had to do something else or go mad. He had taken up the golf, she the dog showing. She had had no idea that she would find the showing, the feeling of competition, so addictive. She loved the thought of being part of a huge countrywide group of people dedicated to dog showing. She was a different person now, she wanted more enjoyment from life, more excitement. This she had found with Simon but Duncan, as far as she knew, didn't know about that. She was still very fond of Duncan and their life together was still very much as it had been, so surely all this upset today wasn't just about cooking a dinner.

'ANOTHER PINT DUNCAN?'

Duncan continued sitting in silence opposite Michael. They had played a round of golf that morning but it had been pretty disastrous, with Duncan playing so badly it was obvious that his mind was on something else.

Michael looked at him. He'd certainly lost a bit of weight lately and he didn't look as well turned out as he usually did. 'How's Fiona and the dogs? Has the litter arrived yet?'

This questioning only brought a slight response from Duncan, who frowned and grunted as he shifted in his chair. Michael realised that there was definitely something wrong. He sat there quietly drinking his beer and waited to see if Duncan would say any more.

After a while, Duncan roused himself, sighed and straightened his back. 'Sorry, Michael, the truth is that the litter has not arrived yet and Fiona is alright – no, the real truth is that I don't bloody know any more how she is or even who she is these days. I don't bloody know the sense of anything.' He took a drink from his glass. 'Why, oh why, couldn't we have had that baby? I keep thinking that if only she had had that child, she wouldn't have wanted the bloody dog. She's changed, Michael, changed out of all recognition since she had that dog.'

Michael frowned. 'What do you mean exactly? Changed how?'

'For heaven's sake, Michael, you and Laura have seen her, she even looks different with that awful hair and those tight jeans and jumpers. When did you last see her looking smart?'

'Well, she certainly looks a bit slimmer and she has changed her hair a bit but she's still—'

'It's not just that though. *She* is different, she's not my Fiona. She's...' He paused, frowning, trying to find the right words. 'I don't know exactly, I can't explain it. Just everything is different.'

They sat on for a while, finishing their drinks, and without saying any more they went out to Michael's car. Just as Michael was about to put the key in the ignition, Duncan said, 'Look, if you're not in a hurry, Michael, I'd like to talk about it. I shall go mad if I don't. You've known us for a long time now and the truth is I don't know what the hell to do; I really don't. It's not just the dogs, it's the house, it's us, it's everything. She doesn't look after the house as she used to, she's always out in the shed grooming the dogs or off to training classes or shows. If she's not doing that, she's on the phone or reading the dog papers or filling in bloody schedules for more dog shows. I can't even have a conversation with her in the evenings like we used to do without it getting switched round to the dogs and she's – well she's not loving as she used to be, if you know what I mean. Honestly, Michael, I just don't know what to do to put things right.'

Michael felt out of his depth. In all the years that they had known Fiona and Michael, their friendship had never been very intimate and he found these revelations to be rather embarrassing. 'Perhaps it's just a reaction to not having a baby?'

'No, that's what I put it down to at first, but it's been a couple of years now.'

'Yes, well, you know what they say, if you can't beat 'em, join 'em. Why don't you take up the dogs as a hobby as well?'

'I did go to a couple of shows at first and I was totally bored out of my mind. I couldn't identify with the show or the people – certainly not the people. They're hardly group one in the socio-economic scale. How can someone like Fiona enjoy the company of people like that? They have all got to be mindless to go to all that expense and effort to win a paltry piece of paper. Fiona has a good brain. Why can't she see all this?'

'Have you asked her?'

'Of course I have, time and time again. All she says is that she finds it stimulating. It makes her feel alive.'

Here the conversation petered out and after a minute or two, Michael started up the car and drove home.

After the children had gone to bed that evening and all the toys had been put away, Michael poured a glass of wine for Laura and himself and sat down. 'Did I have a morning with Duncan,' he said rhetorically.

'I thought that you weren't your usual cheery self when you came home. What was the matter?'

He gave her a résumé of the morning's events and the conversation he had had with Duncan in the car.

'Well, it must be bad if Duncan spoke about it – he's hardly the chatty sort normally, is he? Fiona has never said anything to me but, on reflection, we do talk mostly about children and dogs. She's very keen, you know, on showing them and takes it quite seriously.'

'Obviously, I don't think we should say anything but perhaps you could gently lead the conversation round to Duncan the next time you meet her. You're good at that sort of thing, especially when you want me to do something.' They both laughed and turned the TV on.

An opportunity presented itself a few days later when Fiona phoned to say that the litter had been born and Sally and the puppies – there were four again – were doing well. Laura arranged to go over to see them the following day. After cooing over the puppies and praising Sally, Laura went down to the kitchen, where Fiona had made some tea.

'What lovely puppies. They look so sturdy already. What do you think of them, Fiona?'

'I think that they're better than the first litter.'

'They're so pretty. Did she have an easy birth?'

'Yes, no problems at all, and quite quick, too. You know, if they turn out to be good I might keep a dog and a bitch this time.'

'A dog and a bitch! But, Fiona, you'd have four dogs to look after then; how would you manage with the library as well?'

'No problems, I'm thinking of advertising for someone to come in during the day and exercise them. I shall keep the two new ones in the kennel. Of course, it will mean more grooming for me, especially when they are ready for showing. If the dog does well at the shows and I use him for stud work, then perhaps I shall have to think again.'

'Stud work! Fiona, don't you think that's a bit ambitious?'

'No, I shall get someone to show me the ropes first. People are so very helpful in the dog world, you know, Laura. I want to try it, anyway. It would be so interesting to see the puppies. It's what I want to do, Laura.'

While Fiona had been speaking Laura had been quietly looking round the kitchen and across the hall at the lounge. She didn't think that the house was too neglected but she had to admit that it wasn't quite as it used to be – no flowers in the vase, some dust on the surfaces, cushions not plumped up, books and papers left about. It didn't smell as fresh as it used to. She looked straight at Fiona. 'And what about Duncan? Is he as keen as you in all this?'

'He's got his work and his golf. Quite frankly, Laura, I used to think that we were quite close, on the same wavelength, but really I think that we're poles apart. He's got so staid, so dull, so boring. I've met so many people through dog showing. They travel all over the country; it's wonderful. There is always so much to do, to achieve, to learn and to talk about. I'm sure that you would understand if you could come to a few shows.'

Looking at Fiona while she was talking, Laura began to get the feeling that there was more to this than she was saying. She obviously enjoyed it, that was apparent, but her face was glowing and alive. She suddenly looked younger. There is a man in this somewhere, she thought. I wonder if it could be the one who takes her to the shows. She doesn't mention him much.

Laura suddenly felt out of her depth and sorry for them both. Quickly finishing her tea, she made her excuses and left. That evening she told Michael of her visit and of her fears.

'Um, Laura, I think that we should stay out of this, don't you?'

For the next eight weeks Fiona was rushed off her feet. Her advert had not borne fruit and she had all the cleaning, feeding, exercising and grooming to do herself, as well as her work. She felt exhausted and, apart from doing the washing and the ironing, the house was totally neglected. She did give herself a pat on the back, though, for having the foresight to cook and freeze several dinners so that they could be quickly microwaved in the evening. As far as she knew, Duncan never once went to see the litter in the bedroom. On several occasions he told her not to bother with a dinner that evening, as he would be eating out. She guessed that he was going to his mother's, but she was so relieved that she didn't have to cook a meal that she didn't ask any questions. She would make it up to him when the pups had gone.

When she had sold two of the puppies, she moved the other two into the outside kennel. She had had the run attached to the kennel made bigger while the pups were still in the house. She had tried to discuss this addition beforehand with Duncan, but he had ignored her. The extended run and the path to the kennel had taken up more of Duncan's lawn. He had glared at it when he came home, turned on his heel and slammed out of the house without speaking. He had not returned until around midnight when he had gone to bed without speaking to Fiona, who had waited up for him.

This situation became the norm, with only the most essential things being spoken about. Fiona couldn't wait to start going to the shows again and to chat to people. She was longing to see Simon again. The first show that she had entered was on a Sunday and she asked Duncan if he would feed the puppies for her while she was there. Without looking at her he replied, 'Don't expect me to do anything for those dogs in future. You well know my feelings about them; I do not want them in my house or my garden and the sooner they go the better.'

This presented Fiona with quite a problem. She went to the show, which luckily wasn't far away, and came home as soon as she had finished her class. As she had got BOB, it meant that she wasn't able to stay for the BIS challenge. It was obvious that this was going to crop up again and again so she decided to put an advert in the local paper for someone to see to the dogs when she was at a show.

A girl of fourteen answered the advertisement. She was very fond of dogs but, as her family lived in a flat, she was unable to have one of her own. The dogs took to her immediately and Fiona thought that she would be very suitable. They discussed her duties and how much Fiona would pay her, and she left.

Immediately Duncan came into the garden and angrily demanded to know what was going on. Fiona told him of her arrangement with the girl. His voice got louder and louder as he informed her that this was still his home, not a damned dog kennel, and she could get rid of that girl now. She calmly told him that she had had to do it because of his childish refusal to feed the dogs.

Relations between them were becoming very strained indeed, but Fiona felt that it was all due to Duncan being so unreasonable about her hobby. She felt, too, that he was secretly jealous of the dogs because, up until then she had devoted all her thoughts and time to him and the house.

One evening, as they were sitting quietly watching the television, the phone rang and a voice she did not recognise spoke. 'Hello, may I speak to Fiona McCleod?'

'Fiona McCleod speaking.'

'Hello, Fiona, this is Paul Aston here; do you remember? I judged your bitch at the LKA last year?'

'Hello, Paul, yes I remember you.'

'Well, from the grapevine, I understand that you have been running on a couple of puppies, a dog and a bitch. Is that right?'

'Yes, it is.'

'You sound surprised – the old grapevine is very strong in the dog world, you know. Anyway, why I am phoning is to ask you if you would be prepared to sell me the bitch. You see, I had been running a bitch on and unfortunately her teeth aren't quite right so I'm looking to replace her.'

'I see, well, I don't know. I shall have to consider it.'

'She's shaping up well, is she, teeth, etc?'

'Oh yes, she's very promising I think.'

'Good, well, can I leave you to mull it over? Perhaps you could let me know in a day or two.'

Replacing the receiver, Fiona's mind was in a confusion of thoughts. She hadn't ever dreamed that someone like Paul Aston, a Championship-show judge, would want one of her puppies. She wanted to phone Simon for his advice, but she had never phoned his home before. She hesitated for a moment and then picked up the phone and tapped out his number. 'Hello, could I possibly speak to Simon Philips, please?'

A young girl's voice said, 'Who's speaking, please?'

'It's Fiona McCleod.'

'Hello,' Simon's voice answered. 'What's wrong?'

Fiona proceeded to tell him about her conversation with Paul Aston.

'You jammy beggar.'

'What do you mean?'

'God, Fee, you're still so green. You let him have that bitch, no, better still give it to him. Give it to him and if he does well with it you'll be in line for a ticket when he next judges a champ show. For God's sake, Fee, that's how it works. You scratch my back, etc.'

'But you know that I want to show her myself. I've got so fond of her.'

'You do that and you can forget ever showing under him again.'

'So you're saying that I must sell her, or rather, give her to him?'

'Yes, Fee. Apart from anything else, if it's any good and he shows it, he'll do a damn sight better with it than you could, just because it's him.'

'Oh, Simon, that's so unfair. I know that you're right but I don't like it. Thanks for the advice, anyway. You'll pick me up for the show at the same time, will you? Bye.'

She sat by the phone for a long time, mulling over Simon's words. She knew that it was the right thing to do if she wanted to get on. She knew that in judging and winning there were a lot of considerations other than the dog. It meant compromising her integrity as well, something she had never had to consider before. She now knew that, if she were to succeed in dog showing, some of her scruples would have to be swept under the carpet. Sighing, she realised that she had already done these things by making love to Simon. She picked up the phone again and arranged for Paul Aston to come and see the bitch on Monday week.

Looking out of the window for the fifth time, she realised just how nervous she was about the forthcoming meeting. She found it hard to be devious and had rehearsed her words many times in the past few days. An estate car stopped and then turned into the drive. She watched Paul get out of the car. He was casually but smartly dressed. She hadn't noticed before that he was as tall as Simon. He was more heavily built and fresh-faced. A shaft of sun caught his red hair as he walked up the drive.

'Hello, you found it alright?'

'No trouble, your directions were perfect.'

'Would you like a cup of coffee?'

'I should love one, but could I see the bitch first?'

After giving both the dog and the bitch a thorough examination, and complimenting her on how well she had reared them, he said that he would very much like to have the bitch. They went back into the house and as she poured the coffee she got ready to say her speech. 'I am so pleased that you would consider having one of my puppies to show. It is such an honour that I would like to give her to you.' Fiona could feel her cheeks burning and she felt sick as he looked at her long and hard. Supposing Simon had got it all wrong? What had she done? What would Paul Aston be thinking of her?

'That is very sweet of you, my dear lady, but surely you would like me to pay for her?'

With much relief Fiona said, 'No, no, as I said, I'm really honoured that you like her and it would be good for me if you were to show her.'

'I shall certainly show her, my dear, and may I thank you very much. I shan't forget.'

He shook her hand and smiled. He looked quite different when he smiled, she thought.

Watching him settle the bitch in his car, Fiona let out a sigh of relief and of regret. Well, at least Simon would be proud of her and Duncan would have one dog less to complain about. She would have liked to show her herself but... time would tell.

'I DON'T BELIEVE it. I just do not believe it. How you can stand there and say that you are not going to your own brother's wedding because you are going to a blasted dog show?'

'Come on, Mary, it's only a registry office one and they're not having a do afterwards. Anyway, I've already had a word with Peter and he said that it was okay.'

'Of course, he would say it was okay, but I bet he minds a hell of a lot. You and those bloody dogs. Our whole life has to revolve around their damned needs. They come first every time and sod the rest of us. I'll tell you now I'm sick to death of those dogs and I'm sick to death of you as well.' So saying, Mary stormed out of the kennel, slamming the door in the process. Simon was left to finish grooming the dogs that he was taking to the show.

'And I suppose you'll be picking up that damned woman again,' Mary had returned to deliver this broadside. 'I tell you, if I find that there's anything going on there I'll damn well divorce you and get rid of those bloody dogs.' She again slammed the door as she left.

Simon finished his preparations and gathered up his grooming box, leads, towels and other equipment. He took them indoors and packed his bag for an early start in the morning.

'And what am I supposed to say to everybody tomorrow when they ask where you are?' Mary had come into the hall and was standing there with an angry expression on her face.

Glancing round at her, Simon replied, 'Tell them the truth, I don't mind.'

'Oh yes, and what's that? That you're off for the day with your fancy piece?'

'Don't be ridiculous!'

'Ridiculous! You're the one that's ridiculous, putting those dogs and your bit on the side before your own flesh and blood.'

Simon's face flushed angrily at her words but he did not turn round or reply. Instead, he quietly picked up his bag and box and took them out to the car.

Driving up to the show early the next morning, Fiona was busily telling him how the young dog which she had kept was progressing and how much she was looking forward to bringing him out when he was ready.

'How is the bitch doing that Paul had?'

'Oh, fine. He phoned me with a progress report the other week. He said that she was shaping up quite nicely.'

'Coming from him that means that she looks good. I told you that you'd done the right thing. If he shows her and does well, all you've got to do is wait until he's judging again. I heard on the grapevine that he's down to do South Wales next year, so we'll have to wait and see. You could take the dog under him.'

Always relaxed in each other's company, they chatted on until they reached the show ground. Although the CCs went where Simon had said that they would go, they both were placed quite well in their respective classes and as Simon said to her, considering the judge, they had had a damn good day. Having been to several Championship shows now, Fiona knew many regular exhibitors by sight and realised that they were indeed fortunate. Some never or hardly ever seemed to even get a fifth place and usually went home with nothing.

'Simon, why do some of these people go to these shows when they hardly ever get anywhere at all?'

'Ah, now you've asked me. I've thought about this in the past. I think you'll find that, for a lot of them, they don't understand how the system works so they live in hope. Others, who know how the system works, try to get into it and others come because they've got nothing else in their lives to keep them occupied, or because they're lonely. A few come because they just love dogs.'

'How awful.' She looked around her and wondered just how

happy these smiling, talking people were. Showing wasn't very fair at all, in fact, it was downright dishonest.

On the journey home she was still rather pensive and a bit depressed when Simon pulled into a motel forecourt. He turned to face her and, smiling, said, 'Alright?'

'Yes, perfectly alright,' she replied and kissed him, all thoughts of the show gone.

They booked a room and when Simon shut the door she found that she was shivering in anticipation. He stood looking at her without speaking until Fiona, feeling a little uncertain, asked, 'Is something wrong?'

He shook his head and held out his arms; she went into them and he kissed her with such intensity that it took her breath away. They quickly removed their clothes. Their brief time together could not be wasted.

He pulled her close to him and once again he kissed her passionately. 'My God, Fee, you're beautiful,' he said, as his hands found all the remembered curves and crevices of her body. She smiled and stroked his body until he groaned with pleasure. 'For God's sake, Fee, give me a break.'

Sure of the outcome, they enjoyed their foreplay, with Fiona taking a much more active part than she had previously. No longer reticent, she teased and delayed until they both reached a noisy, laughing climax together. Fiona had never felt so beautiful, so powerful in her femininity. She lay there beside him and realised that she could no longer distinguish between their two bodies; they were as one person.

Simon propped himself up on one elbow and looked at her. 'You do know that I've fallen completely in love with you, don't you?' He smiled, took her in his arms and held her close.

Later, they drove home, wrapped in their own private world. He dropped Fiona and her dogs outside her house. 'I don't want to leave you. Will you be alright?'

She nodded and he started up the engine. She waited until the car was out of sight and went indoors. Duncan was watching a programme on television and did not speak. She took the dogs out to the kennel and settled them in. Going back into the kitchen she shouted to Duncan that she was tired and was going straight to bed. He didn't reply.

As Simon turned into his driveway and switched off the engine the front door was flung open by Mary. 'And what time do you call this? Don't give me that "stopped for a meal routine" because it won't wash. You've been having it away, haven't you, with that bloody McCleod woman?'

'Alright, I won't then, but could we continue this conversation inside the house?'

'Right, so now you're in, I'll say again, what's your excuse this time?'

'I haven't got one, I'm just late.' He brushed past her and put his bag and equipment down on the floor. He then went out again for the dogs.

'Oh yes, see to the damned dogs first. They always come first; never mind about me and Barry and Sharon.'

'Everything's alright, isn't it?'

'Oh, how nice of you to ask, I didn't think you cared.'

As he went out of the back door to the shed he muttered, 'I don't.'

Later, when he was making a cup of tea, she started again, 'You use this place like a hotel. Honestly, if I could win the pools I'd leave you, I really would. And I'll tell you something else. If I find out that you are having an affair with that bloody dog woman, I'll divorce you and it'll be a pleasure.'

'Do you want a cup of tea?'

'I'll get it myself, thank you. You haven't even asked how the wedding went.'

'How did it go?'

'Lovely, no thanks to you. Peter looked so happy and Beryl had a lovely suit on and a real silk blouse. Peter had given her an orchid to wear as a corsage. She looked ever so smart with matching shoes and handbag. It made Sharon and me feel quite dowdy. We all went off to a restaurant after the ceremony. Beryl's daughter came too and we had a very nice meal with plenty of wine. You should have been there, though, you really should. Fancy his only brother being at a bloody dog show. I was really embarrassed. God knows what Beryl must think of you.'

Simon let it all wash over him; he was thinking of Fee.

Sighing, he got up and locked the back door. He asked Mary if the children were in and on hearing that Sharon had gone to bed and Barry was out at a party but had his key, he went to bed and was asleep before Mary got in beside him.

Sunday passed in a similar vein, with Mary whining about everything, as usual. She needed some new smart clothes, she had felt so dowdy yesterday and so did Sharon. They never went out for expensive meals in a restaurant or anywhere else for that matter. Oh no, all the money went on those bloody dogs out there.

It was like a recording, he thought; she hardly ever varied it just added more to it. Walking the dogs along the river bank he speculated on how he could possibly find the money to leave Mary and live with Fee. If only he could, they could start a kennel, a cattery even, right in the heart of the countryside, and build it up until it was a going concern. He could then retire early and they could run the business together. Dream on, he told himself ruefully.

Fiona was busy in the house. Having seen to the dogs, she decided that the house was looking rather neglected and she must do something about it. They had eaten breakfast in silence and Duncan was now out in his greenhouse. Life was getting very awkward, she thought as she hurried round with the vacuum cleaner and duster. With the dogs taking up so much of her time, she just could not fit working at the library and the housework into the time available. She had been late on several occasions recently and she knew it wouldn't be long before Rosemary said something about it. She had taken to doing a lot more convenience meals in the microwave, too. She herself didn't like that, but there wasn't the time to do otherwise. She sighed heavily as she started to clean the bathroom.

Sally was due to whelp again in a week's time and that would make things even worse. If only she didn't have to go to the library. Right from the start of their marriage they had agreed to share all expenses until such time as she gave up work to have a baby. She didn't think that, under the circumstances, Duncan would agree that she no longer had to find her share. She sighed again and carried an armful of washing downstairs to the kitchen. Perhaps if she got up half an hour earlier each day she would manage better.

Her resolve lasted precisely three days because on the Wednesday evening, Sally started to whelp. Fiona had used Mrs Emsworth's young winning dog for this mating and she was very hopeful of the litter. Sally was slower this time between whelping each puppy and, although she only had three, it was almost 5 a.m. before Fiona had her cleaned up and settled down with her new litter. She sat down on the settee and was asleep almost immediately.

Duncan shook her awake at 7.30 a.m. He made her a cup of tea, got his own breakfast and warned her of the time as he left for work. It was no good, she was exhausted and she phoned to say that she would not be in that day. Rosemary took the call and didn't seem too pleased, but Fiona was too tired to worry about it.

She saw to the other dogs, fed and cleaned Sally again, and then went to bed, setting the alarm for 2 p.m. in order to see to Sally again.

The next eight weeks proved to be chaotic and very tiring for Fiona. Although there were no problems with the litter, just the sheer amount of extra work, coupled with her already full workload exhausted her. She couldn't go to any shows and she longed to see Simon. If she could only see him for a few minutes, just kiss him and talk to him. She thought about him all the time.

She got young Christine to come in every weekend to help with the other dogs. This proved to be a great success, as she was a sensible and capable girl and could be left to feed and groom them on her own; and the dogs loved her. She also agreed to come round after school during the week to exercise them. With this help, Fiona managed to keep things going until it was time for the puppies to go to their new homes. Although during the past few weeks she had vowed to herself not to keep any of them, she was so taken with one little bitch that she decided to run her on to see if she would be good for showing. As the second puppy happily went off in the arms of its new owner, Fiona breathed a sigh of relief and shut the door. A decidedly dirty and untidy house met her eyes.

Fiona went on a guilt trip and during the next few weeks spent a great deal of time cleaning, washing and cooking. She was once again punctual at the library and her only worry was that she was not spending time with the dogs, especially the puppy bitch – she had put her out in the kennel and had not told Duncan that she had kept it, banking on the fact that he never went in there. She deliberately did not go to several Open shows that she had entered and the tension between her and Duncan eased a little.

During this time she had plenty of phone calls from other dog exhibitors, saying that they had missed her at the shows and telling her all the latest news and gossip. One evening, the phone rang and her heart missed a beat when she heard Simon's voice.

'Hi, Fee, it's me. Is everything alright? I know we agreed not to phone each other unless it was urgent but, oh God, Fee, it's been weeks and I've been worried about you and I've missed you. I've picked up the phone to call you a dozen times and put it down in case I got Duncan. I didn't know how things were between you and I didn't want to cause any more problems for you. Look, is it still on for next week? I can't wait to see you and hold you. I'll pick you up at the usual time next Sunday.'

Fiona's mind was in turmoil; she had temporarily forgotten that this Championship show was so close. They had agreed months ago that they would go to it. She so wanted to see Simon again but she knew that if she went, it would upset the peace and quiet again with Duncan. With her mind still racing through the various consequences, she said, 'But I haven't had the chance to get them ready. The pups have only just gone.'

'You've got a week – that's enough. Anyway, how are the pups? You haven't told me. How many did you have?'

'They're fine. Actually, I've only got the one now. She had two dogs and a bitch. I kept the bitch – she was so gorgeous that I couldn't resist her.'

'Great, you can tell me all about her when I see you. Bye for now. I love you. See you Sunday.'

Fiona put the phone down. Why hadn't she said that she couldn't go? It was going to make life very difficult again with Duncan. They'd be back to the long silences. Even as she thought it, she knew that she would go. She just couldn't bear the thought of not seeing Simon for weeks. She had to see him, just to hear his voice, to touch him.

FIONA HEARD THE car stop in the drive. She looked at her watch, it was 6.30 a.m. Simon was absolutely on time. Picking up her bag and grooming box, she opened the door and took them out to the car. Simon opened up the tailgate of the estate, put the bag in and then came into the hall to get her table and the two dogs. As they drove out she looked up at the bedroom window, but the curtains were still drawn and there was no sign of Duncan.

Mrs Emsworth was the judge for this show and Fiona was especially excited. Surely she would like her two youngsters, Heather, the bitch that she had kept from the first litter, and Sorrel, the young dog from the second one. Simon had brought Bracken, so they were both keeping their fingers crossed. They all went back to Mrs Emsworth's stock.

As Sorrel was in the Puppy Dog class, Fiona was the first to go into the ring. Mrs Emsworth smiled at her as she put her dog on the table. She was very thorough in her examination of the dog, checking his teeth and skull, his skeletal structure, his feet and coat, but her face didn't reveal anything. When she asked her to do the customary triangle and straight up and down, Fiona was worried that Sorrel wouldn't behave. As she walked back to the judge he started to play about. Fiona quickly brought him back on course. She apologised to Mrs Emsworth, who said that it was alright – she had seen enough of his movement. Fiona waited anxiously while the other puppies were seen and was thrilled when Sorrel was pulled out for the second place. This qualified him for Crufts next year.

Simon did better by coming first in his class, but didn't go any further in the challenge.

After lunch it was the turn of the bitches to be judged. Fiona was almost shaking when she entered the ring with Heather. Simon caught her eye, winked and gave her a thumbs-up sign. She had done very well with her at Open shows, but would Mrs Emsworth like her now? The competition was so much stronger at Championship shows. Fiona kept telling herself not to be nervous in case it communicated down the lead to Heather.

When it was their turn to be seen, Heather walked and stood well and was pulled out into the first spot. Fiona was delighted. It was Heather's very first first at a Championship show. She hurried out of the ring to be given a resounding kiss by Simon. Blushing, she looked round and saw several grinning faces. When all winning bitches were called in for the challenge, Simon told her to go in there and show them how it was done. She was shaking with nerves and wanted to dash to the loo, but kept her head, smiled and, taking a deep breath, encouraged Heather into the ring at a smart pace.

When Mrs Emsworth pulled out the winning bitch from the Open class, Fiona's heart sank but then, after another quick assessment of the other dogs, she came over to Fiona and gave her the Reserve CC. As she and Heather followed the CC bitch around the ring on their lap of honour, Fiona's heart was singing. She was seized by Simon as she came out of the ring and given a bear hug and a kiss. She kissed him back and he said, 'Bloody marvellous, you were bloody marvellous. Congratulations.' Many other fellow exhibitors came up in the next few minutes to congratulate her and Heather. Only one said that she wasn't surprised, because Heather was, after all, partly the judge's breeding, as she smiled and kissed her on the cheek. Fiona felt rather upset but Simon told her not to be so sensitive.

'Don't think that all the bitches are on the end of a lead. If you have a good dog and start winning, you had better be prepared for a lot worse than that.'

They had already decided not to go to a motel on the way home, in view of Mary's suspicions and Duncan's silence. It had been a hard decision to make, but Fiona had reluctantly agreed with Simon that it was best to play safe for a while. On arriving home, she rushed into the house waving her green and white card. 'Duncan, Duncan, where are you? Look, I got the RCC; isn't that wonderful!' Only Sally greeted her. Duncan was not there.

She was sound asleep when he quietly returned home around midnight, and even when he got into bed she did not stir, so she didn't tell him her news until the next morning. His only reply was a vague, 'Oh, good,' which somewhat dashed her high spirits. Nevertheless, she found an old photo frame, put the RCC card into it and hung it proudly in the kennel. As she did so, she remembered that Paul Aston had been at the show and had got a first in the bitch puppy class. She had bred three of the winning dogs there yesterday!

Paul had been one of the exhibitors to congratulate her, saying as he left, 'Come up with Simon, did you? Lucky man.' He winked at her. 'Hope to see you later on,' but she had not congratulated him.

Feeling guilty, she went indoors and phoned him. 'Oh, Paul, this is Fiona McCleod here, I just wanted to congratulate you on your first yesterday.'

'Hello, Fiona, how nice of you to think of phoning. I'm very pleased with her, thank you.' They chatted for a few more minutes, promising to meet up for a drink at a future show.

The days of early summer flew by. Having determined to enter more Championship shows, Fiona was kept very busy with the adult dogs and the new puppy. The relationship between her and Duncan was no better – he now slept in the other double bedroom by mutual agreement. It had come about by his constant complaining about her early starts in the mornings and by her unwillingness to make love to him. She had invented every excuse in the book to avoid it. Duncan wanted her to go to see a doctor but she had insisted that it was just a temporary thing and would pass if he would give her a bit of space. He had very reluctantly agreed and now, it seemed, their only communication was about everyday things. No holiday had been mentioned for this year so Fiona felt quite free to enter more shows. Her feelings of guilt were running at an all-time high now and she tried to push them to the back of her mind.

Many shows she went to on her own because Simon was unable to afford the entry fees for all of them. However, they had both entered for the Welsh show in July and, as the day approached, Fiona was tense with excitement. They had agreed over the phone, Fiona had phoned him at his office, that they would stay overnight at a B&B place to avoid two long journeys in one day; that was the excuse which they had agreed on for Duncan and Mary and for Rosemary at the library, who had not been at all pleased. Duncan had merely grunted when Fiona told him of the arrangements and had walked out into the garden to work in his greenhouse until it was dark. Mary had thrown a tantrum when Simon had told her and a bitter row had developed. Simon was in the middle of decorating the lounge and Mary wanted it all finished before he went. When he told her that she was asking the impossible, she totally lost her temper and screamed accusations at him. Since then she had gone very quiet.

As they drove to Wales, early on a beautiful summer's morning, they told each other of the problems that they were having but, as usual when they were together, their moods lightened and they started talking about the day ahead. As they drove over the Severn Bridge with its spectacular views, the excitement began to build in them. Paul Aston was the judge today, and Fiona would be going in the ring first with the litter brother of the bitch that Paul had had from her. Would he like him? Simon thought that Sorrel was good and should do well.

As Paul walked up and down the line-up before making his decision, Fiona's heart was hammering in her throat and she was desperate to go to the toilet. He's not going to pick me, she thought, Simon's theory was all wrong. He pulled her out into second place. He gave Simon's dog a first in a later class and as he came out of the ring, Fiona said, 'You see, you were wrong. He prefers your dog to mine.'

'You wait, the day's not over yet.'

After lunch, Simon helped her to prepare Heather for her class.

'Now come on, go in there with confidence, let's have a big smile.' Simon gave her a kiss and patted her bottom. 'Go on, they're calling your class. Good luck.'

She was even more nervous now and was worried that it would transmit down the lead to the dog. However, Heather behaved well and Paul pulled her out into the first spot. Later, when she went in for the challenge, she was almost shaking. Was Simon right after all? As Paul looked at each of the class winners in turn, she couldn't bear to look at him. There was a cheer and looking up from the dog she found that she was looking into Paul's smiling face; in his hand was the CC and he was offering his congratulations. She shook his hand and took the card in a daze, tears of happiness filling her eyes.

'I think that deserves a kiss, don't you?' Paul raised his eyebrows as he smiled at her.

She swiftly gave him a peck on the cheek and blushed.

As she and Heather ran around the ring on her lap of honour, her mind ceased to function. She just couldn't believe it. Her first CC. As she came out of the ring she was surrounded by people congratulating her, patting her on the back and shaking her hand.

'Here, give me those, Fee, and get back in there for the challenge for BOB.' Simon pushed her back into the ring.

Heather had picked up on the excitement and was not as settled. Paul gave the BOB to the dog CC.

'Never mind, Fee, you got the CC and that's the most important thing for you. I told you, didn't I? I told you.' He hugged her and kissed her.

'Oh Simon, I almost forgot to breathe, I was so nervous.'

Paul came up to them. 'That is a very nice bitch you've got there, Fiona, and I liked your young dog. Needs to mature a bit, though.'

Fiona was still on cloud nine as they drove to their B&B. Simon put his bag on the floor of the bedroom and produced a bottle of champagne. 'I bought it yesterday to celebrate or to drown our sorrows.'

Laughing, they drank the champagne, toasted the dogs and each other, then, still laughing, they undressed and made love. It had been some time since they had last done so and they both climaxed quickly.

'Let's take the dogs for a walk and settle them down. Then we can have a meal and come back here, and I can spend my time in seducing you all night.'

'Sounds fine to me, as long as I'm allowed to seduce you.'

'Be my guest,' he said, and pulled her up out of the bed.

Arriving home on the Saturday afternoon, Fiona found the mail on the hall floor. She thought it strange that Duncan hadn't picked it up. He must have gone out very early to play golf with Michael. She found another invitation to judge an Open show. She was already booked to judge one this autumn. This one was for early next year. She was just entering it in her diary and on the wall chart in the kitchen when she heard Duncan coming in. 'Hello Duncan, I'm in the kitchen. Did you enjoy your game of golf?'

'Fiona, I want to talk to you.' Walking straight into the lounge, he poured two glasses of whisky.

Standing in the doorway, Fiona said, 'I'm rather tired, couldn't it wait until later?'

'No, it can't. I'm sorry, Fiona, but I can't go on like this.'

'What do you mean?'

'I mean that you have got to stop all this dog business. It's destroying us. Can't you see that? Do you want to see that? I say again, you must stop all of it. The breeding, the showing, all of it.'

'And if I don't want to?'

'Then we'll have to separate.'

'Separate! How can you be so selfish? This is my hobby we are talking about, the first hobby that I've had since we were married, and you demand that I give it up. You have your hobbies – the golf and your gardening. Do I interfere in those? Do I demand that you give those up? No, I don't. What right have you got to tell me that I must stop showing?'

'Fiona, calm down, I have given this a great deal of thought. In answer to your question, I don't have the right to tell you to stop showing. Perhaps I phrased it badly. I should like you to stop showing and breeding because it interferes too much in our marriage and is driving us apart. Also, I'm not happy about you being away overnight.'

'I see, what you mean is that you don't want me to have any

freedom. You just want me to be a housewife. Well, that's not enough for me now. I'm sick of forever cleaning an already clean house. I'm sick of forever cooking meals for us and then watching you eat them. I'm tired of the library and all those silent books. I want to live every day and I can't if you won't let me have the dogs.'

Duncan stood looking out of the window for so long that in the end Fiona said, 'Well, for goodness' sake, say something.'

Turning to face her, Duncan put his empty whisky glass on the table. 'I had no idea that you felt so strongly. Are you telling me that you have never been happy with me?'

'Of course not, you know that, but things have changed.'

'Yes, that's true enough. Will you please think about what I've said, and perhaps we can come up with a solution to suit us both and to save our marriage.'

S IMON AND MARY let the New Year in by arguing about money. Both Barry and Sharon had gone to parties, leaving Simon and Mary on their own. This was so unusual that it felt uncomfortable for them both. Simon sat watching television and drinking bitter while Mary leafed through holiday brochures. The argument started with Mary stating that, now that Barry had his two A levels and had got a job in the local bank, there would only be the three of them to go on holiday. When Simon asked her why Barry would not be coming, Mary replied that he had said that he wanted to go on holiday with his mates. She then went on to say that, as they were the only family she knew who had not been to Italy, now was the time for them to go. Simon insisted that they could not afford it because the new lounge carpet, which she had said was desperately needed, had taken most of their spare cash.

The conversation now took on a well-worn pattern with Mary saying, 'It's not surprising that there isn't much spare, is it? Look at all the money you spend. Dog showing is all money going out and none coming in. If you weren't so damned selfish, we'd all be better off.'

'Can't you for God's sake play another record! I've said a hundred times, if you would only look after the puppies during the day, we could have a couple of litters and that would bring in a bit. Anyway, the studs bring in a bit so it's not all paying out.'

'A bit is right. Nowhere near what you spend out on those damned dogs. What with the food, the vet's bills and those bloody show entries, not to mention the petrol you use getting to and from the bloody shows. It's all pay out, as I said, with nothing left for your family.'

'Alright then, if you feel so bloody poor and hard done by why don't you, for once, put your money where your mouth is and go out and get yourself a job. Then, perhaps, you could have this blasted holiday in Italy and you and Sharon could sit on the beach all day and fry in suntan oil.'

'I don't want a holiday with you if you're going to take that attitude.'

'Good, well, that's settled then, you can bloody well go without me and that will be even cheaper.' Banging his glass down on the floor he got up to leave the room.

'Oh yes, going to see the dogs are we, running away as usual. Well, I will then. Sharon and I will go on our own and what's more I will get a little job. At least I'd have somebody interesting to talk to.'

When Simon came home from the office on the following Thursday, he could see from the smug look on Mary's face that she had something important to say to him. He didn't bother to prompt her because the past had taught him that it was usually only a juicy bit of gossip about a friend or neighbour which didn't interest him in the slightest. He was, therefore, pleasantly surprised when, just after they had all sat down for their evening meal, Mary announced that she had got a job. She would be on the check-out at the local supermarket every morning from Monday to Friday, starting next week. She then announced that she had booked a holiday in Lido di Jesolo in August for herself and Sharon. She went on to tell them how she had noticed that the local travel agency was offering special discounts if you booked early so, when she had got the job, she called in, on the way home, and booked it. She ended by saying, 'So you see, I have put my money where my mouth is.'

Later on, while Simon was in the kennel, Mary's news set him thinking about the year ahead. He was pleased that Mary had at last got off her backside and done something other than whinge. The extra money would certainly ease things a bit, especially now that Barry was working. He smiled to himself; yes, this year was going to be good.

He looked at Bracken. If only he could make him up into a

champion, he might be able to sell him abroad for a four-figure sum. He knew that those in the charmed circle could definitely command those figures for their champions but then, just being in the charmed circle made it easier to make up a champion in the first place. His thoughts continued in a similar vein. It was his first Championship-show judging appointment this year, supposing he could organise a tit-for-tat CC with someone else. He would have to think very carefully over the other Championship judges this year. He sighed, it wasn't how he liked to operate, he told himself, but, desperate times called for desperate measures.

His thoughts then turned to Fee. If money became a little easier he could at least go to a few more shows and would be able to see her more often, though in a way, that made his need to see her worse. He was happy in her company and the more he had of it the more he wanted. He knew that he loved her in a way that was absolutely fundamental to him; he loved her in a way that he had never loved Mary. Had he ever loved Mary? He had been young and lustful, she had been trim and pretty – the rest had been social brainwashing, he thought sourly. Nobody should marry under thirty years old, he speculated. Good God, I was only just beginning to know who I was and what I wanted from this life then.

His thoughts were interrupted by Sharon yelling at the top of her voice, 'Dad, phone.'

Sighing, he left the kennel and went indoors.

'Hello, Simon, I'm sorry to phone you at home but I honestly don't know what to do.' It was Fiona.

'What's the matter, Fee?'

'It's Duncan. We've just had another big row. He said it before but I didn't really believe he meant it, but he has just said it again and gone out in his car.'

'Just a minute, Fee, you didn't believe he meant what?'

'He's given me an ultimatum – give up showing and the dogs or we must separate.'

'God, that's bad.'

'I don't know what to do. Could you possibly meet me some-where – I need to talk this through.'

'Yes, of course; I'm just trying to think when. We've got my brother Peter and his wife coming round tomorrow night. I've entered a show on Saturday so I'll come then. We can spend all day talking if you want. Just tell me where and what time. I'll have to bring the dog, though.'

'That's fine.' They made their arrangements and rang off.

Simon was already there when Fiona walked into the lounge bar of The Foresters Arms. He had already bought a pint for himself and half a shandy for her. He stood up and kissed her.

'Am I glad to see you. Is everything alright? You look worn out.'

'Yes, I'm alright, I'm just so tired. I couldn't sleep the last couple of nights with everything going round and round in my mind.'

'Have you come to any decisions?'

'No.'

'Has he said anything else?'

'No, I've hardly seen him and when I have he has almost ignored me. Oh, Simon, everything is such a mess.'

'Look, Fee, you do know, don't you, that if I could say let's live together I would, but financially, at the present moment anyway, it's impossible.'

'I know that but I can't help wishing that we could.'

'Look, Fee, are you sure that you can't get him to see sense and at least keep the dogs?'

'Absolutely certain. He never really wanted Sally in the first place and now that I have got five more and the kennel in the garden, not to mention Christine who comes in to help at the weekend, he is up in arms about all of them. He says that everything must go except Sally. He has agreed that I can keep her.'

'Are you going to do it?'

'Do you think I should?'

'Of course I bloody don't. You know what I want but my hands are tied, so I have no right to tell you what to do, have I?'

Tears welled up in her eyes. 'Oh, Simon, I can't part from you and I can't part from the dogs either. It's my life now. I am so alive when I'm with you and we are at the shows. It's the excitement, the tension, the interest, it's… but I don't have to tell you, I know that you feel the same. What am I to do?'

'What the hell does he expect you to do with yourself without the dogs?'

'What I used to do before – work at the library, keep the house looking nice, feed him, entertain friends now and again and, of course, play golf with him now.'

'What about a compromise? How about suggesting that you just keep the two most promising dogs and only go to Champ shows. Do you think that he'd accept that? Tell him how much it means to you.'

'Well, I've tried in the past without success, but I'll try again. Why do I have to have such a non-doggy husband?'

'You're not alone; I've known several divorces over the past few years in the dog world and all for the same reason – dogs. It's usually the husband who objects, too. The dog game is very tough on marriages. Perhaps that's why you see so many gay couples in it. They don't seem to have a problem.'

'I must get back. I'll try the compromise, Simon, but don't hold out too many hopes. After all, it's not just the dogs, is it? He'll expect me to be his wife in bed again and that I can never do. I love you far too much.'

He reached out and held her hands in his, and the pain and the love in their eyes as they looked at each other said it all. There could be no compromise on that.

Fiona did some grocery shopping on her way home, which had been her excuse for going out, and then returned, determined to face Duncan with her compromise and get him to let her keep a couple of dogs. She started composing the sentences as she drove home.

Parking the car in the drive, she was about to get the shopping out of the boot when the front door opened and Duncan came hurrying towards her. 'Fiona, the hospital have just rung. Apparently your father collapsed at home last night. It was only when a neighbour called to see if he wanted any shopping that he was found on the kitchen floor. The hospital said that he is comfortable but they thought that you should be there.'

'Oh no, I must go straight away. How long is it since they

phoned?'

'Only about ten minutes. Look, I'll take you in my car. It's better if I drive you. We'll be there in under half an hour.'

While Duncan parked the car, Fiona ran into reception and asked to which ward her father had been taken. She hurried along the various corridors, praying not to be too late. Entering the ward she saw screens around one of the beds. Please, please God, don't let me be too late. Please let me tell him how much I love him, she said to herself as she approached the screens.

A nurse came up and asked her who she was looking for, and then took her to the screened bed. 'I'm afraid that your father is very ill. He hasn't regained consciousness. He is suffering from hypothermia and his heart is very weak. I'm sorry. We are doing all we can.'

Fiona thanked her and sat down beside her father's bed. He looked so still. She wanted him to open his eyes and smile at her as he always did. She badly needed him to tell her that everything would be alright, as he had when she was a little girl. Taking his cold hand and holding it in both of hers, she willed him to live.

Shortly afterwards, Duncan appeared and sat down quietly beside her. She sat there for what seemed many hours in the small private world made by the curtains. A nurse came in to check on him and once a doctor came in. He spoke to them, again emphasising how very ill and frail her father was and not to be too hopeful, using the familiar words that they were doing all they could. At some point Duncan went off and brought her back a cup of tea, but she didn't even taste it. She was lost in a kaleidoscope of happy, childhood memories and was totally isolated from Duncan and the routine ward activities. Pictures floated into her head of happy birthday parties, of sandcastles by the sea, of help with homework, of how strong he had been for her when her mother had died, of so many, many things.

A doctor and nurse appeared again but she did not notice them until Duncan called her name and tried to take her hands from her father's hand. 'Fiona, Fiona, they want us to leave for a while. Come on now.' He helped her to her feet and took her out of the ward.

She was shivering and cold. Her memories had been almost

up to the present day and she was feeling so guilty that she had spent so little time with him over the past few years.

The doctor came out of the ward and over to where they were seated. 'I'm sorry to have to tell you that your father has just died. He did not regain consciousness.'

'THIS IS PLAIN idiotic,' Duncan addressed himself in the mirror whilst putting the shaver round his chin. The past few weeks had been very busy and very difficult for him. He had not only had a lot on at work but also, as named executor, had all the business of sorting out his father-in-law's affairs. In all that time Fiona had hardly said two words to him. At first he had put it down to grief – she had been very fond of her father and his sudden death had shaken her – but he felt that she should, by now, be a bit more friendly and talk now and again. For heaven's sake, hadn't he done everything he could to help her in the early days after her father had died, and at the funeral?

It was true that she had come to her senses and given up the dog showing. It was also true that she had sold one of the dogs and had stopped that wretched Christine from coming in at weekends. She had made a big effort in the house and was certainly cooking more but… 'Yes, but,' he said out loud, 'it's like living with a ghost. It's ridiculous.' Wiping his face and hands, he put on his shirt and went downstairs to find her.

'Now Fiona, we have got to talk. I know that your father's death upset you but this is ridiculous. Talk to me, let me help you.'

'What would you like me to talk about?'

'You know perfectly well what – us!'

'Us? What is there to say about us?'

At this, Duncan got really annoyed and grabbed Fiona by the arms. 'For goodness' sake, Fiona, why are you like this, so quiet, so dead. Are you ill? Are you still upset about your father? I know how much you wanted to speak to him before he died but you've just got to accept it, Fiona. You've got to come to terms with it. Perhaps I could help if you told me how you are feeling.'

'Oh, so you think I'm half dead too, do you? Well, I know I am. The dogs and showing are my life, my love, my fun, my excitement and you are taking them away from me and I don't like what's left. What's the point of having a beautiful garden and house? It's just a showpiece, it's boring and dead and we are boring and dead and it's all your fault. You don't want a woman with thoughts and feelings, you just want someone to cook and clean and be prettily intelligent. You just want someone who will be quietly submissive in bed when you feel the urge to prove your manhood. What happened to fun?'

Duncan sat down heavily as if she had hit him. A long, heavy silence followed and something was irretrievably lost between them.

Simon was putting the finishing touches to Bracken for the Bath Championship Show. He was thinking about Fee – he had done nothing else for weeks now. He had phoned her several times since her father's death, but all she would say was that she loved him and missed him and thought about him all the time but that she had decided to try a compromise over the dogs, at least for a while. She sounded so miserable and lonely. He had asked her to meet him several times and had even threatened to go round to her house when she had refused. He had written several letters to her but she had not replied to any of them. He had phoned her last night and begged her to change her mind and come with him to Bath, but she had still insisted that the only way was to try to make the compromise work. He was terrified of losing her.

Finishing the dog, he closed the kennel and went indoors. Barry was out with his friends and Mary and Sharon had gone to see a film – he had the place to himself.

'Fee, it's Simon. Fee I'm going crazy here worrying about you. Please, Fee, please come to Bath with me. This bloody compromise is not on, it's killing both of us. I love you and I want you with me.'

His call had broken the silence that had existed all day between her and Duncan, and she had been pleased to get out of the room.

'Oh, Simon, I can't say just at this moment. I've had another row with Duncan about the dogs and my mind is in a turmoil. Look, I'll ring you tomorrow.'

'Are you okay?'

'Yes, I'm alright. I'll ring tomorrow.'

'Make sure you do. I love you, Fee.'

As she put the phone down Duncan passed her and went out of the front door. She heard his car start up. Sighing deeply, she went back into the lounge, hesitated for a moment and then poured herself a whisky.

She was lying awake in bed when she heard Duncan's car return. She looked at the bedside clock – it was just gone midnight. She heard him come in and then the house settled down again to its night vigil. It was gone two o'clock when she heard him come upstairs and go into the back bedroom. She must have fallen asleep then, because the next thing she knew was Duncan standing beside her bed with a cup of tea in his hand. He looked utterly exhausted and she felt a pang of guilt as he wearily sat on the edge of the bed.

'Fiona, I've been doing a lot of thinking. I've been remembering how happy we were when we bought this house and all the plans we made. I know that things didn't work out with regard to our family and I think that I understand why you so want the dogs and perhaps, in that respect, I have been unreasonable. I should like you to keep your dogs. With regard to the shows and the litters, however, I can't help but feel that these two things are coming between us and destroying our marriage. Surely you can see this too? Can we please talk about this?'

Fiona said nothing. It had been a very long speech from Duncan and she knew it had been said with the best of intentions, but she equally knew that without the shows and Simon, his solution would never work. After a few minutes she said, 'Alright, I won't have any litters for a while but you must let me go to some shows.'

Duncan looked at her sadly for a while and then nodded his head in agreement. Later that day, while Duncan was out, she phoned Simon to say that she would be going to Bath and would he pick her up. She said that she would explain everything tomorrow. When she told Duncan of her plans she thought that they were in for another enormous row but, although his face flushed and he clenched his fists, he nodded and went into the garden.

She had hardly got into the car when Simon demanded to know everything, but before she could start, he stopped the car and taking her in his arms kissed her again and again.

'God, but that feels better. Now, tell me all.'

Fiona told him of Duncan's decision.

'Does that mean sleeping with him?'

'That wasn't actually mentioned but I've told you, we haven't slept together for a while now. No, it's just that we won't separate.'

'The man must be mad. I just don't understand it; I want to love you every night and in every possible position.'

They both laughed and he started up the car again. The journey passed swiftly with them talking about aspects of the dog scene: wins, litters, gossip, future plans. Simon and Bracken didn't do too well in their class so they were able to leave fairly early. They stopped for a drink and discussed their present situation, and in between kisses it was agreed that Fiona would continue with the compromise for now and see how things panned out.

Duncan was at home that evening and they went out for a meal but, as Fiona couldn't talk about the dogs or Simon, it was all rather quiet and slightly uncomfortable.

So the show merry-go-round started up again. For Duncan it meant loneliness and microwave meals or his mother's at the weekends. For Fiona the sun shone again. Having had time to reflect on the dog-show game while she was away from it, she saw even more of the devious aspects of it, the organised winning, the deals, the unfairness and how one should act in order to achieve, and she was even more determined to succeed. Her goals now were to somehow live with Simon, to be a Championship show judge and to make up a champion, preferably at Crufts.

In order to be a Championship show judge she had to have judged a required number of breed classes at Open shows. She was nearly up to that number so, with the help and support of

Simon, she embarked on a plan. Her father's affairs had still not been finalised but she knew that she was going to be comfortably off soon. Now, when she entered Open shows she always made a point of putting a note in with her entry form saying that she would like to become a member of that society and that she wished to donate money for rosettes and would be bringing a raffle prize. She felt that this would bring her name to the secretary's attention more than just the entry. At the same time, Simon spoke to several show secretaries that he knew, telling them what a good judge she was and how she always got good entries. Over the course of the year, if this ploy was to prove successful, then Fiona would be at least ready to accept a Championship show appointment if offered one.

She in no way felt at all underhand in this exploit because, as Simon said, she had read as many books on, not only the Cumbrian, but every other kind of terrier that she could find. She had attended seminars as well, and now understood the interplay of the bones, muscles and ligaments in producing a good dog with good movement. They equally felt that a large proportion of Open and Championship show judges didn't know or understand the conformation of the dog in front of them but relied more on knowing which person they should put up to benefit them for whatever reason. Needless to say, those people who won like that would always counteract such claims by saying that it was all 'sour grapes' uttered by those who hadn't won.

'What has happened to good sportsmanship?' they would loudly say, with earnest faces. Simon and Fiona's aim was that, when they were both Championship show judges and could, therefore, give four CCs per year, they might be able to exert a little pressure on their own destinies.

Later in the year, her father's house was finally sold and when Duncan was able to tell her just how much she had now in shares and cash, she was amazed. Her first thought was to finish working for the library so that she could spend all day with the dogs. It wouldn't affect their joint mortgage – she could easily pay her half out of the dividends from her shares and Duncan would have no reason to disagree. Quickly following on that, came the realisation that she was now in a position to buy a house of her own if she wanted, and to live with Simon.

She wanted to phone him straight away with the news, but felt that she would have to wait until Duncan wasn't in the house. She felt that she would burst with happiness and was terrified that Duncan would see it in her face. He had brought home a celebratory bottle of champagne to drink to her good fortune, but their evening was interrupted twice with 'doggy' calls. When the phone rang for the third time that evening, and she rushed out of the room, her eyes alight, Duncan put down his glass champagne flute and sighed; even their evenings together no longer existed.

She burst into the room. 'Duncan, that was a secretary with an invitation to judge four Terrier breeds. Isn't that marvellous? What a day!'

He looked at her shining eyes, her animated features, her sheer vivacity and got up and put his arms around her and kissed her. Then his arms tightened around her and she could feel the heat and urgency of his body. she tried to pull away but he tightened his arms around her, crushing her breasts against him. He started kissing her neck and then slid his mouth down to her breasts. 'Fiona, Fiona, please, I love you so much and it's been so long,' he gasped as his hand slipped into her bra and pulled out one breast. 'Oh God, Fiona!'

His hand was now undoing the button on her jeans. She frantically tried to break away from him, saying, 'No, Duncan, no,' but his other arm held her firmly. She pummelled him about the head and for a second his grip loosened. She broke away, staring angrily at his flushed face.

He shouted, 'I want to love you; I've done everything you've asked. You are my wife, for God's sake. I have a right to expect you to make love to me.' He lunged at her but she managed to avoid his arm and ran upstairs shutting the bedroom door.

He followed her and burst into the room, his face contorted with lust and anger. 'I'm fed up with this. It's all take and no give as far as you're concerned. Well, I'm bloody well taking now.'

Fiona was very frightened – she had never seen Duncan like this and suddenly realised what she had put him through in her own selfishness. She stood there completely motionless as Duncan ripped her clothes off. He then pushed her on to the bed, forcing her legs wide apart. He ripped off his own clothes and flung himself on top of her, entering her with force. Thrusting rapidly, he soon climaxed, but stayed on top of her. His weight prevented her from moving. She tried to keep her face turned away from him but he kept grabbing her jaw and forcing her to kiss him, his tongue nearly choking her. She struggled, trying to get away from him, but only succeeded in exciting him again.

This time he took a lot longer to climax and she felt very sore and bruised from his constant forceful thrusting. Her breasts and mouth felt bruised and tears were rolling down her face as, red-faced and gasping, he rolled away from her. She lay there, hardly daring to move until she knew that he was asleep. Then she slipped out of bed and went to the bathroom. She felt dirty.

It was some time before she fell asleep and it was later than usual when she woke up. Duncan was not beside her. She remembered the events of the previous evening and tears came into her eyes. She slipped her dressing gown on and crept out on to the landing. There were no sounds coming from his bedroom or from downstairs. She descended the stairs and came face to face with Duncan.

He couldn't meet her eyes but flushed and said that he hoped that he hadn't hurt her last night but, well... He went out, closing the door.

Fiona phoned the library to say she wasn't well and then, after another shower, spent all day making plans.

D URING THE NEXT few days Fiona was very busy putting one of her plans into operation. She saw very little of Duncan, who left the house early and didn't arrive home until Fiona had gone to bed. On the Friday evening, however, he arrived home earlier, carrying a large bouquet of flowers. He was very surprised to see a caravan parked in the drive. Leaving the flowers on the back seat he went into the house, expecting to hear voices but all was quiet. Fiona was in the kitchen.

'Who's here?' he asked.

'No one. Why?'

'There's a caravan parked in the drive.'

'Yes, it's mine. I bought it to go to the shows.'

'I see. Have you had a ball-hitch fitted to your car?'

'Yes, all organised.'

She and Simon had often spoken about the advantages of going to the shows with a caravan. It not only saved a long journey back on the same day, but they had discovered that a lot of social entertaining went on in the evenings and some wheeler-dealing as well. After that dreadful evening with Duncan, her first thought had been to get away as soon as possible, but then she decided that it would be far more convenient for her to stay there while she put her plans into operation. She had also decided that, for the present, she would not tell Simon what had happened because that too might necessitate her leaving the house immediately. She felt that, at last, she was growing up and behaving independently.

Simon had not been so delighted with her news about the caravan as she had hoped. It was mainly his male pride getting in the way because he was unable to contribute to it financially, but when she told him the extent of her inheritance from her prudent father, he had been very quiet indeed.

She travelled down to Paignton on the Thursday evening when she thought that the traffic would be lighter. When she got to the showground and was shown where to park her car and caravan, she was smiling broadly. She felt that, all on her own, she had really achieved something – buying the caravan, stocking it, which had been a great pleasure, and then successfully driving down to the ground.

A friendly fellow exhibitor came along to help her put up the awning and the pen for the dogs. Having got everything settled, she took the dogs for a walk round the field. As the show had been on that day as well, it was still quite a busy scene. One or two caravans were preparing to leave while others were arriving. The large marquees were quiet and still in the gathering dusk, and Fiona felt rather excited about the coming day's show.

Later, warm and cosy in the caravan, the dogs in their cages in the awning, she mentally gave herself a pat on the back for her own enterprise. It felt rather good to have accomplished something entirely on her own without the aid of Duncan, or Simon for that matter.

Simon arrived at the show on the Friday morning and was most impressed with the caravan; he praised her organising skills. At the show, Simon got a first in his class and then the Res. CC with Bracken, but Fiona didn't get placed with her dog and only got a third with her bitch. They both went back to the caravan site after the judging was over and had a chat to several Cumbrian exhibitors, who were also staying with their caravans.

Later, they went into Fiona's caravan. Simon immediately grabbed her and kissed her.

'Do you realise that we have two whole nights together?' she said.

'Ah, I'm sorry my love, no can do. Mary has refused to do anything for the dogs now so I must get home some time tonight to see to them.'

'Oh, Simon.'

'I know, I know. I'll get something organised.'

They had a meal and talked about the judging. Simon felt that Bob had given him the Res. CC because his first Champ judging at Birmingham was looming.

'Mind you, Fee, Bob's judging again next year as well, so I'd better think about that, too.'

They had been invited to a fellow Cumbrian's caravan for a drink but declined on the pretext of tiredness. Later, when they had settled all the dogs, they opened a bottle of wine and as they sipped their second glass, they caressingly undressed each other between kisses. Just for a fleeting moment, as Simon started to kiss her nipples, Fiona thought of the incident with Duncan and she stopped unzipping Simon's trousers and pulled away from him.

'What's the matter?'

'Nothing, er, n-nothing, just somebody walked over my grave.'

Not having made love to each other since her father's death, their passion was intense. As she knelt on the bed, he entered her and played with her full, hanging breasts. They climaxed quickly and together, laughing out loud with sheer exultation.

A dog barked, which woke them both up.

'Good God, what's the time?' Simon grabbed his watch. 'It's five past bloody midnight, I'll have to go, Fee.'

She slid her hand down his chest and belly. 'Don't do that, for God's sake.' She started to slide her mouth down his belly, twirling his curly hair in her fingers.

'Fee,' he groaned as he grabbed her breasts.

They made love again. Simon finally crept out of the caravan and, wincing, tried to quietly start the car and leave.

Very little gets missed by fellow exhibitors, and they noticed the caravan at the South Wales and Leeds and Bournemouth shows. There were quite a lot of knowing looks and ribald remarks, but none of it was malicious. All scandal and gossip is transient in the world of dogs and Fiona and Simon knew that it would soon be some other event that would set the tongues wagging.

Their main worry at this time was how Simon could stay with her at night. Since Paignton, Mary was now getting very suspicious if he was at all late home. After the Bournemouth show, when it was a very hot, humid night and their lovemaking had been very energetic, they had drifted off to sleep in each other's arms. Fiona had woken at 3.30 a.m. and had woken Simon, urgently. He said that it was far too late to go now and, cuddling her, fell asleep again. Fiona had stayed awake and had made him some tea at six, worried about his reception.

On arriving home late on Sunday morning, Simon walked into the house and was immediately confronted by an irate Mary. 'And where were you last night, may I ask?'

'And good morning to you, too. Yes, sorry about that, the car broke down, fan belt went. I was lucky, really. Ted Roberts saw me on the hard shoulder and pulled over. He took me to a garage and I was able to get another one. Took me ages to change and Ted and his wife kindly offered me a bed for the night.'

'So why didn't you phone?'

'Sorry, meant to but forgot.'

'And you expect me to believe that? Look, you're playing around with that bloody McCleod woman, aren't you? I know it and if I can prove it there's going to be hell to pay. Do you hear me?'

Simon didn't reply but picked up his show equipment and took it out to the kennel. He realised that he was going to have to be very careful from now on. Some women are funny, he thought to himself. Mary had never liked making love right from the start of their marriage. Even on their honeymoon she had been shy – wouldn't take her nightie off, insisting that he turned away as he undressed, and wouldn't have the light on. She had lain there totally unresponsive to his caresses and had not initiated any herself. He had always been very patient with her, thinking that things would improve, but her attitude to sex had never really got any better. After the children had been born she had intimated that she herself wasn't very keen on having any more intercourse, because she found it all rather messy and boring. She didn't want to have any more children but, if he absolutely had to, it would be alright now and again. After all, it was only right to keep her marriage vows.

This had been the status quo for the last fifteen years until he had met Fiona. He'd fancied her straight away but hadn't dreamt that it would get to this. God, but she was wonderful in bed.

Reluctant to go back to the house, he got some disinfectant and washed down the dog run, changed the water in the bowls and checked up on the food situation. When Sharon called him in for dinner, Mary was very quiet as she put the final touches to the Sunday roast. As he was drying his hands, she suddenly turned to look at him.

'Look here, I've decided that you're off the hook this time but if—'

'What do you mean?'

'What I say. I phoned Ted Roberts while you were out with those damned dogs. I got the phone number out of the Cumbrian yearbook. He said that you had stayed there last night when I asked him. I wonder, though, what he'd have said if I had just asked to speak to you? I'll know better next time. Anyway, you can't use that excuse again, can you, or running out of petrol like last time, so just be warned.'

Simon was shaken; things were coming to a head quicker than he had expected. He had not thought that Mary would check up on his story. Torn between his love for Fiona and his responsibilities, it was getting more difficult by the day. Looking across the table at Mary he thought, thank god for Ted Roberts; he must have known about him and Fiona, although he had never said a word. Thank God also that Ted could think on his feet! He certainly owed him a pint when he next saw him.

It was little better for Fiona. She drove the caravan into the drive and went indoors. The house felt and smelled unlived in. There was a long note from Christine to say that all the dogs had been fed, watered and exercised. Sally had been rather upset this morning. She had been dirty in the kitchen and Beryl wondered if Mr McCleod had gone away as well. She was sorry if Mrs McCleod had told her and she had forgotten, but she had put her in the kennel with the others this morning.

Putting down the note, Fiona hurried out to the kennel and found Sally. The bitch was pleased to see her but a little reluctant to go into the kitchen. She obviously still felt upset about being dirty. Fiona hugged her and coaxed her in. She then got the other dogs settled down and went upstairs to shower and change.

There was a note from Duncan on her bed, dated Friday, saying that he would be staying with his parents over the weekend and not to expect him until Monday evening. She was horrified. The dogs had been left Friday evening and all of Saturday afternoon and evening! She felt very guilty. If only Duncan had said before she went.

On Monday evening, Duncan let himself in and came straight into the kitchen, where Fiona was putting the finishing touches to a casserole.

'I shan't be staying for dinner. I've only come to acquaint you with the situation.'

'Oh, but I've cooked. What situation?'

'For goodness' sake, Fiona, don't try to make out that everything's normal. I'm moving out. No, I've moved out as, no doubt, you have already noticed. I'll collect some more clothes etc. later on.'

Fiona, who had not noticed that he had taken some of his clothes, could only reply, 'Moving out?'

'Do me the courtesy of not pretending our marriage isn't over. You know that and so do I. The sooner we finish the better, so that we can get on with our separate lives.'

All that Fiona could say was, 'I'm so sorry, Duncan,' before she burst into tears. She wasn't quite sure why or for whom.

Duncan made as if to comfort her and stopped himself. 'Right, I'll just collect some more of my things then, and be off. Anything urgent, call me at work.'

Tired and still somewhat shocked at the suddenness of it, Fiona stood in the hall until Duncan came down. They made polite, awkward farewells and, as Duncan went out of the door, he turned and said, 'My solicitor will be in touch – I'm sure that we can sort everything out amicably.'

The dinner went uneaten as Fiona sat in the lounge. She had such terrible feelings of having failed Duncan and of letting him down. It was all her fault. Why hadn't she seen before how very different they really were? Why had she taken up dog showing? Why had she fallen in love with Simon? Could she have stopped it? Duncan was a kind man. She frowned as she remembered that awful night again. Look what she had driven him to. She knew that, deep down, it wasn't just her – it was life, it was a set of circumstances – but it didn't stop the feelings of guilt. Duncan had always managed to make her feel guilty.

She looked around at the attractive decor, the matching suite covers and curtains, the Minton statues which Duncan bought her every year for her birthday. All so beautiful, so sterile, as indeed her marriage had been. Why couldn't she have seen it earlier? Why had it taken her so long to grow up, to want to do things herself and not be so submissive? Why?

It was quite dark when, at last, she got up and, locking up the kennel and the house, went to bed. Sleep was quite impossible as memories of her life with Duncan came to haunt her.

She did finally doze off, but after only a couple of hours sleep she woke and decided to get up and make some tea. Sighing, she decided to get on with her life on a daily basis; her mind would not function sufficiently at the moment to know what to do about anything. She put the kettle on and went out to let the dogs out into their run. When she got back indoors the phone was ringing.

'Hello, is that Fiona? Tom Turner here. Look, I think we've been very patient up to now while you've turned your place into a damned kennel, but this is too much. Are you aware that those dogs barked for hours over the weekend and are now barking again and it's only just 6 a.m.? Lord knows what Duncan is thinking of, letting you do this at all? This is a well-thought-of neighbourhood, you know, and I feel it's high time that you started to think of us. If you don't stop this barking, I shall have to report you to the council. It's only our past friendship that has stopped me up to now.'

'I'm so sorry, Tom, I didn't realise that it was so early. I promise that it won't happen again. Apologise to Rosemary for me, please.'

As she replaced the phone she said, 'Well, thank you, Tom; I didn't know what to do but you have just helped me to make up my mind.' She smiled. Tom and Rosemary were such nice people with whom they had always had a good relationship so, if they were upset, then it was time to move on. The thought frightened her a bit and she dearly wanted to talk to Simon, but he would be on his way to work and it really wasn't something to be discussed over the telephone anyway. She decided to go round and see Laura.

'Hello, Fiona. Well, it really is long time, no see. Come in.'

Over coffee, Fiona told Laura the whole story while Laura sat crumbling a biscuit between her fingers. When, at last, she arrived at the events of the morning and the decision she had finally made, Laura looked up with tears in her eyes.

'Oh, Fiona, that's such a big step. Have you really thought it through? I can't believe that you would throw up your marriage and your lovely home for the dogs and this man, Simon. What does he think? Are you sure that he is prepared to leave his wife and children? Do you think that you really know him? Please, Fiona, please think again.'

'Laura, don't you think that I have thought, again and again. You must have seen that things haven't been right between Duncan and me for ages now. I can't go backwards.' She had not told Laura about the rape.

Wiping her eyes, Laura stood up. 'Look, let me make a fresh cup of coffee. This one's gone cold.'

They talked on in a similar vein while yet another cup of coffee went cold, with Laura constantly trying to get Fiona to change her mind. The whole thing made her feel rather appalled at Fiona's behaviour, frightened, and in some way threatened. Surely her marriage to Michael was secure? She thought it was but now, was any marriage secure? She began to get cross with Fiona because of her own uncertainty, and Fiona felt that she had outstayed her welcome. The two friends parted with tears in their eyes and a feeling of loss.

The rest of the day crawled by until, at last, she could phone Simon. Mary answered the phone and Fiona asked if she might have a word with him about Cumbrian Terriers. There was a slight pause but then Mary said that she would call him.

'Oh, Simon, I must talk to you. I know that you can't at the moment, so can you come over?'

'I don't think so.'

'Please, you must, Simon. Duncan has left me and wants a divorce.'

'Oh, I see. Well, I'll try and come over later.'

Suddenly realising that she hadn't eaten all day, she made a sandwich. She had hardly finished eating it when she heard a car in the drive. She ran to the door and flung herself into Simon's arms. 'How did you get here so fast! I've got so much to tell you.' She told him what Duncan had said and about the phone call from Tom.

'You've been damned lucky up to now with the neighbours. Ours are always complaining. That's not the point, though. What do you want to do now? What do you want me to do now?'

'I know what I want to do but I don't know if you'll agree.'

'Try me.'

She told him that as far as she could see there was only one solution, and that was for her to buy another house. If she could get Duncan to agree to sell the house, and with the money her father had left her, she could easily buy a suitable property for breeding dogs.

'Don't you see, Simon,' she went on, 'we could really breed and show then. You want that too, don't you?'

Caught up in her enthusiasm, he discussed all the possibilities with her and was in the middle of elaborating about the sort of place that would be suitable, when he suddenly thought of Mary and looked at his watch – it was after midnight. Hurriedly kissing her, he raced home. The house was in darkness and switching on the hall light, he found a note on the hall table, saying, 'You can sleep on the settee.'

S IMON'S SEPARATION WAS not to be as civilised as Fiona's. He was shaken awake the next morning. As he opened his eyes, he found Mary glaring at him. She then proceeded to scream and shout for the next ten minutes non-stop. He had ruined her life for years with those damned dogs. He thought more of those bloody dogs than he did of his own family. He even thought more of the awful, common low-life who showed dogs – his so-called friends – than he did of his own family. He'd been a lousy husband and father, never earning enough money to provide properly for his family, and what he did earn he spent on those bloody dogs. His trouble was that he was only interested in two things: dogs and sex. He'd been sex mad right from the first day of their marriage. She would never have married him if she'd known what he was like.

At this point in the tirade, Simon got up from the settee and went into the kitchen to make a cup of tea. Mary followed him. 'I suppose this is some cheap, little bimbo, is it, this woman who wants to talk to you about terriers, or is it that bloody McCleod woman? Perhaps you've got two on the go now, you randy sod. I've been suspicious of you for months now. I bet she wants you for a stud, that's about all you're fit for. Dog people are all the same, it's doing all these matings, I think. Gives you ideas. Well, you're not going to get away with it.'

During the course of the morning she phoned her mother and told her that Simon was having an affair; she phoned his brother and told him about it; and when Barry and Sharon appeared, having slept in, she told them as well. His brother Peter had been ordered round to talk some sense into him and when he appeared, looking extremely awkward and apologising to Simon, they both went off to the pub for a drink. Peter had known for years of the situation between Simon and Mary, so hadn't been too surprised at the news. Simon told him very little but Peter could tell even from that that there was more to this than a casual fling.

When Simon got home, having left Peter at the top of the road, both of Mary's parents were drinking tea in the sitting room. They were obviously extremely embarrassed about the whole thing but, prodded by Mary, her father did try to point out to Simon that he had let Mary and the children down very badly and he thought that, for all the happy times that they had had, he should really think about what he was doing. As soon as they had finished their tea, they made a hurried departure so that they could feed the cat.

Once the door had closed behind them, Mary started up her verbal barrage again until Simon could not take it any longer. He told her that he was leaving and would arrange for a divorce. This statement silenced Mary instantly and then she burst into tears and demanded to know how she was supposed to manage. 'You needn't think that you're going to walk out just like that, not after all the years of misery you've given me. I'll tell you something else, your little bimbo needn't think that she's going to get her hands on any of your money. You've got to go on paying the mortgage and looking after us.'

He went upstairs and packed some clothes and his toilet things into a suitcase. Mary continued shouting at him as he put the case into the car and then went into the garden to collect the dogs and all of their equipment. Going upstairs again, he knocked and went into Barry's room. Barry was lying on the bed. Simon explained that he was leaving but would be in touch with him very soon. There were tears in Barry's eyes as he shook his father's hand. When Simon went into Sharon's room, she refused to look at him and continued sobbing loudly. Simon was hurting so much that he almost changed his mind, but one look at Mary's face stopped that and he got into his car and drove away.

The next two weeks were very difficult for Fiona and Simon, with many harrowing incidents. The first happened within days of Simon arriving. Tom Turner phoned again and was very angry this time about the noise the dogs were making, stating that it was louder than ever. Fiona apologised and explained that she was looking after a friend's dogs for a few days. She promised to try to keep them quieter. She had hardly put the phone down before it rang again. This time it was a more distant neighbour. She was not as polite as Tom had been and shouted that, if it didn't stop, she would inform the police and the council. Fiona once again tried to explain about the dogs but it was very obvious that this woman would not give an inch. It was definitely, shut them up now or I'll report you. Fiona rushed out to the kennel with a radio hoping that, if the dog couldn't hear outside noises, they would be quieter. She then shut them all in. She didn't know what else she could do.

Simon returned, having been to his house while Mary was at work, to collect more of his clothes. He had been rather upset to find them all stuffed into litter bags and left in the front garden ready for the refuse collection. Had he gone a bit later he would have lost everything. He couldn't believe that Mary could be quite so vindictive; after all, although their marriage hadn't been a great romance, they had brought up two children together reasonably well and Mary had seemed quite happy, except about money.

On returning to Fiona's house he was presented with another problem. His dogs were very responsive to his commands and soon peace was restored, but they spent the rest of that day talking about their current position and what to do about it. Simon said that this arrangement could only be temporary because it might take a while to sell Fiona's house and, as the dogs were too crowded, it would cause more trouble with the neighbours and he didn't want Fiona to have to put up with that.

A few days later, in the evening, Duncan decided to call in at his house to collect some documents relating to the work he was currently doing and which he would need in the next few days. He put his key in the door, having already noticed Simon's car in the drive, to be confronted with several large litter bags full of Simon's clothes, shoes and books. The sight of these infuriated him – he had only just moved out and she had already moved this man in. It also confirmed his earlier suspicions of a liaison and he was outraged.

Marching into the lounge, he glared at them both and ordered Simon out of his house. Fiona tried to explain but Duncan shouted her down and again ordered Simon out. Simon looked at Fiona, she nodded and he left. As he drove out, he saw Duncan throwing the litter bags containing his clothes and other items into the drive. This would be funny, he thought, if I saw it in a film. He drove to his brother's house and asked if he could stay for a night or two.

In all the years that Fiona had known Duncan, she had never seen him like this. His face was suffused with rage, his eyes blazing as he shouted at her, 'How dare you? How dare you sully my home with your cheap, sordid little affair? My God, how you've changed – mixing with all those people has made you common, cheap and immoral. You disgust me. Thank heaven we didn't have any children. You're not fit to be my wife or the mother of my children. And there was I feeling guilty for forcing myself on you. I suppose he was already enjoying you then, was he? The thought makes me feel sick.'

Fiona ran out of the room, tears streaming down her face. Her whole world was disintegrating. Falling on to her bed she buried her face in the pillow. After a while the banging around stopped and Duncan was gone. When she went downstairs there was a note lying on the table.

In view of your infidelity, I shall instruct my solicitor to proceed with the divorce as quickly as possible. I should also like you to vacate this house and, to that end, I shall also instruct my solicitor to purchase on my behalf your share in the property. I presume that, given the circumstances, you will not object and, as I shall pay cash, this should be completed quite quickly. I should like you to remove all traces of yourself and your dogs from my house and garden when you leave, so that I may arrange to have the house cleansed before I return to it.

D.

She made herself a large pot of tea and sat down in the kitchen; she knew that it was her own actions that had finally brought her to this turning point in her life and that it would have to be her own actions now that would decide her future. How could something as lovely as her love for Simon suddenly appear to be so sordid?

Apart from seeing to the dogs and trying to keep them quiet, she spent the rest of the day looking at the various options open to her – not that there were that many. This was a very big leap into the unknown and it frightened her, but she now had no choice. The phone had rung several times during that long day but, knowing that it must be Simon, she deliberately did not answer it. She needed to be entirely alone to decide her own fate. She did speak to Simon of her plans when he phoned in the evening, frantic with worry by now, but she only said that she was fine. Duncan hadn't stayed for long and she needed a little time on her own to think.

Having asked Christine to come in after school to see to the dogs, she spent the next three days travelling round certain rural areas which she had always liked. The following day she visited her bank manager, her solicitor and then several estate agents, who dealt with the areas in which she was interested. She had been relieved to know that she could afford the sort of property she wanted without having to wait for Duncan's money. She arranged to meet Simon for dinner and told him what she had been doing. His reaction was not quite what she had expected. He was silent for several minutes before he looked at her.

'You're sure this is what you want?'

'Yes, I thought this was what we both wanted.'

'Um, but it won't be ours, it will be all yours. You know how I'm placed financially, I could hardly put a damn thing into it.'

'Does that matter? We don't need it.'

'Yes, it bloody matters to me.'

She could understand how he felt but didn't know what words to say to change his mind. She only knew that he had to be part of her future. 'Look, I've been given several possible properties to look at. Please, at least come with me and advise me. I've got to move anyway and you'll know which would be the best for a kennel.'

He took some time off from work and they went round and viewed the various properties that she had been given. Simon found fault with all of them. Fiona began to wonder if he was deliberately nit-picking so as not to commit himself, and became worried. She had saved the one that she considered best until last, and when they finally found the lane and drove in, Fiona was thrilled – it was just what she had envisaged. It was an old, stone-built cottage, with mullioned windows not too big, set in five acres and with no near neighbours. She immediately exclaimed that this was quite definitely the one, and when Simon again said that it wasn't suitable, they had quite a heated argument.

'Why?' Fiona exclaimed. 'What is wrong with this one?'

'Just about everything. Hardly a fence in sight, no hard standing, no outbuildings except for that wooden garage; in fact, nothing.'

'But the cottage is gorgeous. It's got a lovely front garden. The drive up to the garage is quite big and there is lots of room between the garage and the cottage – enough for several cars to park. Let's just look inside, shall we?'

'Fiona, there's no point; there is just too much work to be done on it.'

They were both stressed over the happenings of the past week and the argument went from bad to worse and got to the point when they both agreed that the relationship could not continue. Fiona went home in tears only to receive more phone calls from the neighbours about the noise from the dogs and Simon returned to his brother's house to be asked if he could find somewhere else because the extra work was proving to be too much for Peter's wife.

Fiona was cuddling Sally and crying when the phone rang again. It was Simon – he was upset, too. They both apologised to each other through their tears. Simon said that he loved her and still wanted to see her but felt that, at the moment, he couldn't make any decisions about anything. He said that he realised that she had to move out soon and that she was still lumbered with his dogs so, if she liked the last house that they had seen, he did honestly think that it could, with a bit of working on, be just what she wanted. They arranged to meet for a drink the next evening to discuss it further.

During the next week she had a visit from someone from the council, concerning the noise from the dogs. She explained her situation and said that they would be moving as soon as she had a house. When he left, Fiona, in desperation, brought several of her dogs into the house. This would at least keep the noise down a bit, even if it meant more cleaning indoors. It would buy her a bit more time.

It seemed that she received a letter from Duncan's solicitor every other day. It hurt her to think how he was even stating what furniture Duncan wanted to retain and what he thought she should have, right down to very small items that she had forgotten about. All of their past years together were being torn apart into small pieces.

One thing did seem to be going her way. She had been to see the cottage again. When she was shown over it by the owner, she was even more determined to buy it. The large, stone-flagged kitchen had an Aga and was a perfect place for puppies; there was also a large brick fireplace in the lounge. Upstairs, there were two double bedrooms, both with excellent views over the fields and woods, and a bathroom that would definitely need renovating but was alright for now. Taking a deep breath, Fiona agreed to purchase it. She went to see the estate agent and a price was agreed. As it was to be a cash purchase and the present owner, a widow, was going to live with her daughter, the agent thought that, with luck, it should be a quick completion.

During this worrying time, all dog showing stopped for both of them, but Simon's first Championship-judging appointment was coming up. The digs that he had managed to find were not very comfortable and he was not sleeping well. Here was the appointment he had been wishing for for many years and he was too tired and dispirited to enjoy it as much as he should have done.

It proved to be a bit of an anti-climax. Fiona went with him and was sad that this show should have come at a time like this. Bob had entered, as Simon had predicted, and Simon did give his dog the CC, which showed that he was at least thinking ahead, Fiona thought. They were both tired afterwards and only stopped for a drink on the way home, neither wishing to talk much.

At last, she received a date for completion in September and was able to organise the removals and tell Simon the good news.

As she was taking very little of the furniture – only, in fact, some pieces that she had brought from her father's house – the biggest problem was the dogs and the kennel. It was decided that she would put the dogs into boarding kennels for a few days, during which time Simon would take down the kennel for the removers. He would supervise a builder to lay a concrete base for it and a large corridor-type kennel, which Fiona had ordered to go in a suitable place at the end of the large garden at the back of the cottage. They had spent hours together deciding where the kennels and the runs should go. They would use her present kennel as a whelping and puppy kennel in the course of time, and the positioning of that had to be worked out for maximum advantage.

They were both caught up in the excitement of it all and past arguments were forgotten. Fiona had wondered if Duncan might come round when she, at last, moved out, but she saw no one and dropped the keys off at his solicitor's. On the evening of the 26 September, with all the dogs temporarily settled into their new quarters, with no curtains at the windows and the few bits of furniture piled around just as the removers had left them, Fiona and Simon wearily erected a new double bed, made it up, tumbled into it and fell asleep in each other's arms.

By Christmas, after much work in all weathers, the kennels were complete and had heating installed. Simon had designed and erected fences for the runs and an exercise paddock. All of their dogs were now happily settled in the kennels, except for Sally, who was still the house dog. They sat by a log fire on Christmas Eve, drinking a glass of whisky and planning their showing and breeding programme for the coming year. They were both extremely tired, but contented, and looking forward to a successful New Year.

I T SEEMED TO have been raining for weeks, thought Fiona as she sat in the whelping shed, listening to the heavy rain beating on the roof. It was 3.30 a.m. and she was waiting for a bitch to start bearing down. She sighed heavily and hunched her shoulders deeper into her old anorak. Everything to do with dogs was so much harder when it was constantly wet. They were wet, their bedding was wet, the runs were wet, her clothes and boots were always wet. She sighed again. They had accomplished so much so quickly up until Christmas, but this damned rain had held up all their plans.

The bitch was very restless and Fiona stroked her head. 'Won't be long now, poppet.' This would be their first litter since coming here and they needed everything to go well. This was her livelihood now and she needed puppies to sell and the dogs to be used for stud. The bitch started to bear down.

She was just cleaning and disinfecting everywhere when the door opened and Simon came in with a steaming cup of tea. 'How's it going? Woke up early and thought that you would be in need of this.'

'She's fine; three dogs and one bitch, all okay. Thanks for the tea. I'll be in shortly.' She had a last look at the new mother busy washing her new family, and left the kennel, shutting the door to keep the warmth in.

She shivered as she walked back down the garden to the cottage, stopping only to admire a drift of daffodils. She was so happy here; the cottage had proved to be perfect for what they wanted. Her only regret was that she had not had any time since they moved in to make a few changes to the bathroom and to pretty up some of the other rooms.

'I'm off now, Fee. There's more tea in the pot. I'll be home early tonight to give you a hand and I must make a start on getting Jay and Bracken ready for the show.'

All showing had ceased when they moved in. Simon had dashed up to Crufts on Terrier day and passed round business cards with their new address on to fellow exhibitors. Simfell Kennels was going to be well known if Simon had anything to do with it. They had chosen to use Simon's prefix for the kennel as his was more established.

Fiona sighed as she put her damp coat to dry near the Aga. The kitchen was her favourite room in the cottage. Always warm, always welcoming, very handy for quick meals, of which there seemed to be many. It had proved invaluable over the past few months of hard work. She had never dreamed that she could turn her hand to putting in fence posts, erecting six-foot-high wire fencing, making and laying concrete, but she had enjoyed every minute of it. She did envy Simon though, going to this show at the weekend. She really missed showing and looked forward to getting someone to come in and look after the dogs soon.

April proved to be a much nicer month for weather and the litter were developing well when Fiona, her day's work done, went in search of Simon in the grooming shed. 'Hi, how are they looking?'

'Good. I'm pleased with them both. I'll load the car before I come in so that we're ready for an early start.'

They had advertised for a kennel maid to help mornings and some weekends, and couldn't believe their luck when a Ruth Baxter answered the ad. A trained veterinary nurse before her marriage, she now had three children, the last one having just started school, and had jumped at the chance to get out for a bit. Fiona desperately wanted to go with Simon to the National Terrier show and Ruth had said that she would look after the kennel on the Saturday while her husband looked after the children.

Fiona had a shower and washed her hair; it was very short now and didn't take long to dry. Her nails were in a deplorable state, but she couldn't worry about that. Going out and winning tomorrow was the important thing now, she thought, as she put some cream on her rough hands.

Settling the two dogs on their bench at the show the next morning, they browsed through the catalogue, surveying the competition in their respective classes.

'Jay'll have his work cut out to beat Harry Thomas's young dog,' said Simon. 'His wife and Marg are great buddies. Bracken stands a better chance and we know that Marg likes him.'

The judging turned out to be much as Simon had forecast – he came fourth in the class with Jay but got a first with Bracken. He was strung up when he took the dog in for the challenge – if they could make Bracken up into a champion it would certainly help in bringing in more money for studs, as well as the prestige of having a champion at the kennel. He was very disappointed when he was not given the award.

'Come on, Simon, you didn't really think that Marg would give it to you, did you?'

'No, I suppose not.'

'What bothers me more is what Betty told us about someone cutting that chunk of hair from her dog at the last show. Who would do that?'

'Just about anyone who wanted to stop her from winning. At least it wasn't dope or poison.'

'You're joking?'

'No, I'm bloody not. If we get near to having a champion, Fee, we must never let it out of our sight for a moment.'

That evening, Simon carried a tray upstairs on which were two glasses and a bottle of wine. As he entered the bedroom, Fiona emerged from the shower and came, completely naked, into the bedroom.

'Do you know something?' Simon remarked. 'You're not only clever and hard working, you're extraordinarily beautiful, too.'

'Flatterer, get out of those clothes and into the shower.'

They stood in the bedroom with their bodies pressed close together as they sipped the wine. They caressed and pleasured each other in several different positions until they climaxed and lay on the bed utterly content. It had been a good day.

For the rest of that year they continued to work extremely hard at establishing the Simfell kennel. They attended as many Championship shows as they could, as well as several Open shows in the area, to get the name known. They sold one of the promising youngsters from the spring litter to one of the big kennels at a very reasonable price. Fiona judged at several Open shows, Simon was invited to judge another Championship show the following year, but still the top wins, the coveted CCs eluded them.

Ruth had proved to be worth her weight in gold. Fiona had been very pleased to have someone to chat to as well; she had missed the female chat of the library. It had also given her a bit more time to spend on the cottage. Through the summer she had attended a few auctions and purchased one or two pieces of furniture. These, together with the new curtains and cushion covers, had totally transformed some of the rooms and Fiona felt a deep sense of belonging now in this old cottage. She now knew it in its winter, spring and summer moods; how the pheasant and partridge came into the garden in the winter looking for food, how the fire wouldn't draw so well when the wind was in a certain direction. What a delight and a surprise it had been one day to walk in the woods with Sally and find a carpet of the deepest blue. How the summer sun shone into various rooms as it travelled round the cottage windows. She was looking forward to seeing it in the autumn. She could look out of the bedroom window every morning for the first signs of the leaves turning in the woods.

One evening, towards the end of November, Simon suggested that they should give a little party to let in the New Year. 'What do you think, Fee? We've got bags of room and I'd help you. It would certainly help us.'

'What a marvellous idea. I haven't given a party for ages and I'm sure the cottage would enjoy it, too. I won't have much time to cook but I can get lots of goodies from the supermarket.'

'I'll see to the booze. It'll go with a swing.'

Fiona smiled, thinking of the hours of careful planning when she had entertained Duncan's parents or a few friends and now, in a few minutes, a whole party was organised. 'I wonder if Laura and Michael would come?'

She hadn't seen them since she came here. She had sent cards and a present to the children on their birthdays and had received a letter of thanks each time from Laura, but that was all.

'Do ask them if you think that they'll enjoy themselves. It's all going to be rather doggy and they won't know anyone else, will they?'

'No. Perhaps I'll invite them another time.'

She continued. 'We've received our first Christmas card, Simon – it's from Harry and Lyn Watson. I must find time to get a load of cards to send.'

'Fine, but make sure you get them personalised and with our kennel name in large letters.'

The doggy fraternity were very good at sending cards and by 15 December they had received sixty-two cards. Fiona had ordered one hundred and was kept busy every evening sending them out. As neither of them had received cards in such profusion before, they felt that, at last, their name was becoming well known. By Christmas Day the walls of their hall and dining room were a riot of festive colour.

On the day of the party it was bitterly cold, with a very sharp frost. In all, about twenty-seven people had accepted their invitation and, after they had seen to the dogs, they were both busy with preparations. By evening, as they locked up the dogs for the night and checked the heating, the frost was thick on all surfaces. As they slithered back to the house Fiona remarked, 'I'm almost too tired for a party.'

Simon put his arm round her shoulders. 'Me too, but a shower and a drink will get the old adrenaline running. You'll see.'

He was right. When the first guests arrived Fiona greeted them dressed in a black dress, which showed her slim figure off to perfection. Several of the men cast a lustful eye over her during the evening and thought what a lucky beggar Simon was.

At about ten o'clock, as she was passing round more food, laughing at a risqué joke that she had just heard, she had to agree with Simon. Everyone was talking, eating, drinking and laughing. All dressed up in their finery, it was hard to recognise some women that she had only ever seen in dog-show gear. In their finery with make-up, a hairdo, high heels and jewellery, they were transformed. Most people asked her how the kennel was progressing and what she would be showing in the coming year. As Simon dispensed the drinks she noticed that he was often in quiet and earnest conversation with several of their Cumbrian acquaintances, and she was dying to know what he was talking about.

On the stroke of midnight, they all raised their glasses and drank each other's health, then joined hands for 'Auld Lang Syne'. Simon kissed her and whispered in her ear, 'I love you, beautiful girl; Happy New Year.'

Then she was being kissed by several of the men. She found that she didn't like this at all and tried to turn her cheek at the crucial moment, but sometimes this was not possible and she had to push them away from her with a set smile. She noticed that Simon was kissing most of the women and thanking them for coming, but at least he was kissing them on the cheek. She then tried this and found that it worked quite well.

When they finally shouted their last goodbyes and happy new years, and closed the door on the blue-white frosty morning, they both collapsed on the settee. Simon exhaled loudly. 'Wow, what a party.'

'Yes, I think everyone enjoyed themselves. What were you talking about so earnestly?'

'Ah, I've learnt a hell of a lot tonight. It was a damned good idea to have this party.'

'So have I, but most of it was gossip.'

'No, I mean important stuff. I'll tell you tomorrow when we're not so tired. But I'll tell you something now, it's done us a world of good to have this party. And by the way, you looked smashing in that dress. If I wasn't so tired…'

Over a late breakfast, he told her that he was being put forward to judge another Championship show and he was also asked if she had her requisite number of classes to be eligible to judge at champ level, because her name might be put forward, too. 'How about that? We'll have a bit of pulling power then, won't we, being able to award two sets of tickets. Must remember, though, that it was Tony who would have put our names forward to the secretary. Oh, and Ted who's judging Midland Counties, said that he would be interested in having a puppy from a litter by Jay. At the right price of course!'

'So, it really was a successful party. Good,' Fiona remarked, tiredly. She was thinking of her father and how much he would have enjoyed the fun. Would he have approved of Simon and of her new life? She was also thinking that she was so glad that she had not invited Laura and Michael – they would not have fitted in. Getting dressed up like that had made her a little nostalgic, she reflected and, shrugging herself into her old anorak, woolly hat, thick socks and wellies, she followed Simon out of the back door into a very cold, white new year. 'Ah well, back to work.'

T HAT JANUARY, THE winds drove down from the north-east across the fields and were bitterly cold. The outside taps froze and some days even the water in the dogs' bowls froze. As neither of them were used to being outside so much in the winter months, Fiona got chilblains and they both suffered from chapped, sore hands. Fiona got a very bad cold and a wracking cough, which would not clear up. Simon also caught the cold. Fiona dragged herself round the kennels every day in order to feed and exercise the dogs, because Ruth was unable to come as two of her children also had bad colds. Fiona was thankful that there were no puppies at the moment. After three days she was utterly exhausted, and when Simon came home he insisted that she see the doctor the next morning. He would take some leave and take over from her, although he wasn't much better than she was. They both ended up at the doctor's the next morning; he prescribed antibiotics and rest, saying that they should go out as little as possible.

The following week, with Simon back at work, Fiona was sitting by the Aga with her cold hands wrapped around a steaming cup of coffee, when the phone rang. She went to answer it, mentally praying that it wouldn't be somebody desperately wanting a stud for today. Normally, people booked the stud as soon as the bitch came into season, but now and again you got somebody, usually a pet owner, who either hadn't noticed that the bitch was in season, or had unsuccessfully tried to mate it to another owner's pet dog and failed. It was cold away from the Aga and Fiona shivered. 'Hello, Simfell Kennels.'

'Hello, hello. Is Simon there, please?'

The caller, a woman, sounded rather agitated and Fiona feared that her thoughts had been correct. 'I'm sorry but he is not here at the moment. Can I help you?'

'Is that Fiona? This is Mary, I must get hold of Simon. Is he at work?'

'Yes, is there something the matter?'

'Yes, I'll phone him at work.'

The phone went dead and Fiona shrugged her shoulders. If Mary ever had any communication with Simon it was usually about money. I expect Simon will tell me all about it when he comes home, she thought, as she slipped on her heavy anorak again and went outside. As an afterthought, she went back indoors and put on the answerphone. Still feeling the after-effects of her cold, she continued slowly with the day's work, pondering, as she did, on the phone call. Both of their divorces had been finalised now, fairly amicably too, so there couldn't be problems there.

As she finished the last run, she gratefully hurried back to the cottage. Slipping off her boots, anorak, woolly hat and gloves, she wandered over to the phone. There were three calls: the first message was a puppy enquiry, Fiona noted the name and number on the pad; the second was from a friend in showing who wanted to know if she could beg a lift to the show next weekend; the third was from Simon. She knew as soon as she heard his voice that something was wrong. He told her that he was at the general hospital and that Barry had been in a car pile-up on his way to work. He didn't know how long he would be there but would ring her again later.

She sat down by the Aga and Sally came up to her and put her head on Fiona's lap. 'Yes, Sal, you know something's wrong, don't you?' The bitch continued to look at her with sad eyes. How badly was Barry hurt? Fiona fondled Sally's head. Poor Simon, she thought, he felt awful when he went to work this morning after that cold; heaven knows how he must be feeling now with this worry to contend with. Again putting on the answerphone, she went out to exercise the dogs.

It was just beginning to get dark as she finished and went back to the warm kitchen. There were no phone messages this time and she began to feel very worried. She liked Barry. Unlike his sister, who had been very unpleasant over the divorce, Barry had often come over to see them and had helped his father quite a lot with some of the construction work.

By nine o'clock there was still no word from Simon, the dinner was cold and she was nervous with worry. When the phone finally rang she hurried to answer it.

'Fee, it's me. Fee, Barry died about half an hour ago; he never regained consciousness.'

She could hear him sobbing, trying to hold back the tears, and she hurt inside with wanting to help and comfort him. 'Oh, Simon, I'm so very sorry. Are you alright?'

'I'll cope somehow. Look, Fee, will you be alright if I stay with Mary and Sharon tonight? They're pretty broken up and I'll have things to do tomorrow.'

'Yes, I'll be fine. You stay for as long as you have to. Don't worry, I'll manage.'

She did a last check on the kennels and locked up for the night. Trying to keep busy she then filled in a couple of schedules for forthcoming shows. Simon had not phoned when she finally went up to bed. Too exhausted and worried to sleep, she lay there for a while, reading. It felt cold and lonely without Simon beside her. She was just drifting off to sleep when she heard the sound of a car and lights dashed across the bedroom ceiling. Pulling on her dressing gown she ran to the window. Some of the dogs were barking, alerted by the noise, and the security light had come on at the front of the house. She raced downstairs, rather frightened now, and switched on the outside lights. Someone knocked on the door.

'Fee, it's me, Simon.'

Looking out of a front window she saw him and, letting out a sigh of relief, quickly unbolted the door. Simon walked in and her heart jumped in her breast: he was deathly pale with dark patches under his eyes and seemed to have aged five years. He put his arms round her and his whole body was wracked with sobs. She could physically feel his pain.

They stood locked in each other's arm's for some time, while Simon shuddered out his misery. Although very cold, Fiona neither moved nor spoke until he finally lifted his head and sighed deeply. Helping him out of his coat, she led him into the warm kitchen. Going into the dining room, she poured him a large brandy. He was shivering violently when she came back and placed the glass in his hand; he nodded but said nothing and Fiona just sat quietly beside him. His sorrow was too deep for words and she knew that, no matter how much she wanted to, she could in no way share it with him. She had never had a child – how could she know what it felt like to lose one?

Only when she was stiff with cold did she say, 'Would you like to lie down for a few hours?'

Again he nodded, and together they went upstairs, leaving all the lights on. In bed, he lay his head on her breast and fell into an exhausted sleep.

When Sally put an enquiring head round the door, Fiona wearily realised that another day, with all its work, was awaiting her. For the first time since moving there, she fervently wished that she was in her lovely, neat house with no dogs to see to. She tried to move without disturbing Simon, but he woke just as she was getting out of bed.

'Hello you,' he smiled, and then memory returned and his face drained of colour. 'Oh God, Fee. He's dead.' Tears filled his eyes.

Together, and in silence, they did all the daily chores. There was an easterly wind driving the rain clouds across the fields and even the dogs didn't wish to be out in it, preferring to stay in the comfort of their heated kennels. Taking off their soaking outer clothes and their wet, muddy boots, they made some lunch and sat by the Aga.

'It's not doggy weather, is it?' Fiona broke the silence.

Simon smiled and agreed. Then, in halting sentences, he told her about the hours he had spent at the hospital, of Barry's horrific injuries and of the doctors trying desperately to save him.

'I was able to sit with him for a while and hold his hand, but he didn't even know I was there. They told me that the injuries to his head were quite severe so perhaps it was best but…' He faltered and started to cry again. '…but…' He could not continue.

Lying in each other's arms that night, Fiona broached the subject that had been troubling her. 'Simon, why didn't you stay with Mary and Sharon?'

There was a long silence until Simon cleared his throat and said, 'We didn't go back to the house for some time after they told us that... that Barry... was dead. Mary was almost hysterical and Sharon not much better. They had to give her something to quieten her down so that I could take her home, and a sleeping tablet to take if she couldn't sleep. They told me to call our doctor if she became hysterical again. When I finally got them to the house, I saw that there were lights on and I was really worried that they had been burgled. I left them in the car and rushed in the back door, only to find some bloke asleep in an armchair. To cut a long story short, he's Mary's boyfriend. She had phoned him from the hospital and he'd been there all evening, waiting for her. She almost became hysterical again when she saw him. Both she and Sharon clutched at him, screaming and crying, and totally ignored me. I made them all a cup of tea, told him about the sleeping tablet and left. I suppose that I ought to phone tomorrow to see how they are.' Sighing deeply, he kissed her goodnight.

Simon's story had made Fiona think of Duncan for the first time in months. She wondered whether he had found someone else.

The next evening, Simon phoned Mary to discuss the funeral arrangements. The boyfriend answered and, after a short conversation with Mary, he came back to Simon with the message that she was too upset to talk to him but would be in touch. Another day passed before Mary finally phoned him. Fiona could hear him speaking to her and he sounded rather annoyed. The conversation was very brief and he soon returned to the kitchen. 'That was Mary. Apparently the funeral is on Tuesday at two o'clock.'

'Where is he being buried?'

'He's not. It appears Mary has made all the arrangements without consulting me. He is being cremated.'

'Oh, are you unhappy with that?'

'No, it's just that she didn't ask me. He's still my son, for God's sake.'

'Do you want me to order a wreath or is it to be a donation?'

'She didn't say but I'd like flowers. Would you do it for me, please?'

On the day of the funeral, Fiona queried whether she should go but Simon insisted that she accompany him, saying, 'Fee, I don't think that I could get through it without you.'

When they arrived at the crematorium, Mary walked up to them and handed Simon some bills. 'I'll send any others on to you. You can't expect me to pay them.'

Simon, too upset to argue, took the proffered envelopes and they went into the small chapel. It was packed with people. Simon recognised quite a few people, some of whom were from the dog world, much to his surprise. There were many young faces there and it was obvious that Barry had been a very popular person. Simon felt a small thrill of pride.

Peter came up and greeted them. 'Are you alright, Simon? Terrible business, isn't it? I still can't take it in.'

'Yes, I'm okay. Fiona's been a lot of help.'

They all sat down to watch Mary crying loudly and holding centre stage.

After the ceremony, as they left the chapel, Peter said, 'You will be coming back to the house, won't you? I understand quite a few are. We thought that we would just pop in for a few minutes.'

'No, as a matter of fact, we're not. This is the first we have heard of it so obviously we are not invited.'

Peter shook his head, kissed Fiona on the cheek and patted Simon on the back. 'Keep in touch, won't you?' he said, and left.

Fiona and Simon spoke to a few more friends and then left as well.

'Did you notice that Paul Aston was there, Simon, and Joan Skipton?'

'Yes, good of them to come.'

The sad news had, of course, travelled the doggy grapevine within twenty-four hours of it happening, and both Fiona and Simon were warmed by the many cards and phone calls expressing sympathy, not only from Cumbrian exhibitors but in other breeds as well. There was a nasty side to dog showing, they reflected, but there was also a nice one.

S PRING SEEMED VERY late in arriving that year; every day was cold, wet and windy. Fiona sighed as she disinfected a kennel. The past few weeks since the funeral had been very difficult. Simon had been quiet and reflective and Fiona felt at such a disadvantage not knowing what it would be like to lose a son. Not knowing what to say, she said nothing. A question that kept coming up in her mind was, supposing he was also upset that Mary had another man in the house. Could he be regretting his decision? Then there was the club show coming up next month; supposing she got a poor entry? She would feel awful. It had been such an honour to be asked to judge it and she had been so pleased but now... She jumped as Simon's arms went round her and he planted a kiss on her neck.

'I've been watching you dawdling over that run; what are you thinking about?'

'Oh, I was wondering what sort of entry I will get at the club show; it will be awfully embarrassing if it is small.'

'Don't be daft, Fee. You're very popular and people know you have done your homework and really studied and understood the standard and the anatomy of the Cumbrian. Of course you'll get a good entry.' He turned her round and gave her a kiss. 'Come on, cheer up. I'm sorry if I've been a bit quiet of late. Let's go out to that Chinese restaurant tonight and we'll have a bottle of wine, too.'

Neither of them said very much as they ate the meal, until Simon put his chopsticks down and said, 'Fee, don't tell me that you're still worrying about that show. For heaven's sake, Fee, you'll be fine.'

'No, I'm not really. Well, only a bit. I'm more worried about you, you've been so quiet since…'

'Yes, I know. I'm sorry, Fee. It was a bit hard to take and as for that bloody wife, sorry, ex-wife!'

Fiona smiled, her fears gone.

At the end of the week she received a catalogue showing her entries for the show and they were good. As the day for the show was a Saturday, Simon drove her to the venue.

'God, I'm so nervous, Simon. Supposing people don't turn up?'

Laughing, Simon drove into the car park. 'Look, there are loads of people here.'

'Do you think my outfit's alright? Perhaps I should have worn something else.'

'You would look lovely in anything and nothing. Especially nothing.'

His reply did not help to calm the butterflies in her stomach.

'So many big breeders are here. What will they think of my judging?'

'You know what to do. They'll think that you've done a good job. Now get in there.'

As she entered the ring with her steward, her brain felt numb. She took off the jacket she was wearing, got her pen out of her handbag and asked the steward to call in the first class. As soon as she touched the first puppy, all her nerves disappeared; she was happy. When the very last class was over and the last prizes given, she received a tremendous clap. She then knew that, once again, Simon had been right.

They started showing the dogs again and making great plans for the future. They still had not made up a champion though. Simon had got the expected Championship-judging appointment and Fiona was proposed to judge her first Championship show in the following year, subject, of course, to the breed clubs and the KC approving it.

That summer brought them a most promising litter and Simon was full of plans for their show career. When his friend Bob gave their dog Jay a first and the Res. CC, they were both over the moon. The puppies were making good progress and they felt that, at last, their hard work and planning were beginning to pay off.

One day, Fiona put the phone down and called to Simon, 'Ruth has hurt her back and won't be able to come in this weekend. That means that I won't be able to come with you to Driffield.'

'That's a damn shame. You'll still have young Jenny to help you.'

'Yes, but don't forget that I'm taking the puppies out to that Open show on Saturday. I must go – they've hardly been shown and they are already out of minor puppy.'

'Hell, I'd forgotten that we had entered that too. It's going to be a busy couple of days.'

Fiona set off at 7 a.m. on the Saturday. Not having slept too well, she was feeling somewhat sorry for herself, but cheered up as she drove into the car park and saw one or two familiar faces. Not having been shown because of Barry's death, she was very pleased when one of the puppies responded well in the ring, won its class and went on to win Best Puppy in Breed. The other one showed rather badly and only managed a VHC or fifth – it obviously needed a lot more time spent on it at ringcraft training sessions. Fiona had to wait until much later to take the winning puppy bitch into the ring to challenge other Terrier puppy winners for best puppy in the Terrier group. She stepped out, smiling, and was delighted in the way the puppy responded again. It obviously enjoyed the atmosphere of the ring. Fiona was more than satisfied when she was pulled out second.

The next day, with Simon at Driffield, Fiona was kept busy in the kennel but found time to help young Jenny pin up the rosettes that Sapphire, the puppy, had won the previous day. She looked at them and hoped that this was the beginning of a successful career for Sapphire. After all, she was a descendant of Sally. Would this one be her first champion? She was hastily getting something ready for their evening meal when she heard Simon drive in. She looked out of the kitchen window and he waved his hand as he went to put the dogs in their kennel. He hadn't phoned her during the day so she knew that he could not have done as well as he had hoped. As he came through the kitchen door she had a hot cup of tea ready for him.

'Thanks love, it's been a long, hard day and I'm damned tired.'

'How did Bracken and Jay get on? I thought that you might have phoned me.'

'Sorry, I nearly did. We didn't do too badly. Jay got the dog CC and BOB.'

'What!' shrieked Fiona. 'How did you do in the group?'

'We came third. Honestly, Fee, he went round that ring like a good'un. I was so proud of him.'

Simon only just had time to put his cup down before Fiona flung herself into his arms. 'You horrible man; fancy not phoning me with such wonderful news.'

'What, and miss out on a cuddle like this?'

'Oh, Simon, his first CC. Now we want two more and we have our champion. Isn't that marvellous?'

At his next Championship show Jay only managed a first so when, at 4 a.m. on a cold morning in December, they set off for the last Championship show of that year, they were both very tense. Ruth had stayed the night and would be seeing to the kennel so they had no worries on that score but, nevertheless, they were both rather quiet on the journey up. Simon was concentrating on his driving and trying not to think of the day ahead. Fiona was wondering if the judge, their old friend Paul Aston, would like Sapphire. He had done rather well with the bitch that he'd had from her so she was hoping that he would see some similarities in Sapphire.

By the time it came to Jay's class, Fiona had already been to the Ladies twice, she was so tense. Jay showed well and won his class. The steward called in all the unbeaten dogs for the challenge. Simon's hopes rose as he looked round at the other winning dogs. Jay looked as good, if not better, than any of them. On the outside of the ring, Fiona was having similar thoughts, but also had her fingers crossed. There was complete silence as, once again, Paul looked at every dog. He then went to Simon and handed him the CC. Those round the ring applauded as Simon and Jay did their lap of honour. Fiona ran up to them and kissed both Simon and Jay, tears of happiness running down her face.

All the hard work had been worth it. Jay now had two CCs.

Fiona suddenly realised that she was in the bitch puppy class with Sapphire and minor puppy was already in the ring.

She hurried off to prepare her. The puppy bitch class was called by the steward and she went in with Sapphire.

Cumbrian Terriers had become more popular in the past few years and numbers in the ring had risen. There were fourteen other puppies here and some looked rather good.

Paul smiled as she put Sapphire on the table. 'Hello, Fiona. How old is she?'

'Eleven months.'

Paul studied Sapphire's conformation. 'A triangle, then straight up and down please.'

Fiona and Sapphire walked smartly round the ring. Paul pulled them out into second place. Fiona was pleased because this qualified Sapphire to go to Crufts next year. Fiona's euphoria lasted all afternoon and even though the bitch CC beat Jay for BOB, she didn't mind at all.

They were both feeling very tired as they drove home. Simon took the first stint and Fiona drove the rest of the way. When they arrived home they were so pleased to see that Ruth had everything under control. The money they paid her was worth every penny. She had even put a casserole in the Aga for them.

Simon came in. having seen to the two show dogs. 'Um, that smells good.'

'Yes, Ruth made it. I couldn't thank her enough.'

They ate the meal in the warm kitchen. It was only when they were in bed and Fiona couldn't sleep that she realised that Simon had been surprisingly quiet about the CC. She lay there in the darkness for a while and gradually the warmth made her drowsy; she turned over and put an arm around Simon, cuddling close to his sleeping body.

The next day, several of their close friends phoned to congratulate them on the second CC. Fiona watched Simon as he took some of the calls. He didn't seem as pleased as she thought that he'd be – he obviously had something on his mind. That evening, with all the work done, they sat by the fire, having opened a celebratory bottle of wine, and relaxed.

Fiona yawned and stretched. 'What a weekend. Sapphire doing

so well first time out and Jay's second. Have you enjoyed it?'

'Yes, I have. It does make next year's prospects look hopeful, doesn't it? It's time all our efforts started to bear fruit.'

'People have been very nice about it, although I've no doubt that many will have been saying things that were less complimentary.'

'No doubt, and there will be those who will not want us to make him up. Just let them start knocking him and they'll have me to answer to.'

Could he be worrying about that? No, Simon was more than capable of dealing with the nasty side of showing. She realised that she was just going to have to wait for Simon to tell her what was wrong. They sat together on the settee, drinking the wine and watching the flames gradually die down.

She was just getting drowsy when she heard Simon quietly say, 'You know, Fee, I wish I could pick up the phone and tell Barry about Jay and his two CCs. Right from when he was a little boy I always promised him that one day I would make up a champion.'

A WEEK LATER, with Christmas almost upon her, Fiona was frantically writing out Christmas cards. They had already received more than she had anticipated and the excitement of LKA and Jay's second ticket had quite upset her schedule. Having written what she hoped was the last card, she was just starting on a list of presents still to buy, and the food list, when the phone rang. To her surprise, it was Laura.

Fiona was pleased to hear her voice. Their friendship had suffered when Fiona had moved away to live with Simon. Michael and Laura had never accepted an invitation to visit them at the kennels in all this time, and they had never invited her and Simon to visit them.

After the usual pleasantries and enquiries Laura said, 'I'm really phoning because I have two wonderful bits of news for you. One, I'm going to have another baby. Isn't that wonderful? It was confirmed last week; both Michael and I are delighted. And two, when Duncan and Barbara came round last week... Oh, I did tell you that Duncan had married again, didn't I? No? Oh, I thought I had. Well, when they came round to dinner last week they told us that Barbara was expecting. Duncan was absolutely over the moon.'

Fiona could not reply for a moment or two – she felt as if someone had just hit her very hard in the stomach. She tried to collect her thoughts but her mouth was so dry that, even had she been able to think of something to say, she would not have been able to speak.

'Hello, Fiona, are you still there? I suppose I've rather surprised you.'

Finally Fiona managed to say, 'Yes, Laura, you have somewhat. I didn't even know that Duncan had remarried.'

'I wondered if perhaps he had told you. It was in September. I don't know if you knew her – she was the secretary to Duncan's partner. It was a very quiet ceremony, only a few friends.'

'No, I didn't know about it and I didn't really know her.'

'She is very pretty – a bit younger than Duncan. We should have our babies within ten days of each other. Isn't that remarkable?'

'Yes, it is. Well, congratulations to you both. Thank you for phoning. Bye.'

Fiona stood staring at the phone for several minutes. The news had brought back all those unhappy memories when she and Duncan had tried and tried to have a baby. That it should have happened so quickly with someone else made her feel angry, angry and very inadequate again. She wondered if they were living in 'her' house, and that made her feel even angrier. Realising that she was icy cold and trembling, she made her way to the kitchen and sat down.

Why was she so angry? She was happy with Simon. She was living the life that she wanted. True, she would never have a child now, but there were many other compensations: Simon and the dogs. Did she really mind if they were living in that perfect house? No, she had her cottage. In fact, she was pleased in a way that Duncan, at least, would get the child he had always wanted.

What had upset her was the obvious pleasure that Laura had got from telling her. She was her friend; she knew how much it would upset her to hear this news. How could she be so unkind? Why did she have to be so unkind? Fiona gradually got her emotions under control and when Simon came home she was able to tell him the news quite calmly while they ate dinner.

'And how do you feel about it?' Simon asked quietly.

'Alright now. It was a bit of a shock at first and then I felt very angry but now... well...' Fiona shrugged her shoulders. She did not continue, and Simon looked at her for a second or two but said no more.

Christmas Day that year was rather quiet, with each wrapped in their own sad thoughts. They had told Ruth and Jenny that they did not have to come in until the New Year if they didn't want to, when they gave them their Christmas presents the previous day, so they were both kept pretty busy all over the Christmas period. They had both agreed that they must have a repeat of last year's New Year party as the last one had been such a success. They had invited even more friends and enemies from the dog-show scene this year so they were soon immersed in preparations.

On the evening of the party Fiona, bathed, dressed and made-up looked with surprise at her reflection in the cheval mirror. 'Hard work must be good for you,' she told the slim woman in the close-fitted, black dress. Her breasts were still firm and her waist neat, her skin tones were good and her hair still thick. Most days, she reflected, she hardly had time to look in a mirror to comb her hair. I must keep up my skin care for Simon, she vowed.

'Admiring ourselves are we?' Simon's voice interrupted her thoughts. Standing there naked, towelling his hair, his tall leanness still excited her, making her tiredness drop away and her eyes sparkle.

'Well, if nobody else admires me...'

'What, at this moment I fancy you rotten. See for yourself, wench.'

Laughing, she tried to escape his arms. 'No, no, don't touch me, I'm all ready for the party. Go away, you brute.'

He kissed her and the passion began to rise in them both.

'I'm going, Simon. I'd love to stay but I have a party to organise. I'm going.' Laughing, she kissed him on the cheek and ran out of the room. As she went downstairs she smiled. It was very reassuring to know that Simon still found her so attractive.

The party was obviously a great success, she thought, a few hours later, as she plied various people with food. The cottage was full of the noise of talk and laughter. She had overheard several interesting snippets of conversation and wanted to hear more: who was having an affair with whom, who had slept with a forthcoming judge, so should get the ticket; who dyed their dog's hair and had their dog's teeth straightened; who had mated a bitch and then said that it was their other stud dog, who everyone knew was absolutely knackered and was past mating anything, poor devil; who had lent someone their holiday home; who always gave someone several bottles of whisky or a crate of wine before a show. Fiona's mind was buzzing with so many questions that she would like answered. She reflected, not for the first time, as she went out for more food and to wash some glasses, on the extent of this dog world that she was now a part of. It was really a massive industry, the commercial side alone, with its tremendous variety of tinned foods, complete foods, biscuits, snacks, supplements and medicines; its scissors, brushes, combs, beds, bowls, leads and kennels; its cards, stationery, pedigree forms, stud books, posters and ornaments. She gave up, her mind too tired to think of more.

Suddenly, an arm went tightly round her waist. 'Do you know, Simon, I hadn't realised just how involved the dog world really is.'

'And I hadn't realised until now just how gorgeous you are.'

Fiona whirled round to find Alan Burgess smiling a little drunkenly at her. Alan, she knew, was a member of the Kennel Club and, it was said, was very well in with several Championship-show secretaries; his wife was on the committee of one of the shows. Simon had said that it was almost a certainty that he put forward judges' names for several of the shows and it would be unwise to upset him.

With this in mind she smiled and said, 'You startled me, Alan. I hope you are enjoying the party. Would you like a cup of coffee? I've just made one.'

'I'd much rather have you some time.'

'You flatterer, Alan.' As she said this, she smilingly moved out of his arms. 'I must be a good hostess and ask if anyone wants a cup of coffee.'

He lurched towards her. 'Well, how about a little kiss on account first.'

Fiona thought quickly. An outright refusal would annoy him and Sapphire needed CCs. She picked up the tray of cups and held them in front of her, which made it impossible for him to hold her. Leaning forward, she gave him a quick kiss on the lips and hurried into the lounge.

At midnight, as the chimes rang out for the New Year, Fiona made sure that she was standing next to Simon. When everyone was kissing each other and wishing each other a Happy New Year, Fiona managed to meet up with Alan when he was still with his wife. She gave them both a kiss on the cheek but, as she kissed Alan's cheek, he turned his head slightly and whispered in her ear, 'I'll give you a ring and we can continue our little conversation.'

Rather startled, Fiona just smiled and moved away.

Simon seemed a bit quiet as they tidied up and got ready for bed but Fiona, thinking that it was tiredness, didn't query it. The next day though when he was still quiet, she asked him what was wrong.

'Oh, it's just something that Paul said to me last night. I don't know what to do about it.'

'What, Paul Aston? Well, tell me. Is it something to do with us?'

'Yes and no, not us exactly. We were talking, as you do, about forthcoming shows and what we would be showing and what we hoped to win, when he suddenly asked me if we owned the kennels jointly.'

'Whatever did he want to know that for?'

'Well, if I was the owner or the joint owner he would... he would arrange for me to be proposed to... to join the Masons.'

'Join the Masons! What has that got to do with showing the dogs?'

'God, Fiona, a hell of a lot when it comes to winning and judging.'

'You're joking.'

'I'm bloody well not. I've known this for ages but never ever thought that I would be asked, so I've never bothered to say anything. It's all supposed to be a well-kept secret.'

'I can't believe it. I mean, I knew that it happened a lot. Duncan is a Mason and I know that it helps him in his business but... dog showing! No, I can't believe that.'

The subject was dropped and Simon did not mention it again, but during the next few days it occupied Fiona's mind considerably. They weren't married. Simon had never mentioned marriage and she wasn't sure that she wanted to get married again. Would it be wise to let him be joint owner? It was all her money that had set it up in the first place. It was really only the interest on her shares that kept it going. Could she let him be joint owner of the kennels but keep the property in her name? Why was she thinking like this? If only her father had still been alive she could have talked it through with him. She decided to make an appointment with her solicitor.

It appeared, having spoken to her solicitor, that, with a little juggling, this could be achieved. The business known as Simfell Kennels could be in their joint names but all the property would remain in her name only. She had great reservations about telling Simon what she had decided. Supposing he saw it as a lack of trust on her part. Was it? She didn't really know herself why she didn't want to make Simon a joint partner of everything. She chose to tell him what she had done one evening as they sat by the fire. For a long time Simon sat looking at the flames licking around the logs and said nothing. He cleared his throat.

'I think that, under the circumstances, that is a wise thing. I think that owning the business side of the kennels will do just fine. You know I would never abuse my position, don't you, Fee. It will help us though, you'll see.'

It was decided to let the solicitor draw up the necessary agreement and no more was said about it.

At the beginning of February, one of the bitches having a first litter, had a difficult labour which finally resulted in a Caesarean section. All but one of the five puppies lived but the bitch would have nothing to do with them. This meant that they had to be fed every few hours, day and night, with an orphan feeder. After the first week Fiona was utterly exhausted. Simon had been doing a lot of her work when he came home so that she was free to keep making up the feed and feeding 'The Gang of Four' as they called them but she was still tired. She managed to get through the second week, helped by Sally who cuddled and licked them as if they were her own. It was inevitable that, sitting by the warm Aga during the wee, small hours, tending the puppies, her thoughts kept returning to the baby of Duncan's that his wife Barbara was carrying. Was it moving now? Did Duncan put his hand on her swelling belly and feel it? Were they planning to decorate the nursery and picking names out of a book? Oh God, she thought, why wasn't it me? She felt so cheated. She said none of this to

Simon though, because she didn't want him to think that she was unhappy; she wasn't.

B Y THE TIME the litter was weaned, both Fiona and Simon, who had taken on most of her other kennel work, were worn out and irritable. The nights where Fiona had to keep getting up to feed the litter had drained her energy reserves and Simon found that the extra work in the evenings made him tired and depressed. The weather had not helped either with a late fall of snow which had caused even more work. They had had several disagreements and their relationship was somewhat strained.

Thoughts of Duncan's forthcoming baby still troubled Fiona. She knew that, now that she was well into her forties, it was very unlikely that she would ever conceive. Privately, she had wondered if such great lovemaking as she had with Simon just might have made the difference, but time was no longer on her side and she was having a small identity crisis. This had caused her to be a little less keen to make love. She knew that she loved Simon but felt unable to tell him of her silly secret hopes, and without a satisfactory reason for her lack of interest, fell back on the time-honoured excuse of tiredness, which was, in part, true.

Crufts was on the following Sunday and they had spent all week working on Jay and Sapphire so that they were in peak condition for the show. Their hopes for the show were not very high because the woman judge, who had been in the breed for many years, was known to be 'facey', putting up the dogs of old friends wherever possible.

Ruth arrived at 6 a.m. on the Sunday morning and they set off for the show.

On arrival, they studied the catalogue to see how many

'friends' were in their classes.

'Doesn't look too hopeful, Fee, for either of us, but you never know.'

His prophecy proved to be true, with Jay coming fifth in his class and Fiona and Sapphire getting thrown out with nothing.

'Don't be too disappointed, Fee. Remember that future judges might have noticed how gorgeous she is.'

As they tiredly drove home, they talked about Simon's second champ show coming up shortly, about the future possibilities of the new litter and about the gossip, the jokes, the moans and the fiddles they had heard or talked over with other exhibitors.

Suddenly Simon said, 'I wish to God, Fee, that you'd tell me what's been bothering you lately.'

'Nothing, I'm just tired.'

'Come on, love, I know you're tired; so am I, but there's more to it than that, isn't there? Are you regretting being with me?'

'No, Simon, no. Please don't think that. It's nothing really, only me being silly and womanish.'

'And what does that mean?'

'Well, if you must know, I can't get Duncan's baby out of my mind. I'm jealous.'

'Um, I see.' Simon said nothing further and the matter was dropped.


Spring turned to summer and it was time for Simon's second Champ show appointment. After answering the phone for the second time one evening, Simon came back into the kitchen. 'Well, it's getting more difficult by the minute.'

'What is?' asked Fiona, hauling dog blankets and towels out of the 'dog' washing machine.

'I've just had an interesting conversation with Alan Burgess. You know he and his wife came to the party.'

'What did he want?'

'Well, I should hazard a guess at a CC. He is suggesting that he puts my name forward for the committee of the Cumbrian Club and has vaguely hinted at a possible overseas appointment.'

'Could he do that?'

'Oh, yes, he has the contacts. It just means that I'll have to put up that bitch of his. Thank God that Paul has a dog.'

'Paul? Do you mean Paul Aston?'

'Who else? You know that he gave Jay the ticket and told me that he would be coming under me. Oh, Alan said would I give you his best wishes.'

Fiona fell silent. It had been a hard day and it was not over yet. Alan hadn't phoned her and she thought that he had forgotten about the incident at the party – he had been rather drunk.

Other more important matters had been occupying her mind through that day. There was so much money that had to be paid out when dog showing: travelling costs, show entries, food, extras for the dogs, and no prize money. She had been rather surprised, when she had received her latest bank statement that morning, at just how much it had gone down. The money they made on the odd boarding, the puppy sales and the stud fees in no way balanced the books. She thought that she would have a chat to Simon about it after his show. When she thought of all the 'little people' who showed dogs as a hobby, had a couple of litters, and would never stand a chance at the 'big time', she felt very sad. So much time, effort and money spent on a hopeless cause.

'It's not fair, is it, Simon, that the little people don't stand a chance of getting a CC?'

'Yes, they do; the odd one is allowed to make up a champion. It makes it all look more genuine and...' The phone rang again.

Alan phoned her on the following Tuesday. 'Hello, is that Fee? Alan Burgess here. How are you, my dear; well, I hope? I was just ringing to suggest that we lunch together tomorrow. I know of a very nice country pub that serves excellent food. Would you be free?'

Fiona was quite taken aback. Damn, damn, damn, she thought. What the devil was she going to do now? If she said no it would undo all the progress that they had made. He'd see to it that her name and Simon's was mud with all the people that mattered. On the other hand... 'Hello, Alan, how nice of you to remember. Yes, I'd love to meet you for lunch. How do I get to this wonderful pub?'

She changed her outfit for the third time. God, she thought,

I'm so damned nervous I don't know how I want to look. Not sexy, that's for sure; nothing tight, not much make-up and no perfume.

The pub turned out to be old and timbered and, as she walked into its dark interior, Alan got up to greet her. 'Hello, my dear.' He kissed her on the cheek. 'So glad you could make it. I took the liberty of ordering you a drink.'

He's pretty sure of himself, she thought, rescuing her hand from his rather damp one. His fair hair was perfect, not a hair out of place. I wonder if it's a wig, she thought. His blue eyes smiled into hers and she realised that he was still holding her hand. 'Thank you, Alan, that was very thoughtful.'

Over the meal he spoke about dog matters, mainly bragging of his importance and influence in the dog scene, of his contacts at the Kennel Club and how well he was entertained at overseas appointments. He went on to remark on what a nice bitch Sapphire was and how he hoped that she would become a champion.

When the coffee was brought to the table, he again took her hand and looking into her eyes he told her how much he had looked forward to their meeting and how he didn't want it to end.

Here it comes, thought Fiona.

He suggested that they leave her car here and go for a drive in his, so that they could continue their conversation. Good God, she thought, the mean old devil wants me to make love to him in the back of his car!

She looked at her watch; any moment now, she thought. 'That would be lovely, Alan. The country is so beautiful at the moment.'

He called for the bill and, as he did so, her mobile phone rang. 'Hello, oh, hello, Ruth. Yes, oh no, I'll come straight away.' She looked at Alan. 'Alan, such awful luck. That was Ruth, our kennel maid. One of the dogs has hurt himself while exercising. I'm afraid I shall have to go and take him to the vet's. I'm so awfully sorry.'

Alan's face went red with annoyance but he smiled and shrugged his shoulders. 'Ah, well my dear, these things happen.'

They walked out to her car and she turned and kissed him on the cheek. 'Thank you again, Alan; I'm sorry that I've had to end it so abruptly but...' She shrugged her shoulders and kissed him again, and got into her car. She didn't laugh until she was well away from the pub. Good old Ruth, she had rung at exactly the time she had told her to.

She went with Simon on the day of his appointment and, as he entered the ring dressed in his best suit and looking very confident, she felt a surge of pride. She wandered round the ringside, pausing now and again, hoping to hear spectators' comments on his judging. On the whole it seemed quite favourable. She knew, from the type of dog he was putting up, that he was doing what he wanted and putting up the good dogs, whoever was on the end of the lead. He did put Paul's dog first in the Open class and then gave him the dog CC. Fiona didn't mind that, because Paul's dog was very handsome.

An arm went round her waist. 'Hello gorgeous, how are you?'

It was Alan Burgess again. 'Do you agree with your better half's judging? But he isn't your better half, is he? You're a free agent.'

'Hello, Alan. Is your wife here? I must dash, I'm dying to go to the Ladies and there is sure to be a long queue.' She hurried away in the direction of the loos.

She was seething. So that's how all the men see me, is it? A free agent. She felt degraded. It hadn't entered her head that they would still be the subject of gossip. Is that what they think when they come to our parties and drink our wine? She shut herself in a cubicle and found that she was shaking. Was that what was expected of her to get a champion dog herself? As if on cue, she heard two women come into the toilet.

'My God, how the hell did he have the gall to put that ghastly dog up?'

'You know how, Dot has been very accommodating.'

'You mean...'

'Yes, didn't you know? She told me all about it. When he judges they stay at a hotel. She says that he is a hoot. They have to do it like dogs.'

'What do you mean?'

'You know, on their hands and knees; he does everything that dogs do. Do I have to spell it out? Apparently, he even barks!'

Both women burst out laughing.

Fiona stood there and waited until they had each gone into a cubicle, and then made a hurried exit. Heaven forbid that anyone should talk about her or Simon like that. She desperately wanted to make Sapphire into a champion but one had to draw the line somewhere.

She returned to the Cumbrian ring in time to see Simon judging the bitch classes. One or two fellow exhibitors came up and spoke to her. A couple came up and introduced themselves, wanting to buy a puppy for the show ring. A German couple talked to her about buying an older dog for stud work.

Time passed and it was soon time for Simon to pick the bitch CC. He walked down the line of winning bitches and stopped at Alan's bitch. Fiona held her breath; she knew that he had to pick it out but she really wanted him to ignore it. When he gave Alan the CC, she did not clap, but when he picked out a bitch which she knew he had admired before, for the reserve CC, she clapped and cheered. She steeled herself to congratulate Alan. He, of course, took the opportunity to kiss her on the lips.

'How kind of you, my dear. I'll give you a ring shortly and then we can really celebrate my win in style.'

Simon was a little quiet on the way home and Fiona did not tell him about Alan or about the conversation in the toilet. She had intended to tell him about it and gauge his reaction, but somehow it didn't seem the right time.

As the days warmed and life became a little easier, their relationship almost returned to its usual level of happiness. Success seemed to bring more success. Simon was proposed by Alan to go on the committee of the club and accepted. Fiona was doing quite well, with Sapphire getting several firsts at Championship shows. Jay got his third ticket from another of their partygoers, which gave them their first champion at the kennels. As Simon came out of the ring, they immediately had an offer for him from an overseas buyer, which was in four figures.

It was tempting but they refused, saying that they would let him have one of Jay's very promising puppies that they had been running on. At last they felt that they had arrived. The name of Simfell was catching the attention of people overseas, as well as in

England.

Simon lifted Fiona off her feet and swung her round. 'We've done it, Fee. We've bloody done it. A Simfell Champion.'

Fiona was feeling over the moon. Her ambitions and hopes were materialising; she would even be a champ show judge herself next year. All their dreams were coming true. It was great, but still, at the back of her mind, the shadow of the forthcoming baby hung over her. She was counting the days. Simon watched her as she sat quietly some evenings, obviously lost in her own thoughts. She would often sigh deeply and then get up to busy herself with some chore or another. She had not mentioned the baby again and he was certainly not going to mention it.

Fiona was due to judge several breeds at a dog show that was also part of a big agricultural show and Simon suggested that they asked Ruth to come in for the weekend so that they could take the caravan. Due to the pressure of work, they had not used the caravan for some time. Simon decided to park it in a caravan site near to the show, rather than at the show itself, so that they could have a little more privacy.

Fiona enjoyed her judging engagement and afterwards they wandered round the show together. She laughed when a sheep suddenly took off with its owner in tow, and Simon squeezed her hand. 'Fee, it's so good to see you relaxed and happy. I've been a bit worried about you lately. All work etc… Let's go out for a meal tonight.'

Over dinner that evening Simon raised his wine glass. 'Here's to the most beautiful judge I know. What's more, I intend to get to know her a lot better before the night's out.'

She burst out laughing and they touched glasses and drank the wine.

Every nerve was tingling as Fiona lay on the bed. Simon had slowly kissed every part of her body and was now caressing her. She cried out as she climaxed and he quickly entered her, so that they could mutually enjoy each other. With Simon cuddling her, she was just about to go to sleep when he suddenly took his arm away from her. She felt him get out of bed and stumble around but, thinking that he was going to the toilet, she said nothing.

She was just snuggling down into the pillow when she heard him say, 'Blast and damnation.'

Sitting up and turning on the light, she was confronted with Simon, stark naked, hopping round on one foot and holding his other foot. This is not how I planned it,' he said.

'Planned what?'

'This.' He held out a small, red box.

Opening it, Fiona saw that it contained an antique sapphire ring.

'I chose a sapphire because you were wearing blue the first time I saw you. Will you marry me, Fee? Before you answer, I must point out that it's only for your money, not because I love you with every bone in my body.' He slipped the ring on her finger and kissed her and she knew that it wasn't for her money.

He didn't notice that she hadn't replied to his question.

After that short break they were back on their old footing, until one day when the phone rang as Fiona was preparing the food for the dogs. It was Laura's voice.

'Hello, Fiona, it's me. I've got some wonderful news. At last, we have a beautiful, little girl. She was born three days ago and we are going to call her Amanda. The boys are dying to see her and Michael is over the moon. Can't stop looking at her. He says that she looks just like me.'

Fiona swallowed hard and managed to congratulate her.

'Oh, yes, and Fiona, Duncan's wife had a baby boy a week ago now. They are going to call him Donald. He is…'

Fiona put the receiver down and stood looking at it. The phone rang again but she didn't answer it. Mechanically, she fed the dogs, collected and washed the bowls, got into her car and drove off into the country.

So there was, at last, going to be a baby in the nursery, her nursery. How could Duncan call him Donald – that was the name that they had chosen for a boy. She sat there for several hours as she deliberately thought about the baby. After a while, she began to realise that, now that it had happened, in a way, she was more at peace with herself. She could relax and be pleased for Duncan if she tried hard. She would send them a congratulatory card. With a sad little smile, she looked at her sapphire ring for a moment then started up the engine and went home to the cottage, Simon and the dogs.

'MICHAEL, I'M SO glad you're here,' Laura said as he came into the ward with even more flowers.

'What's the matter? Is Amanda alright?'

'Yes, yes, we're both fine. I've been sitting here feeling terrible all afternoon.' She smiled and patted his arm. 'Don't look so worried. I don't mean that I feel ill, rather that I feel guilty. I think that I have been very cruel and thoughtless.'

Michael looked at her worried face. 'To whom? Now, you know that you shouldn't be upsetting yourself; it'll affect your milk.'

Laura smiled. 'Now that's the voice of experience.' She then proceeded to tell him about her phone call to Fiona and how Fiona had put the phone down abruptly; how she had tried to talk to her again but Fiona had not answered.

'Come on, Laura, what did you expect? It must have been a bit of a bombshell for her.'

'I know, I know, I'm stupid. I so wanted to tell her about Amanda; I'm so proud of her. After all, we have been friends for a long time and—'

Michael interrupted her. 'We haven't been that friendly for the past year or so, have we?'

'No, and that makes me feel even more guilty. I've been very mean and thoughtless and she didn't deserve it.'

'Look, don't worry about it any more. I'll give her a ring when I get home this evening and sort something out.' He then proceeded to tell her how the boys were looking forward to her coming home the next day and how he had been coping with the cooking.

'I gave them scrambled egg this morning for breakfast and they all burst out laughing. I'd put sugar in it instead of salt!'

Laura smiled and Michael was pleased to see that she looked less tense.

Later that evening, after the boys had gone to bed and peace had returned to the house, he decided to phone Fiona. It was only then that he realised that he didn't even know the number. Finding it in the book that Laura kept by the phone, he dialled the number and Simon answered. He asked if he might speak to Fiona and while he was waiting he too felt guilty about the fact that they had never even seen her since she had moved. At first, with Duncan confiding in them so much and with his playing golf with him, it had seemed in some way disloyal to see Fiona as well. Coupled with that was the sheer physical difficulty of going to see them with the boys. He knew that he was only making excuses for his neglect of her, though, so when she spoke he stammered a greeting.

'Michael! Is everything alright?'

Feeling even more guilty at the surprise in her voice, he quickly reassured her that all was well. He then explained how upset Laura had been when he visited her and how frightened she was that she had upset her old friend. 'She was almost in tears at her thoughtlessness.'

'I must admit that, under the circumstances, I was rather upset when I heard about Duncan's baby, but I think that I shall be able to come to terms with it. As for Amanda, I'm delighted that you have a daughter. I know how much you both wanted a little girl.'

'Well, thank you, Fiona, that's very kind of you. She is rather special. As soon as we are settled into a routine you must come and see her and us. It's been far too long since we saw you. I know that Laura feels the same way. Oh, and Simon too, of course.' With obvious relief in his voice, he made his farewells and rang off.

She lay there, looking at Simon as he slept. Was it possible, she wondered, to be able to really tell someone how much they meant to you? It was as if the birth of Duncan's baby had been a watershed in her life and she had shut that door for ever. Now she was even more determined to succeed in the dog world, not only to please Simon but also to fulfil herself, by making Sapphire into a champion. She had taken Sapphire out of her bag when she was born and reared her ever since. She knew that Simon thought Sapphire good enough in her own right, but did they now have enough influence for her to also make up one – short of sleeping with someone like Alan Burgess, or paying someone in cash, to do it. Time will tell, she thought, as she quietly slipped out of bed and put her dressing gown on.

Between taking Sapphire to every Championship show that she could manage, campaigning two more youngsters at Open shows and rearing two litters of puppies that autumn, they had accepted an invitation to visit Laura and Michael. The day was a great success. It seemed that, as soon as Fiona stepped over the threshold and saw the familiar jumble of coats half hanging on their hooks and the pile of shoes on the floor, the past couple of years had never happened. Laura, looking her usual plump, happy, disorganised self, had burst into tears as she flung her arms around Fiona and hugged her. Michael and Simon shook hands and had got on surprisingly well.

The new baby, Amanda, was adorable and Fiona almost shook as she cuddled the small, warm, talcum-powdered baby in her arms. She looked up to see Simon quietly watching her and smiled. She soon handed the small pink bundle back to Laura. No looking back now – that part of her life was over. During the afternoon, she sadly watched Simon playing football in the garden with the boys, knowing that it must have brought back memories of Barry for him, and she sighed deeply as she thought, not for the first time, how lovely it would have been if they had had a child. Taking a deep breath, she went into the garden to join the others in the fun.

The rest of the day passed swiftly and pleasantly and Fiona felt at peace as they drove back to the cottage.

They had decided to make the crossing to Ireland for the Championship show in October. Having struck up quite a friendship with some of the Irish exhibitors, one couple had offered to put them up for the night if they wanted to attend the show. Taking the caravan to various shows had proved to be very useful. It was the custom to meet up with other exhibitors in the evenings and have a few drinks. A lot of wheeler-dealing went on at these get-togethers as well as horse-trading, character assassination and gossip. It was how they had got this invitation to stay in Ireland. Both Liam and Maureen were champ judges and the fact that Maureen was also on the committee of one of the Irish Championship shows was a bonus. This friendship would be to their mutual benefit.

They were fairly hopeful of a good outcome from this show, because they had given Sue Mason, the judge, a free mating with Jay earlier in the year. They had also let her have a puppy that she had admired, at a very reasonable price. Knowing all this, Fiona's competitive spirit, which had become much stronger of late, was well to the fore. She surveyed the opposition and was sure that she would win.

Sapphire performed very well and she took the first. Later, in the challenge, Sue gave her the bitch ticket, Sapphire's first. Fiona shook Sue's hand and thanked her. She looked around at the other exhibitors with pride, no longer feeling any qualms about whether she had won honestly or not. Winning was the name of the game and if the little people didn't know or learn the rules then that was just too bad. She and Simon had worked damned hard and planned for this – others got CCs this way so why not them? She had won fair and square; Sapphire was magnificent and deserved it. She felt that she proved it to all by later coming third in the Terrier Group.

Simon had bought some champagne and they gave several well-wishers a drink. Saying goodbye to their hosts the next day, they returned to the kennels to find that Ruth and Jenny had put up a congratulations banner over Sapphire's kennel. Apparently Simon had rung them with the news.

'Just you wait,' Fiona said, 'we'll need a "Champion" banner there before long.'

At Midland Counties she again got the bitch ticket, the judge being on the Cumbrian committee with Simon. Fiona was so pleased. She could think of nothing else but getting that third CC and making Sapphire into a champion. Every evening she discussed with Simon where her third CC was coming from and how it could be achieved. She threw herself with even more energy into the work at the kennels.

Sometimes, when Simon was working on a dog in the kennels, preparing it for a show or exercising it, he worried a little about the change in Fiona. Her womanliness and gentility, her naivety had so appealed to him, and he felt that it was slipping away. He had seen this happen so often in other women who were dedicated to showing, but he hadn't thought that it might change Fiona. She was so much more intelligent than a lot of them; he hoped that she would get that third bloody CC and then perhaps she would get back to normal; that included making love more.

Once again, they invited friends from the dog world, more than ever in fact, to their New Year's party. Fiona worried a bit about just how much these do's were beginning to cost. Simon always insisted that they were worth it but... She also worried about what she would say to Alan Burgess if he started to get amorous again and invited her out to dinner. However, she was saved any decisions about that when his wife phoned to say that they would not be able to come because he had gone down with the flu.

The party was, once again, a great success and Fiona looked forward to the end of the evening. Everyone drank so much and ate everything in sight – the cost was going to be exorbitant. She hoped that Simon's wheeler-dealing would have made it worthwhile and Sapphire would be a champion.

She did not get the ticket at Manchester, the first big show of the year, and was very down about it. Simon was really beginning to worry about her. She seemed to be changing even more, not bothering about her appearance, constantly on about the cost of things; she had even had a row with Jenny the previous weekend and had the poor kid in tears.

In March he received a letter from Mary to inform him that she had now remarried and wished to sell the house. He showed it to Fiona. 'Good news, isn't it? I'll get the solicitor on to it right away. It'll make our lives a bit easier financially. We might be able to take on more help so that you can have more time to yourself.'

'It'll be nice not to have a drain on the bank reserves, but I really don't need any more help. Do you mind her getting married again?'

'Not one bit, just feel sorry for the poor bugger. Hope he's got plenty of money and is deaf into the bargain.'

Fiona got her first Championship-show appointment confirmed for early the following year, which pleased her tremendously, but she did not seem able to get that third CC. She seemed to spend more and more time with the dogs and could talk of nothing else. Their relationship began to change slightly – she seemed preoccupied and disinterested in anything other than showing. Another invitation from Laura and Michael was turned down because it interfered with showing. She no longer bothered to change out of her working clothes and was too tired to go out for a meal or a drink. She grumbled about every bitch, two-legged or four, who beat her for the ticket. Even Paul Aston had remarked to Simon at the last show that Fiona did not seem to be her usual self and asked if there was anything the matter. Simon was worried that he was losing her to showing; he'd seen it happen to others and he sure as hell was not going to let it happen to him. He decided to do something about it, something drastic.

Some weeks later, after yet another disappointing show, Fiona woke one Saturday morning to find that Simon was already up. She hurriedly dressed and went downstairs to find the table laid and breakfast ready.

'Sit down, all the dogs are let out and have fresh water.'

'Couldn't you sleep? Are you alright?'

'Perfectly alright. I did wake up a bit early and saw that it was such a beautiful day that I just had to get up. Now eat up because we are going out.'

'Where? We haven't got a dog show.'

'I'm not telling. Just get into your glad rags.'

'Glad rags! Now you've got to tell me, I don't know what sort of glad rags to wear.'

'Anything really, something pretty. Anyway, you always look smashing in everything.'

'That's very complimentary but not much help.'

'Alright, I'm wearing my best suit. Does that help?'

'Your best suit! Now you really have me worried. What have you got planned that needs a suit?'

She showered and chose an outfit that she had only worn once before. Putting on her make-up she watched Simon in the mirror to see if she could get any clues, but it proved a fruitless exercise. As they got in the car, Ruth and Jenny both came from the kennels to wave them off.

'That's odd. Do they know where we are going?'

'Yes.'

'Oh, then it's something doggy and I've got all dressed up for nothing. For goodness' sake, Simon, please tell me where we're going, please.'

'It's no good sweet-talking me. My lips are sealed.'

In no time they arrived at a building in the town and Fiona was astonished to see Peter and Beryl, and Laura, Michael and the children all standing outside. The women had hats on and the men were wearing buttonholes in their lapel.

'Oh, no, Simon, it can't be. You can't. I haven't... You haven't... Oh no!'

'I'm sorry, Fee, I have and I'm bloody terrified that you'll say no. Will you? Will you marry me?'

'But we can't, I haven't...'

'We can, I'll explain it later. But for now, will you please get out of the car and marry me?'

For a few worrying seconds she said nothing but sat there, looking down and frowning.

'This is so embarrassing,' she said, and then, turning to Simon, she smiled faintly. 'As long as you don't expect me to give you all my worldly goods and a CC.'

Laughing together, they got out of the car to join the others at the registry office. Laura and Beryl came forward to kiss Fiona and Laura gave her a posy of flowers. The men shook hands.

Thank God I put this suit on, Fiona thought as she walked into the building. Why has he done this? was her next thought.

The service started and Fiona looked around the room. What a come-down from my first wedding. She recalled the beautiful, white dress, the flowers, the guests, her mother and father, Duncan's parents – his mother had worn an enormous grey hat with trimmings – the hymns, the choir boys, the bridesmaids in blue, the... Her thoughts were interrupted by Simon taking her left hand in his. Startled, she looked at him, realising that she hadn't heard a word of the service.

Simon had even arranged a small reception at the local hotel. During the meal, Fiona looked at the posy Laura had given her and at the assembled company. They were all chatting away and laughing. Laura's boys had loaded their plates with food and were busily enjoying it; Simon and Michael seemed to be in deep conversation.

Peter came towards her. 'Fiona, I'm so pleased to be here. Can I say that Simon is a different person living with you. Don't get me wrong – I mean it in the nicest possible way.' He faltered, suddenly embarrassed. 'He's like he was when we were young. You have made him really happy. I hope that you are as happy, too. We are so pleased for you both.'

'Thank you, Peter.' Fiona kissed him on the cheek. She suddenly realised that she, too, was a very different person now. She had been so naive, so unworldly; how could she have let Duncan keep her so innocent of the world? Simon had certainly shown her what the world was really like.

'We're off now, Fiona; sorry we can't stay longer. We haven't had time for a good chat. Do come and see us again soon, won't you – Amanda is growing so fast.' Laura kissed her on the cheek.

'Yes, of course, and thank you for coming. I really do appreciate it and the posy.' As she was speaking, she thought how very tired and pale Laura looked but put it down to the extra work the new baby must have made.

Ruth and Jenny were full of questions when they got back and Simon had a bottle of champagne to share with them. Later, when Simon had done the last check on the dogs and they were ready for bed, Fiona said, 'Right, now that we are on our own, I have questions for you. What made you decide that we should get married? How did I come to sign for that registry office wedding and what wheeler-dealing were you organising with Michael at the hotel after the meal?'

'It was a bit underhand. I'm sorry for not telling you. To be honest, I suppose I was frightened that you would say no and I did it because I love you.'

'But how did you do it?'

'I slipped it in with two show forms and you signed all three. Would you have said no if I had asked you first?'

'I don't know, but I know that I don't like the underhanded way you did it. And what was all the chat with Michael about? More secrets?'

'Yes, well no; it's all to do with this Mason business.'

'I see. It's to do with the kennel business, you mean. Well, I think I'm beginning to see.'

AFTER THE WEDDING, Peter and Beryl started to come down for the day, usually a Sunday as it was the quiet day at the kennels. Both Fiona and Simon had been pleased at this innovation, Simon because Peter could often give him a hand with a repair job and Fiona because, now and again, she felt the need of female company. Her relationship with Simon had not really improved since the day of the surprise wedding and she was always glad of a chat.

'Forgive me if you think that I'm interfering, but you seem a little strained today. Did you not like Peter and me coming for the day?' Beryl put down her cup and looked at Fiona. 'I know how busy you must be.'

'Oh, please don't think that; I'm glad you came and I know that Simon really looks forward to seeing Peter again. He likes another man about the place. Barry... Barry used to come at first, before the accident, and Simon was pleased to see him. It's the same with Peter. They get on so well, don't they?'

'Yes, they are close. I was an only child myself and longed for a brother or sister. I've never asked, Fiona, do you have any brothers or sisters?'

'No. I was an only child, too. I wanted a sister. Well, really I wanted to be a twin. I have always thought that identical twins have a certain magical quality about them: a wonderful togetherness.'

'Do you find it lonely living here without neighbours?'

'No, not really; there is always something that needs doing and the days fly by. I've got Sally – she is always with me – and the other dogs are great company.'

'Well, you know the old saying about all work and no play. I hope that you and Simon get some time to relax together.'

'Oh yes, of course we do.'

Beryl smiled and finished her tea. She had been a little concerned ever since she had seen Fiona's face as she got out of the car at the registry office. Unlike Peter, she was always aware of any atmosphere and she had felt it the last couple of times that they had seen Fiona and Simon. If there was something wrong though, it was obvious, Beryl thought, that she didn't want to talk about it.

Fiona was just pouring them another cup of tea when Simon and Peter came into the kitchen.

'I hope you've saved some for us,' Peter said, smiling at Beryl. 'I must say, Fiona, that you've got some lovely dogs out there. Simon has been telling me of your latest successes: both now judges at the top level, one champion dog and another in the offing. Marvellous. You've both made a wonderful success of the business.'

'Thank you, Peter,' Fiona responded. 'Yes, we have, although it's been very hard work. We do share the business in name but, of course, I still own the actual property.'

There was an awkward silence broken by Beryl looking at her watch.

'Peter, look at the time. If we don't go now we shall be caught up in the rush hour on the motorway. Thank you both for a lovely day. We'd love you to come and see us when you can. We'd love to see you and you can have a rest.'

When they were driving home, Peter turned to Beryl. 'What do you think that was all about, just before we left? Fiona's remark about the property?'

'Don't tell me that you didn't notice that there was an atmosphere between them all day?'

Peter shook his head.

'Oh, you men. You never notice anything.'

As Peter's car went out of sight, Fiona and Simon stopped waving and turned to go indoors. He grabbed her arm.

'Fee, what was that all about?' he said angrily.

'What?'

'You know, what you said to them about you still owning the property.'

'Well, I do.'

'And who's disputing it? No one; so why was it necessary to say it. Look, Fee, this has gone on long enough and I for one am getting pretty fed up with it. We have got to sit down and sort this out, whatever it is. You've been cold and distant ever since we got married. If you didn't want to get married, I wish to God that you had said so at the time.'

'I didn't have much chance, did I?'

'So that's what's been at the root of all this. Look, Fee, I'm very sorry that I sprung it on you like that. I thought that you would be pleased. It was meant to be a lovely surprise, but now I bloody well wish that I had left things as they were.'

'And so do I. Oh, it was a surprise. But I didn't like you asking me to marry you just so that you could own a business and become a Mason!'

'Bloody hell! Is that what you thought? Now let's get one thing straight here. I did not marry you to get the bloody business. Do you hear me? I don't want the bloody business or the bloody house. I want you. Haven't I made it plain enough? For God's sake, Fee. I love you. I wanted to marry you because I wanted you to be my wife.'

'Well, what was all that scheming with Michael at the reception then, if it wasn't about the Masons?'

'Scheming with Michael at the reception? If you must know, he was sounding me out about how I would feel if, at some time, he and Laura were to have a holiday and we looked after the children. He wondered how you would feel about it, whether it would upset you or not and he also wanted to know my feelings on the subject. Satisfied now?'

Fiona stared at him for a minute. 'Why didn't you tell me this before? Why does he want us to have them? Is there something wrong with Laura? Does he want us to have them soon? Why—'

'Just hold it right there. As far as I know there is nothing wrong with Laura. Their parents aren't fit enough to look after them all and he didn't specify any time. It was just an enquiry. I didn't tell you before because you have hardly been in a good mood, have you, and... well, to be honest, I didn't know if it was seeing the children at the wedding which had upset you.'

'Then I'm sorry, I misjudged you.'

'Yes, you bloody well did; about the house, about the wedding and about Michael.'

'Well, you must admit that it looked like that.'

'Not in my book it didn't. And now ma'am, if I am well and truly forgiven,' he picked her up in his arms, kissed her and carried her into the house, 'don't you think that it is time that we started our honeymoon? Come on, wench, up those stairs.'

Simon was currently concentrating on showing a couple of Jay's offspring, and was having quite a bit of success with them. Several of the judges who had been to their parties had looked upon them favourably, and they also arranged to take other judges out for a meal before or after the show.

This had been Simon's latest idea and it seemed to be working. Fiona did worry a bit about the cost of these elaborate dinners etc., but consoled herself with the thought that it might lead to that third CC for Sapphire, which was still eluding her. She had almost given up hope of getting it. She wanted to mate her soon; they had had several overseas buyers interested in a puppy from her, but only if she was a champion. Anyway, they could ask more for the puppies, so it was important that she got that third CC. She and Simon had poured over the list of judges for the last few shows of the year, but they were not very hopeful. The only favourable one was Alan Burgess who was judging the very last Championship show of that year. Time was running out for Sapphire.

The days are certainly getting colder, thought Fiona, as she came in from feeding the dogs. She saw that there was a message on the answerphone. It was from Laura, asking them if they would like to come over for the day, before she got bogged down in the Christmas rush. She sounded as if she had a heavy cold.

'Hello, Laura, it's me. You sound as if you have an awful cold.'

'Oh, I have. I seem to keep getting them. Must be run down.'

'Well, are you sure that you want us to come?'

'Yes, you know that the children love to see you and they have quite taken to Simon. They keep asking when you'll be coming again. We'd love to see you, too. Do you know that we haven't seen you since the wedding? You can see all the photos that we took.'

'Fine, well, let's arrange a date.'

They went to see them a fortnight later. Both Fiona and Simon were struck by Laura's appearance. She looked so pale and tired but, although they had several occasions when they were on their own and Fiona asked her how things were, Laura never admitted that anything was wrong. As Simon remarked on the way home, Mary nearly went up the wall rearing two children and Laura had four. She must be on the go all day, so was it any wonder that she looked tired?

'Did Michael say anything about her?'

'No, he just said how hectic Christmas was, having to find presents for them all and that it made a lot of extra work.'

'Um, all the same, I think I'll phone her again soon, just to see how she is.'

It was the penultimate show of the year. Neither Simon nor Fiona were very hopeful of doing much. The judge was a handler and it was a well-known fact that he only put people up whom he thought would put him up at future shows. It meant a lot of money for him.

Fiona was walking round the stalls, looking for a present for Simon, when she bumped into Alan Burgess.

'Hello, my dear,' he said, quickly kissing her on the lips. 'I wondered if I would see you here. I wanted to invite you out to lunch again. We still haven't had a chance to really get to know each other, have we? It was such a pity that it got cut short last time. How about Wednesday week?'

She wanted to wipe her mouth but felt that that would look too rude. Her mind was whirling. She couldn't turn him down flat; he would not only throw both their dogs out at the forthcoming show but would vindictively tell other judges that they were not to be put up. She knew that that happened. She had seen other people totally blackened and ostracised for not playing the game – they never won again and they didn't get judging appointments. One poor woman, to whom this had been done, tried to commit suicide. Fiona certainly did not want this to happen to her and Simon: he would never forgive her. She would have to accept and try to think of another ploy to wriggle out of the sex bit. Smiling, she looked up at him. He wasn't bad looking really. He had worn well, in fact, she knew one or two of her fellow exhibitors who would have liked to be in her present position.

'I'd love to have lunch with you again, Alan.' Smiling at him, she thought, and that's what it will be – lunch only, if that is possible.

'Good. I shall look forward to seeing more of you, my dear girl. Same time and place?'

Fiona noted the innuendo as he looked into her eyes and held her hand; what the hell am I going to do this time? she wondered.

They managed a trip to see Peter and Beryl, taking their Christmas presents with them. It was a most enjoyable day – Beryl was a very good cook and Peter a good raconteur. Between them they made the hours fly past.

As Fiona prepared to leave, Beryl came up to her. 'Call me an interfering busybody if you like but, as one only child to another, I know that something is troubling you and I don't think it's Simon. If you ever want a chat, I am here and I do know when to keep silent.'

Fiona kissed her on the cheek. 'I wouldn't dream of calling you that. Thank you for asking, though. Honestly, everything is fine, we've been so busy these past few weeks and I feel a bit tired; I've been overdoing it perhaps.' She looked at Beryl's kindly, homely face for a moment. 'And it's very nice to have a sister.'

Beryl looked at her pale face for a moment and then smiled and nodded her head. 'Well, you take it a bit easier then. We're coming up to Christmas and that always means more work.'

Simon and Fiona were in the kitchen two weeks later and busy making sandwiches and flasks to take with them for the last show of the year.

'Are you sure that you want to come, Fee? I could manage the dogs on my own. I do wish you had gone to see the doctor when I asked you to.'

'Don't fuss, Simon, I'm fine, really. I've just been a bit under the weather; too many late nights with that new litter, I expect, and getting ready for Christmas as well. Anyway, this is Sapphire's last chance and you know she always goes better for me.'

'Okay, if you say so. Well, Alan has drunk enough at our parties – he ought to give us a first, anyway. If he doesn't, we won't invite him again.' Simon laughed. 'Unfortunately, they have already accepted the invitation.'

The show was at the NEC and, as they entered the rapidly filling building, the excitement built up in them as usual. Acknowledging friends and fellow exhibitors as they walked along the rows of benches, Fiona was so tense that she wanted to dash to the Ladies. As soon as they had settled the dogs in their cages, she did just that. Tina Smith and Jenny Brown, two fellow competitors, were in the queue in front of her. 'Hi, Fiona. Who do you think is going to win today?'

'I haven't the faintest idea but I hope that it's me.' After she had been to the toilet she put on some make-up. She hadn't slept too well and there were dark shadows under her eyes. She had been too tense to sleep. Would she get that illusive third today or not? She put a bit of blusher on her pale cheeks.

Judging started and Simon prepared the young dog for his class. As he predicted earlier, he did get a first with him. As the morning wore on, both he and Fiona were wondering if Alan would do any more for the young dog – Simon with hope and Fiona with dread. If he gave the dog the CC or the Res. CC, would he give her anything? She couldn't bear to look as Simon went into the ring again for the challenge. She opened her eyes as people started to cheer. Looking towards the ring she saw, with relief, that it wasn't Simon.

Alan now went to have his lunch and she and Simon sat on the benches to have their sandwiches. Fiona had a job to swallow the food, she was so nervous, and didn't fancy eating anyway. Again, she had to go to the toilet. She put on a bit more blusher and some lipstick and went back to prepare Sapphire. The other bitch classes seemed to take hours and hours and Fiona was almost shaking with nerves and felt sick, when, at last, the Open Bitch class was called in. There were nine other bitches in the class.

When it was Fiona's turn to put her dog on the table, she did not look at Alan as he went over the bitch. 'Hello again, my dear, lovely to see you.' She couldn't speak; she just swallowed hard and smiled. Sapphire walked well and in no time she was back in the line. She was looking down at Sapphire when the woman next to her said, 'Go on, he's calling you out.' Fiona looked up and stumbled out to the middle of the ring: she had been given the first!

Now was the challenge. Her heart was beating so fast that she could hear it pounding in her ears. She felt faint. Alan took the green and white cards and looked at the bitches again. He walked up to Fiona and, as he handed her the CC, the precious third one, he kissed her on the cheek. Fiona blushed furiously; she hated him kissing her in the ring in front of everyone like that. She looked over to where Simon was standing; he was looking rather serious. She ran round the ring on her lap of honour as people clapped and cheered her success. Then people were patting her on the back and shaking her hand. She had done it. She had made up a champion herself, bred by her, and raised and trained by her. At last, she had achieved her ambition, had fulfilled herself. As she walked out of the ring towards all those smiling faces, she was looking for Simon's face. Where was he? He always greeted her as she came out of the ring. She saw him at last, standing by the bench stroking Samson's head. She hurried over to him, flung her arms around him and kissed him.

'I've done it, Simon, I've made her up. It feels so marvellous. I'm so thrilled, over the moon, walking on air, aren't you? We now have two champions in the Simfell kennel.'

'Yes, congratulations.'

'Do sound a bit more enthusiastic, then.'

Before he could say any more, she was distracted by more friends coming up to congratulate her. Laughing excitedly, she turned again to see Simon still standing there, looking down at the floor. Suddenly the old Fiona returned and she looked at Simon standing there and at Sapphire, and the new Fiona was frightened and no longer elated. Why wasn't he pleased? Wasn't this what he wanted? Wasn't this what she had always wanted? She had achieved her goal but now what came next? The smile and the crowds and the noise faded as she fainted.

S HE OPENED HER eyes as the sounds of the show rushed back to her senses, and she looked up at Simon's anxious face. Paul Aston was there and Mrs Emsworth. Why were they looking at her like that? Suddenly the recent events of the day filled her mind and she struggled to get up.

'I'm sorry, I must have fainted. I've never done that before. You must think I'm an awful fool.'

As she was speaking she tried to stand up. Simon helped her to her feet. 'I'm alright now, really. It must have been the shock of winning.'

Mrs Emsworth brought her a chair and made her sit down while Simon poured her some coffee from their flask. Paul said, 'Well, if you are alright now I'll get back to my dog.' She drank the coffee and took hold of Simon's hand.

'Ah, that's brought a bit of colour to your cheeks. Call me if you want me.' Mrs Emsworth smiled and went back to her bench.

'Oh, Simon, I do feel a fool. I was just so pleased to make up Sapphire into a champion.'

'Yes, I suppose that's what it was. You feel alright now?'

'Yes, fine.'

'Well, you don't look it. I'll go to the bar and get you a brandy.'

Fellow exhibitors started to come up to shake her hand or give her a kiss on the cheek and congratulate her. She felt very tired and stayed sitting down but, nevertheless, revelled in the acclaim. This was the moment she had been waiting for ever since she first started showing Sally. It had seemed an almost impossible dream then but it was now a reality. She suddenly remembered that she hadn't challenged the dog CC for BOB.

'Simon, what happened about the Best of Breed?'

'Don't worry about that. Joyce Brown took Sapphire in for you but he gave it to the dog. Look, I think that we ought to go home now. I'll start packing up.'

Fiona got up and, while Simon took the chair back to Mrs Emsworth, she started to pack the dog grooming kit away in its box. He came back, quickly packed everything on to the trolley, and they left.

Simon said very little on the way home. As they came up the drive, Ruth and Jenny were there and eager to hear the news. They gave a cheer when Fiona told them of Sapphire's win and hurried back to the grooming shed to get out the 'Champion' banner and put it up.

'We have two champions in the kennel now,' Ruth said, her face alight with pleasure.

They then all trooped indoors for a congratulatory drink of wine. Later, sitting by the fire, Fiona felt exhausted and went to bed early. She was sound asleep when Simon eventually came to bed. He stood looking down at her for a moment and, shrugging his shoulders, got into bed.

After the excitement, life resumed its normal pattern. Fiona still felt tired and wondered if she could be anaemic. She would go to the doctor's after Christmas was over. There was more to organise this year as Peter and Beryl were coming for Christmas Day. Beryl had invited them for Christmas dinner but, of course, it was impossible to leave the dogs, so they were coming to them.

The food and drink for the New Year party had to be arranged as well. Fiona, still feeling tired, found it hard to concentrate on everything. Looking at her face in the mirror one day, she thought that she looked dreadful and put on some blusher. She wondered if it could be the start of her menopause and decided to have a word with Beryl at Christmas.

Christmas Day was cold and bright and, after a pleasant meal and a couple of rather nice bottles of wine, the men went to see to the dogs and the women to clear the table and make coffee.

'Beryl, do you mind if I ask you a rather personal question?'

'This sounds interesting. No, I don't mind; fire away.'

'Have you started your menopause and, if so, how did you know that you had started?'

'Ah, you are wondering if you have started yours? Well, I think it can vary quite a bit between individuals but for me my periods became irregular.'

'Oh, do you mean that you missed some altogether?'

'No, why have you?'

'Yes, but only one and I've been feeling awfully tired.'

'Yes, I thought that you had been overdoing it a bit. How much overdue are you?'

'About three weeks now, I think. No, it must be nearer four now.'

'Is it possible that you might be pregnant?'

'Oh no.' She proceeded to tell Beryl of her previous attempts to have a baby. 'So you see, it's pretty impossible.'

'Improbable, but not impossible. I think that you ought to see the doctor just to get yourself checked over, if nothing else. Promise me that you will.'

'Do you really think so? After all this time? No, it's not possible.' Fiona gave her a swift hug and a kiss on the cheek. 'It's so nice to have a sister to talk to.'

'Promise me that you will go, though, and let me know what he says.'

Her appointment to see the doctor was on the 3 January. As she came out of the surgery it started to pour with rain. She stood still for a moment, quite oblivious to the fact that she was getting soaked through. She was trying to decide what to do next. Should she go home and see to the dogs; that was what she should do, but she didn't want to. Should she phone Simon? No, I don't want to tell him like that. She could phone Laura, but no. She would phone Beryl... no. She continued to stand there for several minutes more until the cold rain started to run down her neck. Then, making up her mind, she got into the car and went back to the cottage.

After she had hurriedly fed and watered all the dogs, she shut them in their kennels, changed and, phoning Beryl, asked if she could come over for lunch.

As Beryl opened the door to her, Fiona burst into tears. 'Oh

Beryl,' she sobbed, 'the doctor thinks I'm pregnant. What am I going to do? It must be a mistake. I can't think straight any more. I'm happy and frightened at the same time. You've got to help me.'

Driving home later that afternoon, her thoughts were still in turmoil. 'Oh, God, why now?' she spoke out loud. 'Why now, after all this time. What was Simon going to say? It was something that they had never contemplated. Suppose he was angry and didn't want it? She pushed that thought to the back of her mind but it kept coming back. I've got all the kennels to look after and that takes me all my time. I'm too old to manage both.' With this sobering thought, she drove on in silence for a while. 'Well, you know, I suppose that I could get someone in to look after the kennels for a year, and women of my age do have babies very successfully now but even so… what am I going to do?'

'Are you alright?' Simon was sitting by the fire, drinking a cup of tea before going to bed. 'Are you going down with a cold or something? You've been restless all evening.'

'No, I haven't.'

'Well, you certainly seem a bit vague. Have you got something worrying you? Weren't you supposed to see the quack today?'

'Yes, I did go and see him.'

'And?'

She had been wondering all evening how to broach the subject. She had not previously said anything to Simon about the missed period – now two – not wanting to worry him. She had dreaded that it could be cancer or something equally horrible. She had no idea how Simon was going to react to this news.

'Well, come on. What did he say?'

'I'm going to have a baby.'

'What! You're joking?'

'No, I'm two months pregnant.'

After one piercing, brief look at her face, Simon sat looking at the fire as the minutes ticked away. Fiona was on the verge of tears. What was he thinking? Why didn't he say something? After several more minutes of total silence he said, 'Are you sure? I thought that you said that it wasn't possible.'

'I didn't think it was, not after all this time, but the doctor was pretty sure this morning. I'll know for certain when the test result comes back.'

'Why didn't you say something before?'

'I couldn't believe it was possible. I thought that it might have been the menopause or even something awful. I didn't want to worry you.'

'And you're two months, you say?'

'About two months. Oh, Simon, please tell me what are you are thinking. Are you pleased or not?'

'How the hell do I know what I'm thinking? You drop a bombshell like this and...'

He said no more and after a while he went out to check on the dogs. Fiona sat by the fire and tried to gather her thoughts. She had tried to imagine how Simon would react to the news but in no way had she expected this silence. Was he pleased or not?

He did not come back to the house for over an hour and when he did it was only to say that he felt tired and was going to bed. Did she want a drink as he was making one for himself? Fiona answered that she would make one later.

After he had gone upstairs, she sat and sobbed. How could life be so cruel so perverse? Upset, tired and mentally exhausted, she fell asleep by the fire.

She awoke when Simon shook her arm. 'Come on, to bed; it's cold down here.'

She followed him upstairs and, undressing, got into the still warm bed. Oh, please, she thought, please put your arms around me and tell me that you love me.

Simon, however, just lay there with his hands behind his head, looking at the ceiling.

At some time, in the early hours of the morning, she woke up to find Simon standing by the bed with a cup of tea in his hand. 'I'm off now. I've let the dogs out into their runs. See you tonight.' Before she could say anything, he had gone out of the room.

She struggled through the morning, feeling tired and slightly nauseous. When the phone rang, she hurried into the hall. 'Hello, is that you, Simon?' but it was Beryl's voice on the other end.

'Hello, Fiona; hope I haven't disturbed you but I was

wondering how Simon took the big news.'

'Oh, Beryl, it was awful! He just went absolutely quiet and has hardly spoken to me since. I'm at my wit's end here. I don't know what to think.'

'Now, calm down, Fiona. It must have been just as big a shock to him as it was to you and you did have a bit of forewarning. He's very likely trying to take it all in. After all, it would make a big difference to your lifestyle, wouldn't it?'

'I suppose you're right.'

'I'm sure that I am. You'll see, he'll have had all day to think about it and will want to talk about it tonight. After all, it is a big decision to make, isn't it?'

Fiona felt better for the chat with Beryl, and spent the afternoon preparing one of Simon's favourite dinners. Simon came home just as she had put a bottle of wine to chill in the fridge. 'Hello darling, had a good day? Dinner is almost ready.'

As she put her arms around him to kiss him she felt him stiffen and all her confidence melted away. 'Oh, Simon, please talk to me. Don't you want this baby of ours?'

'This baby of ours? How the bloody hell can I be even sure that it is *our* baby?'

Fiona gasped; she felt as if Simon had just hit her in the stomach. Staring white-faced at him, she whispered, 'What do you mean?'

FIONA SAT DOWN unsteadily as Simon stormed out of the room. She heard the car start up and drive away. Taking a deep breath, she tried to calm herself. Of course, of course, everything was falling into place now. Simon's behaviour ever since she had won the last CC under Alan, his silences, his unfriendliness. He hadn't made love to her since then and she had thought that it was concern on his part. In fact, she had to admit that she had been so concerned about her health and having to struggle through each day feeling so tired, that she had assumed that he was just worried about her too, and perhaps about the business. She had been a bit apprehensive of how he might take the news of a baby. She had thought that perhaps he would not want to have another baby at his age or he might be worried about how it would affect the running of the kennels, but what she had never thought was that he might think that it was not his baby, that it was – whose – Alan's?

Until now, she had put that day completely out of her mind. It just never happened. It had not been her in that hotel room but someone else. She sighed deeply. Now she had to face up to it and she had to tell Simon what had happened that afternoon.

She had met Alan at the pub that day and they had had a meal together as they had the previous time. She had hardly noticed what she ate because she was desperately trying to think of a way to get out of the situation without destroying her chance of a CC. She nearly choked when, as she was drinking her coffee, Alan took hold of her hand and told her that he had booked a room for them at a nearby motel. As he drove her there she was almost at the point of telling him to forget the whole thing – no win was worth it – when she thought of Simon and how, ever since she had known him, his aim had always been to succeed in the world of dogs. If she didn't do this, they would be finished.

Getting out of the car and walking into the hotel, Fiona had been red with embarrassment and had stared at her feet until they went upstairs to the bedroom. She kept telling herself that it was just something she had to do to make her darling Sapphire into a champion. She knew that it happened a lot in dog showing; it didn't mean anything and Simon need never know.

As Alan, having locked the door, put his arms around her and kissed her, forcing his tongue into her mouth, she froze, her arms at her side, one hand still clutching her handbag. Suddenly, pushing him away, she gasped, 'Alan, not so fast, you take my breath away.'

'Ah, so you're a tease, my dear, but I'm afraid that I've been waiting for this moment for a long time. Now come on, my dear, get those clothes off and let me look at that lovely body of yours. Perhaps we'll have time for you to tease me later.'

With her heart pounding like a drum she said, 'I won't be a moment,' and went into the bathroom. She couldn't bear to look at herself in the mirror as she quickly undressed and slipped on a silk dressing gown, which she had brought in a bag. Taking a deep breath, she opened the door and went into the bedroom. Alan had stripped down to his underpants. Fiona quickly averted her eyes.

'Won't be a minute, my dear, just lie on the bed.'

She lay on the bed and closed her eyes but quickly opened them when he swore. He had his back to her and was fiddling with something in front of him. Oh, my God, thought Fiona, her mind awhirl; he's putting on a condom. Why ever didn't I think of that? What a fool I am. Thank God he is more experienced than me.

Alan turned and came towards the bed. 'Now, what have we here?' he said as he undid the cord of the dressing gown and exposed her body.

She could see that he was instantly aroused as he bent to caress and kiss her breasts. She closed her eyes as his hands wandered all over her.

'Now, come and stand by the bed, my dear, so that I can

212

appreciate all of your gorgeous body.'

He again started to kiss and lick and caress her all over.

Suddenly, he stopped. 'Quickly, my dear, lie on the bed, quickly.'

She had so shut her mind to what was happening that, for a second or two, she didn't move.

'Quickly, come on, quickly.' Alan almost pushed her back on to the bed and jumped on top of her. 'God, damn and bloody blast,' he said and collapsed on top of her. 'Bloody, bloody, blast.'

Fiona, realising what had happened, was first overcome with relief and then the laughter started to bubble up inside her. She was so busy trying to stop the giggles that she hardly heard him say, 'My dear, you must be so disappointed. I'm afraid that your beauty just proved too much for me this time. I'm so sorry.'

She managed to control herself enough to say, 'Oh, please Alan, I do understand.'

She lay there for a minute as Alan quickly removed the condom.

'Now, let's have a little play together, shall we, and you can tease me in any way you want. I'm sure that you will soon have the desired effect and we'll be alright the next time.'

'Oh, Alan, I'm so sorry but I can't stay any longer; I have someone coming to look at a puppy.' She then excused herself and went back to the bathroom. Shutting the door, she hugged herself with delight at the outcome. Thank goodness that had happened – she didn't feel so defiled. Even so, she was longing to have a good, hot bath.

When she came back, Alan was dressed and sitting on the bed, having a cigarette. He exhaled and looked at her. 'Now, my dear, I'm sure that I can rely on discretion on your part. You wouldn't want to tell anyone about what happened this afternoon. I can assure you that this sort of thing has never happened to me before.'

'You can rely on me, Alan, not to breathe a word to anyone.'

'Good girl. Now, I shall look forward to seeing you at the show. You will be there?'

'Oh, yes Alan, I'll be there with Sapphire.'

'Good. Well then, mum's the word. Until the next time then,

my dear.'

Fiona shivered and realised that, as she had sat there, the fire had got very low. Simon had not come home yet so she couldn't lock up and go to bed. She put another log on the fire. What had happened to make Simon think that the baby wasn't his? She had certainly not said a word to anyone and she was pretty sure that, under the circumstances, Alan wouldn't have gone around bragging to his cronies. Could someone have seen them going into the hotel? It felt so sordid even to think about it now. What madness had possessed her? She had seen quite a few people change dramatically when they got caught up in the desire to win but she hadn't realised that she, too, had changed that much.

Her thoughts were interrupted by the sound of Simon coming in through the kitchen door. He said nothing and went upstairs to bed. By now, too miserable to move, she put another log on the fire and settled down for a nap.

She awoke to the sound of Simon preparing his breakfast. He came in with a steaming cup of tea, said, 'I'm off now', and shortly left the house.

All that day, while she was working in the kennels and the house, she was trying to think of ways of broaching the subject again with Simon. If he did know about her and Alan, what could she say? How could she explain her behaviour? On the other hand, if he only suspected something had happened because of Alan's reputation of giving his girlfriends CCs, what could she then say to him? She wanted to tell him the truth to ease her conscience, but knew that it would destroy their relationship.

When Simon came home that evening he was so silent and withdrawn that her courage failed her and bedtime came without a word of discussion or explanation. Fiona slept fitfully and felt exhausted when light began to show through the curtains and the radio burst into life. Breakfast was almost silent, Simon merely asking if she had slept well because she looked awful.

Once again, she tackled the chores of the day, her mind full of imaginary conversations with Simon. Late that afternoon, as she was preparing the dinner, the phone rang. Her spirits rose: it must be Simon calling her, as he often did, to say that he was leaving work and did she want anything bringing in? She hurried into the hall, not bothering to turn a light on, and fell over the sleeping form of Sally.

The phone had stopped ringing when she hauled herself up from her knees. Thank God nothing's broken, she thought. Sally came up, looking a bit embarrassed and wagging her tail submissively. 'It's alright, Sally, it wasn't your fault. I didn't hurt you, did I?'

She continued preparing the dinner. Conversation that evening was a bit better, although it only centred around the dogs and a forthcoming show. Nevertheless, she slept much better that night and felt more cheerful in the morning. Simon couldn't have any proof or he would have said something by now. If she kept quiet it would all blow over. Singing to herself, she started washing down the runs with disinfectant and a broom.

'Hello, Mrs Philips. Hello. Are you there, Mrs Philips?' The woman didn't know what to do. She had definitely booked the stud for 11.30 and Mrs Philips had confirmed it when she had rung earlier. Putting the bitch in the car, she went back and rang the bell again. When there was no reply, she hesitantly went round to the back of the house, hoping that a guard dog would not suddenly appear. Knocking at the back door, and calling out again, she could hear a dog barking inside but nobody came. Taking her courage in both hands, she started towards the kennels where she could hear dogs barking. Surely somebody must be around; somebody must be working up there and would know where Mrs Philips was to be found.

As she neared the runs, she could see someone lying on the ground. 'Mrs Philips?' The figure did not stir. 'Mrs Philips, are you alright?' Hurrying now, she opened the run and knelt down. 'Mrs Philips, can you hear me?'

She was frightened to move her so she rubbed her hand and spoke to her again. This time there was a slight moan and the woman opened her eyes.

'I must have slipped; help me up, please.' As she did so, the woman put her hands to her belly and groaned, 'Oh God, no, no. Please, you can't, please.'

'Mrs Philips – it is Mrs Philips, isn't it?' The woman nodded.

'Can you walk? Shall I help you to the house?

'Please, and then would you phone for an ambulance; I think I'm having a miscarriage.'

After the woman – she identified herself to Fiona as Mrs Bennett – had phoned for an ambulance, Fiona asked her to phone Simon and tell him what was happening, and then to phone Ruth to ask her if she could come and stay at the kennels until Simon could take over. Mrs Bennett then made Fiona a cup of tea.

'Oh, Mrs – I'm so sorry I've forgotten your name, oh yes, Mrs Bennett – I'm sorry about all this,' she smiled weakly. 'And you only came to have your bitch mated and… Look, phone later on; I'm sure that Simon will do the mating for you. Oh, that sounds like the ambulance.'

Later that afternoon, despite the efforts of the doctor, she lost the baby.

She was put into a very small side ward and the curtains were drawn round the bed. Simon came in but she pretended to be asleep. She wanted nobody and nothing. She was retreating into herself for safety. Her mind could not take in and accept the enormity of what had happened so it rejected it. Soon, the sedative took effect and she did sleep and had no knowledge of Simon, with tears running down his face, saying as he kissed her cheek. 'I'm so sorry, Fee. Why you, why should it happen to you? I love you so much, Fee.'

She slept right through that long night but Simon didn't. Full of self-recrimination, he sat by the Aga through the night. Mrs Bennett, somewhat reluctantly, had come back in the evening for the mating of her bitch to Jay, and Simon had been able to thank her for all her help to Fiona. She had replied that she was so sorry that they hadn't been able to save the baby. Earlier, he had thanked Ruth for coming in. She had burst into tears when she heard the news. 'Poor Fiona, I had no idea that she was pregnant. She would have made a lovely mum. She's so good with the puppies.'

Simon remembered these words and cried again. Why had he been so bloody rotten to her? Why hadn't he trusted her? She wasn't like these women in dog showing who would sleep with anyone to get a bloody CC. He did admit, sadly, that she had become a lot tougher and harder since she had started showing dogs. A lot of women did, but – for him to think that she could have slept with Alan Burgess – no, this was all his fault. He shouldn't have taken any notice when he heard Jim and Andy talking at the ringside when Fee won her CC.

As Alan had given her the big green card they had smirked and looked at each other saying, 'Ho, ho, so that's Alan's latest conquest. I'd heard that there was someone new.'

It had made him furious at the time but he should have trusted her. He should have taken a hell of a lot more care of her too, even though he had to admit, he himself had not really wanted a baby. He felt that it would have interfered with their life too much. They were too old now. Not that he would ever tell her that. No, it was all his fault, he shouldn't have let her carry on with all the kennel work.

He dozed off finally, only to wake up an hour of so later, with Sally pushing her nose into his hand. 'Hi, Sally. You missing her too?' He rose, feeling tired, old and defeated.

FIONA HAD BEEN awake a little earlier than Simon. Waking out of a deep sleep, she was trying to analyse the sounds she was hearing, when the events of the past day flooded in on her and she turned over with a groan and pulled the sheet up to her face to blot out the world.

Just then a nurse pulled back the curtains and said, 'Hello, Mrs Philips. Are you awake now? I've brought you a nice cup of tea.'

She struggled up and took the tea from the nurse.

'How are you feeling?' Fiona looked at her: she was only young, she couldn't possibly know how she was feeling. 'Oh, alright, thank you.'

The nurse drew the curtains back and Fiona saw that there were only two other women in the ward. They both nodded and smiled at her and she nodded back. Not wanting to talk, she finished the tea and lay down again with her face to the wall. She refused food, saying that she was not hungry, and when Simon came in that afternoon, she again pretended to be asleep. She didn't want to talk; she didn't want to think; she didn't want to know.

When the doctor had seen her on his rounds, he had explained to her what had happened and had advised her to sit up. Later, the nurses had insisted that she must sit up and that she should eat something. She reluctantly sat up but kept her eyes shut most of the time.

She was sitting in a chair when Simon came in the evening. 'Hello, Fee,' he said, bending over to kiss her. Her lips were unresponsive. 'How are you feeling now? The sister said that, as soon as you are eating, you can come home. Ruth and Jenny send their love and Sally is missing you.'

She looked at him with tears in her eyes; of course, Sally, the fall. Everything fell into place and the pain of the loss of her baby made her sob. Once she'd started, she couldn't stop.

A nurse came up and drew the curtains round them. Simon knelt on the floor and put his arms around her shaking body. 'Oh my darling girl, I'm so very, very sorry. It's all my fault.' Fiona shook her head but couldn't speak for the sobs tearing at her throat. The nurse came back.

'Perhaps, Mr Philips, it might be best if you left now and we will give her something to help her sleep.'

When she awoke it was morning and the tea trolley was being wheeled into the ward. She sat up and drank the proffered tea. She felt so miserable, so victimised and so alone. As she still had a slight temperature, the doctor decided that she should stay for another day and again advised her to eat something. At lunchtime she did manage to eat the food, and in the afternoon, sat in the chair looking through a magazine that Simon had brought. She knew that he would not be coming until the evening as the vet was coming to give several of the dogs their booster shots.

'Hello, Fiona.' She looked up to see Paul Aston.

'Paul! What are you doing here?' He looked slightly embarrassed.

'Well, you know what the doggy grapevine is like. I heard about – that you weren't too well – and phoned Simon. He said that he couldn't get in to see you this afternoon so I thought that I would come and bring the time-honoured grapes.'

'But it must be twenty miles or so for you to come here.'

'Oh well, I didn't really have a lot on today.'

She looked at his face for several seconds. There was kindness, humour and sadness there.

'Well, thank you for coming anyway. Do sit down. Why aren't you at work?'

'I work from home now, have done for the past year or so.'

'I didn't know that. You're an accountant, aren't you?'

'Yes, for my sins.'

'So why did you decide to work on your own?'

'Oh, you know, I bought this old cottage a few years back now meaning to do it up and never did, so I thought that I might if I worked from home. I've made a start on the kitchen. The dogs like me home as well.'

While he had been talking, Fiona was remembering that he had bought that cottage quite a long time ago; in fact, they hadn't been there very long when his wife just left him without a word. Ran off with a friend of theirs to America, so the grapevine had it.

'You must invite us over to see it when it's finished.'

'Good idea, I'll do that. Well, I'll go now. Take care of yourself.' He held his hand out and she shook hands with him, finding an odd sort of comfort in his large, warm hands.

How funny, she thought, I've known him all this time and that's the first time that I have really spoken to him. 'Thank you very much for coming, Paul, I really do appreciate it.' Tears started to well up as she watched him leave the ward. Just for a brief moment she had forgotten. She retreated again into her grey world of nothingness where she didn't have to think.

'Yes, well, I'm sorry that I didn't let you know before but it all happened so suddenly and there has been so much to do. Well then, you will come up and see her? I'm sure she will want to see you. She might talk to you, Laura.'

Laura replaced the receiver and turned to Michael. 'Oh, Michael, such sad news. That was Simon. Apparently Fiona was pregnant and she has just lost the baby. How can life be so unfair?'

'Good heavens, after all this time. Poor devil. How is she taking it?'

'According to Simon, not too well. She doesn't want to see anyone or talk to anyone and she doesn't want to eat.'

'Well, it must be a bitter pill for her to swallow, especially now that Duncan and Barbara have a child. She really has had some rotten luck. It must be very hard to accept.'

Laura's hand flew to her mouth. 'Duncan! Don't suppose Simon will have told him. I'd better phone him.'

'If Simon hasn't told him, have you thought that he might not want him to know?'

'Why ever not? I don't suppose, being a man, that he has even thought about it.'

'Well, on your own head be it, Laura.'

She dialled Duncan's number. 'Hello, Barbara, it's Laura. How are you? Oh, good. Would it be possible to speak to Duncan?' She stood by the phone hearing Barbara call to Duncan and then heard his footsteps coming. 'Hello, Laura, what can I do for you?'

'I've got a bit of sad news which I think you should know. Have you heard from Simon?'

'Simon?'

'Simon, Fiona's husband.'

'No. Why, is there something wrong?'

'Well, he phoned me to say that Fiona had been pregnant and had a miscarriage and lost the baby.'

There was such a long silence on the other end of the phone that Laura said, 'Hello, Duncan. Are you still there?'

'Yes, er… yes, I'm still here. I'm just trying to take in what you've just told me.'

'Isn't it awful news? I feel so sorry for her. I just thought that you should know. She is devastated, Simon said.'

'Yes, thank you, Laura. Thank you for letting me know. Goodbye.'

Duncan walked slowly into the lounge where Barbara was sitting. He sat down heavily in an armchair and rubbed his forehead with his hand.

'Have you got a headache, Duncan?'

'No, no, my dear; I've just had some unpleasant news.'

Barbara questioned him no further, she had quickly learned that Duncan could not be drawn and would tell her in his own good time. Having been a secretary she had learned to curb her impatience and to think of something else in the meantime.

He cleared his throat and squared his shoulders. 'That was Laura on the phone to say that she has heard that Fiona has had a miscarriage.'

'Fiona! Your first wife?'

'Yes.'

Unsure of what to say, Barbara said nothing and after several minutes of silence decided to go and check if Donald was asleep. When she came back downstairs, Duncan was still sitting where she had left him. Lost in thought, he didn't even look up as she re-entered the room. After several more minutes of silence, she said, 'Look, Duncan, this has obviously upset you. Do you want to talk about it?'

'No, I'm alright. It just brought back some rather painful memories. I was wondering whether I should send some flowers?'

'Yes, if you want to,' Barbara replied, although she did not want him to.

'Yes, well, in that case, I will. Perhaps I'll take them over.'

'Do you think that's a good idea?'

'Perhaps not. I'd better phone Laura back and get the address.'

Laura and Michael had been talking about Fiona and about all the work there was to do in the kennels.

'Look, Laura, why don't you take Amanda with you and go and stay there this coming weekend. If she is coming out perhaps Simon would be pleased to have some help.'

'What about you and the boys?'

'We'll manage fine. Why don't you go Friday morning and stay until Monday?'

'Well, I am so very concerned about her. If you can manage, then I'll go. I'll phone Simon now and arrange it.'

When she came back into the room she told Michael that Simon would rather she went after the weekend.

Fiona smiled and thanked the nurses as she left the ward. Simon held her arm as they walked along the corridor and out to the car.

'Soon have you home.'

'Yes.' She said no more as they drove along.

Simon, who was still feeling guilty about the way he had treated her, felt a little uncomfortable with this quiet, withdrawn Fiona. 'The dog grapevine looks to have been working well. Quite a few cards have arrived for you and Ruth and Jenny have made you a cake. The dogs are all well and Sally has really missed you.'

Sally, she thought, my darling Sally. If only I hadn't fallen over her. She was convinced in her mind that that was the cause of the miscarriage, although the hospital had said that there could have been any number of reasons for it. She bit her lip to stop the tears from forming in her eyes; she had resolved that she must just get on with her life as it was and not cry for what she could not have.

She had not noticed that Simon had turned into the drive and was surprised when the car stopped. Ruth and Jenny came out of the kitchen door to greet her and she had to bite her lip very hard when they said how good it was to have her home again. They all went into the warm kitchen and Sally ran up with her tail wagging furiously, and licked her hand. It was too much for Fiona and the tears ran down her face as she sobbed.

Simon thanked Ruth and Jenny for all their help and they left quietly. He poured Fiona a cup of tea and made her sit down at the big pine table. 'Come on, Fee, drink this,' he said as he put his arm round her shoulder. 'Come on, love.'

Without speaking, she wiped her eyes and dutifully sat down and drank the tea.

'Laura, she's like a ghost wandering round the house. She's hardly saying a word, and isn't eating much either. She just sits and looks out of the window, stroking Sally.'

'You think it's alright for me to come? I mean, bringing Amanda with me? You don't think that it will be more upsetting?'

'Honestly, Laura, I don't know. She's got to talk to someone and let it all out. I'm hoping that she will talk to you. Could you come fairly soon?'

'Right, I'll be there in the morning.'

Putting the phone down, Simon went into the kitchen where Fiona was sitting by the Aga. 'That was Laura; she'll be coming tomorrow morning and staying for a couple of days.'

Fiona looked up at him.

'I'm sorry, Fee, but I must go to work tomorrow. I'll let all the dogs out and feed and water them. Don't do any cleaning or anything. I'll do it when I get home. They'll be perfectly alright.'

'I'm sure that I'll manage, Simon. There is no need for Laura to come.'

'She wanted to, and we both feel that you could do with the company.'

'Why?'

'Well, you've been a bit down since you came home.'

'I've told you, I'm alright now. I'd rather she didn't come just yet.'

Simon phoned Laura again and explained the situation.

'I expect it's Amanda,' Laura replied, 'it's quite understandable. Look, I'll get a friend to look after Amanda and just come for the day. How's that?'

When Laura arrived the next day, she was quite shocked at Fiona's appearance. Pale, with dark circles round her eyes, tight-lipped and silent, Laura suddenly realised the extent of the devastation the miscarriage had caused for Fiona. A miscarriage was bad enough – she knew other women who had lost a baby – but this, for Fiona, was surely the end of the road: all hope gone. She felt her throat tighten and was suddenly lost for words. 'Hello, Fiona. Thought I'd pop over to see you.'

'Yes, thank you for coming.'

That set the tone for the day, which proved to be a hard one for Laura, with Fiona insisting that she saw to the dogs on her own. While Fiona was out, Laura made them both some lunch, but Fiona sat there silently eating her sandwich, Laura chattering away about inconsequentials, trying to lift the feeling of gloom and despondency in the room.

When Simon arrived home in the evening, she was more than relieved to get into her car and drive home. Simon came out to see her off.

'Thank you, Laura, for coming over. Did she talk to you?'

'I'm afraid not. She has hardly said a word all day. I'm really worried about her, Simon. I think you should get her to your doctor.'

After the children had gone to bed that evening Laura phoned Duncan again. She told him of her day with Fiona and how much she was concerned about her.

'How is she physically?'

'Not too bad, all things considered. Although Simon did a lot of the kennel work before he went and told her not to do anything, she went out there and worked until lunchtime.'

'Oh, so she's not too bad then. Well, thank you for letting me know, Laura.'

The following Tuesday, Fiona had just walked into the kitchen, glad to be out of the biting wind. Her hands felt numb with cold as she filled the kettle and placed it on the Aga. She was just blowing her nose when she heard a car stop at the front of the house. Blast, who the devil could that be. The front door bell peeled and pushing her still cold fingers quickly through her hair, she went to answer it.

'Hello, Fiona, thought I'd come round to see how you are,' Standing there, a large bunch of flowers in his hand, was Duncan.

Startled thoughts cascaded through her head. How did he know where to find me? What must I look like? My hair is a mess and my nose is running again. I've got my old working gear on. But all she said was, 'Oh, Duncan, I'm so very pleased to see you.'

He looked at her familiar face – so pale and drawn – and stepped forward. He held out his arms and, as she automatically stepped into them, with a sigh, he shut the door behind them. They stood like that for several minutes until she gave another big, shuddering sigh and looked up at him.

'I somehow knew that you would come. You are the only one who could possibly know how I am feeling.'

'Yes, Muppet, I think I've got a pretty good idea.'

She took the flowers and buried her face in them. 'They're lovely. Come into the kitchen, I was just about to make some lunch.'

He followed her into the big, untidy kitchen full of dog towels, blankets and magazines, and quietly reflected on the difference between his pristine kitchen and this.

They sat in the kitchen after lunch for several hours and Fiona poured out to him all the emotions and feelings that she had had since she lost the baby. Watching Duncan's face as she spoke, she knew that he was living it with her, just as they had shared their other disappointments in the past. He would know how wonderful the realisation had been when she found that she was pregnant. She didn't tell him how complete she had felt, how whole, how exalted, but she did tell him about Sally and how she felt that the loss of the baby was her fault and how she couldn't cope with that knowledge.

Until then, Duncan had not spoken, but when she started to cry again, he reached across the table and took both of her hands in his. 'My dear Muppet, you can't go on torturing yourself in this way. It may have had nothing to do with the episode with Sally. You mustn't ruin the rest of your life. Have you told Simon how you feel?'

Fiona looked away and shook her head.

'Well, don't you think that you should? I know that I'm a fine one to tell you that. I, who didn't really confide my feelings to you.'

They looked across the table at each other and a warm understanding passed between them; they both smiled.

Duncan then squeezed her hands. 'Alright, now?'

She nodded and, looking round the room, suddenly saw that it had gone dark; she got up to switch on the light.

'Good heavens, is that the time? I really must go – Barbara will be wondering where I am.'

'She knows that you've come to see me?'

'Oh, yes. She sent her kindest regards.'

D UNCAN'S VISIT HAD helped Fiona more than he knew. She still felt tired and depressed about her present life and could not find enthusiasm for anything, but at least the guilt that she had been feeling about her past treatment of Duncan had been somewhat assuaged by the knowledge of how happy he was and how proud he was of his son. His son – how those words hurt; she started to conjecture about how her life would be now if she and Duncan had had children. Would she have been happy? She just couldn't say. Sighing deeply, she started on the day's chores.

She was still in the same frame of mind when, some days later, as she was exercising some of the dogs, she heard a voice calling to her and turning round saw Beryl waving and walking up from the cottage.

'Hello, Fiona, thought that I would pop over to see you. Hope I haven't come at an inconvenient time.'

'No, it's lovely to see you. I was only exercising some of the dogs. Won't be a minute.'

Beryl waited while Fiona put the dogs back into their runs and together they walked back to the cottage. While Beryl took her coat off, Fiona put the kettle on the Aga.

'I know that I've come unannounced but to make up for it I've brought some gorgeous sticky, creamy, chocolaty buns. Thought that we could treat ourselves. Not that I should.' Beryl grinned and smoothed down her hips. 'But you look as if you should eat them all. Are you sure that you're eating properly?'

Fiona laughed and poured the water into the mugs. 'I'm fine now, quite recovered.'

After a bit of chit-chat Beryl suddenly said, 'As your self-appointed sister, Fiona, I want to say that I do know a little of what you have gone through and if you want a sympathetic and confidential ear...'

'Thank you, that's very kind of you, but I'm alright now, really.'

'Forgive me, but you're not. I lost a baby some years back now, but I can still remember how I felt at the time and I know damned well that you don't get over it as quickly as this. In fact, you never truly get over it.'

'Oh, Beryl, I didn't know. When was this?'

'No, well, you wouldn't. It was some time ago now, during my first marriage but, just now and again, I still think of her. Your loss is so recent that I'm quite sure that you haven't got over it. How is Simon taking it?'

With the mention of Simon, Fiona's determinedly cheerful facade broke down. She looked at Beryl's kind, sympathetic face. 'Oh, Beryl, it's not just the baby, it's all sorts of other things as well. I suppose that it was really the dog showing that started it; you see, when Duncan and I couldn't have a baby I bought a dog – Sally...'

Once started, she couldn't stop. She told Beryl of her fears about Simon's reasons for wanting the marriage, how she had been tricked into it and, though Simon had reassured her, that she still had doubts deep down that he had married her to secure the business. She told her how very ambitious Simon was to succeed in the dog world and about the little and big things that they did in order to win at the shows to further this ambition; how she had willingly gone along with it, pushing away her doubts about the fairness of it all. Finally, she told her about the afternoon with Alan Burgess and about Simon's comment about whether the baby was his.

Beryl said nothing all the time that Fiona was speaking but when she stopped, she quietly got up and put her arms around her. 'Oh, my dear girl, you've been carrying this around with you all this time. No wonder you look so ill.' Going to the Aga she made two more mugs of coffee.

Sitting down again and looking at Fiona's taut, pale face, she said, 'Have you told Simon about all this?'

Fiona shook her head. 'No, not all of it. We did discuss the wedding arrangements – he said it was meant as a nice surprise – but we haven't really talked about Alan Burgess and the baby.'

'What! Are you saying that he might think that it was this Alan Burgess's baby?'

'I'm not absolutely certain what he thinks. He knows Alan's reputation and I did get the CC, so I imagine he put two and two together.'

'What a mess. I had no idea that dog showing was like this. Naive of me, I suppose. After all, it is a competition but, Fiona, you must sort this out with Simon and as quickly as possible. Don't let it fester away; you must tell him how you feel about the showing and why you did what you did with Alan.'

'But I can't. I'm so ashamed of that now. I don't know what possessed me to do it. I'm afraid that he won't understand and that he won't want me if I don't show the dogs with him.'

'You mustn't value yourself so poorly, Fiona. I would swear that he adores you. This is just a hiccup but you must sort it out, and quickly. I don't condone what you did, but I do understand why you thought that you had to and I'm sure that he will.'

Beryl stood up and put her coat on. 'Look, I must go or I shall miss the train. Now, promise me that you will talk to Simon; from what I know of him and from what Peter has said, I'm sure that he will be reasonable. Bye now. Take care of yourself and do give me a ring if you want to talk some more. I promise you I shall not repeat anything of what you have told me today.' She gave Fiona a kiss on the cheek and left.

Fiona, buoyed up by Beryl's warmth and friendship, resolved to talk to Simon, but when he came into the kitchen that evening he immediately started to talk about the forthcoming mating of Sapphire, who was now in season, and her rehearsed speech died on her lips. They talked about the dog that they intended to use and Fiona found that even she felt a little excited about the prospect of her lovely Sapphire having puppies.

The following evening, sitting by the fire, she plucked up courage, suddenly looked at him and said that they must talk about the baby. Simon did not meet her eyes and did not reply.

Feeling more nervous, now she blurted out, 'The baby was yours, not Alan Burgess's.' Simon looked at her then but still remained silent.

'Simon, I can't stand this any longer; for goodness' sake, will you please talk to me?'

'I am talking to you, we've been talking most of the evening.'

'Please don't prevaricate, you know what I mean. We must talk about the baby.'

'Prevaricate; my, we are using big words.'

Tears stung her eyes, but she brushed them away; it took her a few minutes to get her voice under control.

'Simon, the baby is yours, was yours, I mean. It was not Alan Burgess's.'

Simon started to get up out of the chair. 'Who said that it was? I didn't.' He started to walk out of the room.

Seeing this, Fiona quickly got up and stood in front of him. 'No, you stay here and listen.' In a rush of words she told him about the afternoon with Alan in the hotel room.

When she stopped speaking Simon replied, 'Alright, so the baby wasn't his, but it could have been, couldn't it?' The cold anger showed in his voice. 'You went there to do it, didn't you? How many others have you tried to get CCs with?'

Fiona gasped and stepped back. She opened her mouth to speak but said nothing, too upset for her brain to form any words in her defence.

Simon took the opportunity to get his coat and go out to the kennels.

For the next half hour, Fiona tried to come to terms with the image of herself as Simon saw her. I'm not like that; he knows I'm not. But the events of the past few years kept crowding into her tired mind. She *had* been unfaithful to Duncan, but that was because she loved Simon so much. Beyond all common sense and reason, she had had to love him. It was so very different, he must know that. She shifted in her chair and prodded the fire into life again.

Images kept surfacing in her mind of that hotel room and of Alan standing there with that condom on. She shuddered. Thank God they had not had proper intercourse, she couldn't bear it now. But, she had to admit that she had gone there to have it. It had all been for the love she had for Sapphire and for Simon, and wanting the best for them but... It was no good; she had been unfaithful and for a piece of card and a rosette! She must have been mad. Her self-esteem, already low, took another knock. She couldn't cope with this image of herself.

Wearily, she got up, made a drink and went to bed. She was asleep when Simon eased himself into the bed and he was up when she awoke the next morning.

That weekend they were entered for an Open show in a nearby town. Simon was up and preparing the dogs early on the Saturday morning. He came in to breakfast and told her that he thought it best for him to go on his own as it would be a tiring day for her. She started to protest but he quickly got up and said that he was off. All day, she wandered round doing her best to look normal to Ruth and Jenny, but she was in a turmoil inside.

Suddenly, she rushed upstairs; he had said that he was off! She looked in his wardrobe and drawers and sighed with relief – nothing had gone. Her head ached with worry. What could she do to put things right between them? When he came home in the evening he told her that he had had a good day, the two dogs had behaved well and Opal had got BOB.

A pattern was now established and for the next two months Simon spent a lot of time in the kennels, always came to bed late, usually when she had fallen asleep, and went to the shows on his own. It gave Fiona time to recover fully from the miscarriage and to re-appraise her life. She had changed so, both physically and mentally, since coming to the cottage and living with Simon. Why hadn't she seen it before? The trouble with dog showing was that it was so demanding a hobby, that the months and years rushed past at an alarming rate. No time for friends or other hobbies, no time even for yourself.

'Beryl, I'm so sorry that I haven't rung before; the time seems to fly by. I would so love it if you could come over one day soon for a chat. I'd love to see you.'

'I could just do with a day in the countryside. How about I come over next Wednesday?'

On the morning that Beryl was coming, Fiona hurried

through her kennel duties and even had time to change out of her working gear and make a batch of scones before Beryl arrived.

'Hello, Fiona. You look nice; much better than when I last saw you. What a delicious smell there is. Have you been baking?'

Beryl's greeting helped Fiona to relax. 'Oh, Beryl, thank you so much for coming; I really need to talk to you.'

'Fine, make me a cup of coffee, give me one of those scones and you'll have my full attention.'

Fiona looked at Beryl's rather plain face framed in a riot of greying curls, her deep blue eyes which seemed to hold a wealth of intelligence, the laughter lines which told her happy disposition, and knew that she really did have a good friend here. She told her what had happened since she had last seen her, how Simon had reacted to the news that she was so sure that the baby had been his and of his behaviour since.

'Remind me, how long has this been going on?'

'Over two months now.'

'And you haven't mentioned it again?'

Fiona shook her head. 'He was right, Beryl – I did go there, didn't I? Even I am ashamed of myself. I must have been mad. You see, showing gets to you. It seems to take you over. The only thing that is really important is winning. Simon is always saying that.'

'Um, well, as Simon understands this dog scene far better than I, he must understand the feelings that made you do this thing. Do you think yourself that he is in any way to blame?'

'No, I feel that I am to blame. I went too far and I've hurt him badly. I just want things to be as they were and I don't know how to make it happen.'

'I'm sorry, Fiona, but I don't know what to say to help you. Only you two can find the solution. Do try to break the deadlock. You must remember that he is suffering as well and yet he hasn't gone. That must mean something.'

A week after their conversation, a week in which Fiona tried on several occasions to talk to Simon and to tell him how her feelings about showing had altered, he always quickly changed the subject, preferring to talk about forthcoming shows, which dogs to enter into them or which bitches they should be mating next.

At least, she thought, it was something and in time he would listen to her. The truce did not last long, however, because the following Friday Simon went to a Championship show on his own, even though she had said that she would like to come. Tired and bitterly disappointed at this setback, Fiona did not complain as he drove off, but instead suddenly began to feel very angry. If he was so upset and disgusted with her, so ashamed to be seen with her, why didn't he leave? She thought she knew the answer to that question.

'THEY REALLY DO play well together, don't they?' Laura said to Barbara. It had become the custom for Laura and Michael to go to tea with Duncan and Barbara one Sunday in the month and then have them to tea two weeks later. It enabled the two young children, Amanda and Donald, to play together, and their parents to chat. Laura had got on extremely well with Barbara ever since Duncan had first introduced her as his future wife. She was very interested in children, enjoyed cooking, as was evident from Duncan's increased girth, and was an excellent knitter. Laura, who was quite hopeless at knitting, admired her skill and found her easy to talk to about any homely subjects.

Duncan and Michael came in from the garden where Duncan had been showing him all the plants he was growing in his greenhouse.

'We told the boys that they could stay out there a bit longer, Laura.'

'Yes, that's fine, Duncan.'

Barbara got up to lay the table for tea. 'Shall we feed the youngsters first, Laura?'

The two women busied themselves with the preparations.

'Has Duncan been to see Fiona again?'

'No,' Barbara replied as she buttered the bread. 'He only went the once but he has phoned her once or twice since to see if she is alright.'

'Do you mind that, Barbara?'

'No, not at all. He didn't say much when he came home that day but from one or two things that he has said since, I think that he got a bit of a shock when he saw her.'

Laura's curiosity was instantly aroused at this remark. 'Oh, in what way?'

'Her appearance, mainly; he was shocked at the way she has let herself go. Her mannish haircut, her lack of any make-up, her hands and nails. You must remember how she used to look, Laura.'

'Yes, but she does run a kennel.'

'He also remarked on the untidiness of the house; in fact, he said that it all looked rather grubby. He said that she had always been so neat and tidy in her appearance and in the house.'

'True, but she does work hard. I don't suppose that she has had much time for housework. I didn't think that it was too bad when I went there. But, yes, she is very different now from when she was with Duncan. Much harder and down to earth and I suppose a lot less feminine. I do sometimes wonder which is the real Fiona?'

The women settled the two youngest children down and gave them their tea. Later, when everyone had eaten and they were sitting talking, Duncan asked Laura and Michael if they had ever regretted having a dog while the children were young. They both replied that Dee was a wonderful addition to the family and that they had never regretted buying her for one minute.

'Ah, I'm pleased to hear that. I've been discussing with Barbara whether we should have a dog as a companion for Donald.'

'Oh yes, were you thinking of getting a retriever then? I could give you the name and the telephone number of the person who bred Dee.'

Duncan looked at Laura for a moment and then, looking away, said, 'Well, actually I had thought of a Cumbrian Terrier. As you know, I have some knowledge of what it is like to have one in the house and I do know that Fiona is expecting a litter shortly.'

'Oh well, yes, it's a good idea. You do know what they're like in the house. Have you spoken to Fiona about having one?'

'No, it was her telling me about the litter she was expecting. It's her champion called Sapphire who is the mother-to-be. That gave me the idea of having one. I mentioned it to Barbara and she was entirely in agreement.'

They chatted on for a while until Amanda began to get a bit fidgety, whereupon, Laura and Michael decided that it was time for them to leave.

On the way home Laura said, 'Isn't life funny? Duncan and Fiona's problems were all about dogs and now here he is thinking of buying one. Do you think that he wants one because it's one of Fiona's or does he want it because Sapphire is a champion?'

'Who knows?' said Michael as he turned into their drive. 'I just hope that history doesn't repeat itself.'

'Oh no, I don't think so, Michael; Barbara is very different from Fiona.'

'She's not that different from Fiona when we first knew them.'

That evening Duncan phoned Fiona and told her that he would like to have a puppy. Rather surprised, Fiona said that three were already booked but, depending on how many Sapphire had, he could have one if there was one suitable. She enquired if he wanted a dog or a bitch. He said that he and Barbara had discussed this very thing and had decided that a dog would be better than a bitch – less bother. Fiona smiled to herself and agreed.

Both Simon and Fiona stayed up with Sapphire when she gave birth. She had four puppies without much trouble but it soon became obvious that there was a problem with the fifth. After Sapphire had strained to deliver the puppy without much success, they phoned the vet. They then rushed her down to the surgery where he confirmed that a puppy seemed to be stuck and that he would have to do a Caesarean section, and fast. He was efficient and swift and shortly brought out a large male puppy, who was not breathing, and then a smaller bitch puppy who was rather lethargic but still breathing. The vet's priority was to see to the mother. He gave the puppies to Fiona and Simon and told them to dry them off, massage them and give them oxygen. Fiona's little bitch responded to treatment but Simon, who had the dog puppy, only managed to get it to gasp once or twice and that was all.

Having seen to Sapphire, who was by now beginning to come out of the anaesthetic, the vet had a quick look at the puppies. He was pleased with the bitch and thought that she would make it but he shook his head over the dog and said that he was sorry but… Simon carried Sapphire back to the car and Fiona tucked the puppy in with the four others. They had brought them in a big cardboard box with a hot water bottle underneath thick blankets, which had kept them warm and safe.

Once back at the kennel, they settled the still dozy Sapphire down to fully sleep off the anaesthetic. Meanwhile, they settled the five puppies under an infra-red lamp and fed them with tiny drops of milk. Dawn was just breaking as they walked back to the cottage to make a cup of tea.

Sighing, Fiona took her coat off and turned to Simon. 'Oh, Simon, I was so worried about Sapphire. Thank goodness she's alright. She is alright, isn't she?'

'Yes, she should be okay. He did a damned good job. Very neat stitching. Pity about the dog pup, though – he looked damned nice.' He looked across at Fiona, whose eyes were filling with tears.

'Oh, Simon, he looked so small and lonely I...'

He moved and took her in his arms. 'Don't cry, we've got five puppies. Some people lose the lot.'

The comfort of his warm, hard body against her after the past weeks totally overwhelmed her emotions and she clung to him and cried into his warm jumper.

Suddenly, he moved her away. 'Come on, Fee, pull yourself together. I'll put a shot of whisky in our tea. That'll warm us up.'

Fiona felt so alone as he moved away from her and busied himself with the tea. He was obviously still blaming her for everything and that simply wasn't fair. He was the one who had told her about the seamy side of dog showing. He was the one who had kept telling her that winning was what was important. If he was so ashamed of her, why did he stay? Had she been right all along to question his need to own the kennel? Her tired brain whirled round these ever-present thoughts until she felt giddy. She sat down and took the proffered tea with a sigh.

Sapphire quickly improved and was soon suckling and cleaning her five puppies. There were three bitches and two dogs and they were very pleased with them.

'I think that we've got a future winner or two here you know, Fiona,' Simon remarked as he looked down at the little family. 'That was a bloody good mating. I think that we can charge a good price for these.'

'Yes, they do look promising and Sapphire looks wonderful after her ordeal.' She watched him for a moment looking at the pups. What is he thinking? He talks of the future as if there is nothing wrong, as if nothing has happened, and yet he still won't speak about us. 'I think that we should keep that little bitch there, the smallest one of the three; to me she looks very like Sapphire did, but it's early days yet.'

'You're right, Fee, she does; we'll keep an eye on her.'

One of the two dog puppies was smaller than the rest of the litter. After six weeks, when he was still small, Simon, who all along had been reluctant to let Duncan have a puppy, agreed that he could have that one but insisted that Fiona charge him the full price. 'After all, it may not be up to show standard but it's damned well bred and he's lucky to get one.'

Fiona bit her lip. This was double standards again as far as she was concerned and she was not happy about it but, to stop another argument with Simon, she phoned Duncan to tell him that he could have a puppy. There was a small silence when he heard the price.

'My goodness, that seems an awful lot more than we paid for Sally.'

Stammering, Fiona replied, 'Yes, yes um, well, the mother is a champion. You know, Duncan, you don't have to have it. We'll no doubt have some more puppies later.'

'No, no, that's alright. I was just a little surprised at the price, but I suppose it's like everything else these days. No, I agree to the price. Now, when can we have him?'

Fiona suggested that he should come up first and see the puppy before he made his final decision. He asked if she would mind if he were to bring Donald and Barbara. She instantly replied that it would be quite alright, but as she replaced the receiver she panicked. She would have to look at Donald. Over the years that she had been married to Duncan, she had often imagined what their son would look like and now, in part, she would know. She immediately began to think up reasons why she would not be able to be there. Why had she said that he could have a puppy? She just hadn't thought it through. She could ring now and say that there had been a mix-up and that they were all sold. Yes, that's what she would do. She could say that Simon had forgotten to tell her. She walked over to the phone and hesitated. Wasn't she being deceitful and unfair to Duncan again? She had to start facing up to life and being responsible for her own actions. She picked up the phone and dialled the number of the local hairdresser. She had been letting her hair grow since the miscarriage and it badly needed styling.

By the time the Saturday for the visit arrived, the kitchen and lounge had been cleaned from top to bottom. Fiona had had her hair styled and had been rubbing cream into her hands and face every night. Simon had noticed these preparations but had not commented on them. When she heard the car stop, she rubbed her cheeks, bit her lips and opened the door smiling, although her heart was pounding in her throat.

She saw Barbara first, a shortish, plumpish person – nothing special at all. Fiona watched as she opened the back door of the car, got a little boy out of his harness and stood him on the ground, holding his hand. Fiona felt pain as she looked at 'her' little boy. He had Duncan's colouring and Duncan's eyes, she noticed, as she walked towards Barbara with her hand extended.

'Hello, Barbara, how nice to meet you; and this must be Donald. Don't you look like your daddy? Now, would you like a cup of tea first or would you like to see the puppy?' She was on familiar ground now, her selling routine.

They all walked up to the puppy-rearing shed. 'Now that they are seven weeks old they're not with the mother, but I'll show her to you later.' She pointed out which puppy they would be having, showed them Sapphire and then took them back to the cottage. She quickly put the kettle on the Aga and showed them into the lounge. 'Now, I've made some soup. Would you like to have some lunch?'

Duncan looked across at Barbara who frowned slightly. 'Thank you, but we really can't stay. Donald has to go to a little friend's birthday party this afternoon.'

Fiona was disappointed. She had made scones and cake, some-thing she hardly ever did now, and had been looking forward to the company and being able to look at Donald. 'Of course, I understand. Well, shall we say that you will pick up the puppy in a fortnight's time?'

'Yes, that seems alright. It will give Barbara and me time to prepare for the little chap. Er, do give our regards to Simon.'

Fiona saw them into their car and then turned back to the cottage. She let out a deep sigh, suddenly feeling wrung out. She thought of the little boy and sighed again. 'I wonder if my little boy would have been as handsome as that. Well, Sally, that's something I shall never know. It's no good, I must put the past behind me and get on with my life. Now, what needs doing?'

The following Saturday, when Simon was, once again, at a show, Paul Aston came to collect the bitch puppy that he had booked. Ruth and Jenny were busy in the other part of the kennel, and after he had seen his bitch puppy, she invited him into the kitchen for a cup of coffee. They sat talking about various dogs and show people, forthcoming shows and the various judges who would be judging them, until Paul looked at his watch.

'Good heavens, where's the time gone? I'd better be off. I have so enjoyed our conversation, Fiona. Thank you. And by the way, I do like your hair like that. It reminds me of the first time I met you.'

'Oh, thank you. I have enjoyed our chat, too. There never seems to be time at shows to have a pleasant talk, does there? It's all so frenetic. Look, I've got some home-made cake and stuff. Let me make you a sandwich.'

'How can I resist home-made cake. I'd love to stay.'

Fiona bustled about and they sat down in the kitchen and talked while they ate a sandwich.

Paul was just finishing his second piece of cake when the door opened and Simon yelled, 'Fee, I'm home. It was a fiasco. The bloody judge didn't have a bloody clue what a good Cumbrian should look like, he... Oh, this all looks rather cosy. Has my wife been entertaining you well, Paul?'

Paul, unaware of the innuendo, replied, 'Hello, Simon. Nice to see you. Yes, I've been enjoying some home-made cake – a real treat for me.'

'Oh yes, and what else has she been treating you to?'

Paul, feeling the tension in the room, and realising what

Simon was implying, got up and said, 'Um, I really think that I must go. Got to feed the dogs. I'll just collect the pup, shall I?'

Fiona, who had not said a word until now, got up from the table and pushed past Simon, who was still standing in the doorway. 'I apologise for my husband's behaviour, Paul; if you would like to come with me we can make sure that you get the right pup.'

Paul, excusing himself, slid past Simon and followed her.

When she re-entered the kitchen Simon was sitting at the table eating cake.

'You arrogant pig. How dare you speak to me like that? How dare you make those sorts of accusations about one of our friends?' She swept the cake from out of his hand. 'You know damned well that Paul came here today to collect his bitch puppy. Out of common courtesy I invited him to have a bit of lunch. We were having a pleasant chat about the dogs and...'

Simon swung round to face her. 'Yes, I can imagine that it was pleasant. Where have you arranged to meet him so that you can both enjoy an afternoon's screw to make sure of your next CC?'

For a split second she stared at him and then she slapped him round the face. 'Simon, I...' Words were tumbling through her head at such a rate that she could not speak for a moment or two. She watched as the imprint of her hand appeared on Simon's cheek and then, with a strangled sob, she said, 'Oh, what's the point? You've convicted me already. How could you?'

She ran out of the room and he heard her run up the stairs. He did not move as he heard her going from room to room, but when he heard her coming downstairs he grabbed a newspaper and started to read it.

She came into the room. 'I have made up the bed in the spare room and shall be sleeping there from now on. I should hate to sully your body with the touch of a convicted whore.'

F OR THE NEXT two weeks Fiona and Simon hardly spoke unless it was in connection with the dogs or the kennels. She found sleep very difficult, missing the comforting warmth of Simon's body, and her mind seemed to have a life of its own in the early hours of the morning. She constantly churned over the events of the past few months and sleep evaded her. Tired, and with little appetite, she went about the work of tending to the dogs and Sapphire's litter. The litter was her only pleasure. The wriggling warmth of their little bodies as she cuddled them and their playful antics brought a smile to her lips.

Duncan, Barbara and Donald came to collect their puppy. Surprised and disturbed by her pale face and her looks in general, although she made a big effort and invited them to stay for lunch, they declined and made their excuses.

Just before he got into the car, Duncan hesitated for a moment. 'Is everything alright, Fiona? Only, you look...'

'Yes, I'm fine, thanks, just a bit tired. The pups have been a lot of work but, as yours is the last to go, I can have a bit of a rest now. Thank you for asking, though.' She smiled and waved at Donald as their car went down the drive.

Going back into the kitchen, she made herself a cup of tea. Yes, she thought, I do need a rest. I can't go on like this, I shall crack up. She suddenly remembered that, only the other night, unable to sleep, she had been looking through an old photo album of her father's and had found some old pictures of a holiday that she had spent with her parents at Ilfracombe, when she was eight years old. The images of happiness had calmed her mind and she had fallen asleep with them in her hand.

Fiona stood up. She had come to a decision. Slipping on her anorak, she grabbed the car keys, locked the door and drove into the nearby town. Two days later, having made all the necessary arrangements, she informed Simon when he came home that she was going away for a holiday. He started to say something but she forestalled him by saying, 'And before you make any snide remarks, I am going away on my own and should you wish to check up on me, I shall give you the name and the telephone number of the hotel.'

'I see; and how am I supposed to manage this place on my own?'

'I have made arrangements with Ruth to come in every day. She was pleased to have the extra money. Of course, she won't be cooking for you or looking after the house: only the dogs.'

She spent the next few days ensuring that everything would run smoothly and deciding what clothes to take with her. As she closed the door on the Friday morning, she had tears in her eyes. Stopping at the end of the drive and looking back at the cottage, she wondered whether she would come back here to live with Simon or not.

Friday night was spent at a hotel in Bath, and although she did not sleep very well, she was eager to get on the road the next morning. As she neared Exmoor, her spirits began to rise and a little of the excitement she had felt as a child began to sink into her mind. She stopped the car, opened a window and looked once again at the moor with its short dark grass and gorse bushes. Its quiet dignity in the hazy morning mist and its feeling of timelessness brought peace to Fiona. She drove on to the coast with a feeling of excitement and adventure as she had all those years ago.

After she had booked into the hotel, the same one at which she had stayed with her parents all those years ago, she decided to go for a long walk and re-acquaint herself with the town and the seafront. The hotel had been modernised quite a lot and was still recognisable, but would her other memories still be intact?

That evening, she retired very early and fell asleep almost immediately.

The weather was pleasant for early summer and Fiona spent

most days walking or just sitting on the beach. She always took a book with her to read but found the air so gentle and relaxing and the sound of the waves so thought-provoking that she seldom read more than a page or two, preferring to rethink past events in the light of her present situation. She rediscovered the pleasure of going to the theatre, something she hadn't done since living with Simon. She ate a Knickerbocker Glory in an ice-cream parlour and bought presents for Simon, Ruth and Jenny.

She realised how immature she had been for most of her married life with Duncan, happily allowing him to make most of the decisions; always assuming that he knew best, that his ideas were more sensible than hers. She had remained exactly as she was when she married him and had not gone on maturing. Only when she had been forced to face the truth of her seeming inability to have children had she started to grow up. Dog showing had expanded her horizons slightly and loving Simon had certainly shown her that she had a far more passionate nature than she ever thought she had, but he had also shown her what life was really like in the real world of dog showing and that was where she had made her mistakes.

She had led such a sheltered life with her parents and then with Duncan, protected from looking at people as they really were and how they often behaved. How could she have got to her age and been so unworldly, so stupid? The scene in the hotel bedroom with Alan kept resurfacing in her mind; for God's sake, she hadn't even thought of condoms! How had she allowed herself to get into that situation? Who was to blame? Herself alone? Simon? Dog showing? Ambition? Look at the deals they had done, the parties, the meals, the presents, buying in puppies at exorbitant prices to please the judge concerned, giving free studs, giving away good puppies to future judges: the list went on and on. Was all this worse than going to bed with Alan? Surely it was the same wheeler-dealing in another guise. What about the Masons? They all used it to further their ends. How could Simon be happy with everything else and yet so condemning of her? It was double standards caused by his masculine pride. That was the past. The question uppermost in her mind now was the future.

As the brief holiday came to an end, Fiona took one last walk along the beach and whispered a thank you to the sea. She had decided to make the journey home in one day, stopping for lunch somewhere. As she neared home her need to see Simon and the dogs grew and she stepped out of the car in the drive, smiling. She had phoned Simon when she had stopped for lunch and told him to expect her but he did not come out from the cottage when she got out of the car and she retrieved her suitcase from the boot. All was quiet and her smile gradually faded as she walked towards the kitchen door. Sally was in the kitchen and rushed up to her, furiously wagging her tail and jumping up to lick her hand, obviously delighted to see her. Of Simon, there was no sign.

'Hello, Sally, have you missed me, old lady? I've certainly missed you.' She fondled the dog's head as she spoke but her eyes were looking around at the kitchen. All was neat and tidy and there was a note standing by the teapot. It was in Simon's handwriting. 'Have gone to the pub. See you tomorrow.'

Her previous contentment and happiness disappeared as she read the terse note, and after she had unpacked her suitcase and made herself something to eat, she felt lost and lonely. Picking up the phone she dialled Ruth's number. 'Hi there, Ruth, I'm back. How was everything? How is Sapphire's pup?'

'Hello, Fiona. Did you have a lovely time? All the dogs are fine and Amethyst is wonderful. I'm sure that you have another champ in the offing but I expect that Simon has told you all this.'

'Oh, yes, yes. Well, I'll see you soon and thank you, Ruth. Bye.'

She put the phone down sighed and picked it up again. 'Hello, Peter, how are you? I was wondering if I could have a word with Beryl?'

'Certainly, I'll get her for you. How are you keeping, and Simon?'

'Fine. Oh, hello, Beryl, it's me again. Sorry to bother you, but do you think that you could pop over some time during the day for a chat. Any time next week and the sooner the better, please.'

'Right, I see. I'll be over next Monday, okay?'

After an almost silent weekend spent with Simon, Fiona was so pleased to see Beryl's homely, smiling face that she flung her arms round her. 'Oh, Beryl, it's so nice to see you. I can't thank you enough for coming so quickly.'

'No trouble at all. I'm always pleased to see you, and it seems as though you have a lot to get off your chest. Now, get that kettle on for some coffee; I've brought two Danish pastries for us.'

Two cups of coffee later, and after Fiona had brought her up to date with the problems between herself and Simon, Beryl said, 'So what answers did you come up with while you were in Ilfracombe?'

'Basically, I decided that I love Simon and the dogs but I'm not suited to dog showing and I want to give it up.'

'And you haven't as yet told Simon of your decision?'

'No, Beryl. I'm just terrified that he'll no longer want me. I'm frightened that he only wanted me for the kennels after all.'

'Good heavens, girl, he is head over heels in love with you. Anybody can see that. Why else is he so upset about your dalliance with Alan?'

The phone rang and when Fiona came back into the room Beryl was looking out of the kitchen window. Turning round, she said, 'Fiona you can't give all this up. You have a wonderful life here and you thrive on it. For both your sakes, tell him how you feel and then go from there.'

'And suppose I'm right and he doesn't want me?'

'We'll cross that bridge when we come to it.'

After Beryl had left, Fiona washed up their cups and plates and decided that she must make Simon listen to her decision tonight, regardless of the consequences.

After dinner that evening, when Simon was about to go out to the kennels as he usually did, Fiona stopped him. 'Simon, please will you sit down; there is something important to us both that I must say.'

He turned, one hand already on the door. 'What?'

'Please, sit down, please.'

When he reluctantly complied, she quickly sat down, facing him across the kitchen table. 'Simon, I know that I hurt you very much over Alan Burgess and I…'

Simon got up from his chair.

'No, please listen to me. I came to a decision while I was in Ilfracombe. I want to give up dog showing altogether.'

246

When Simon remained silent she hurried on.

'I can't bear it any more, all the lies and deceit and the cheating and the... all of it; it is so unfair and unkind and I don't like how it has changed me.'

'Don't be so bloody high-minded all of a sudden. The lies and the deceit – it's a competition, same as the rest of life, and that's what happens. You've got to join 'em in order to beat 'em. That's where the buzz is, the adrenaline rush. Don't bloody tell me now that it's not you. I've seen you when you've beat all the other buggers. Bloody hell, look what you did to make sure you won. That was cheating if you like. Cheating on me!'

He got up to leave but she grabbed his arm. 'Don't go. Look what about if I do the breeding and everything and you go to the shows on your own? Or I could come to the shows and just watch.'

'What sort of bloody marriage would we have then? The whole point of being together was to show together, remember? We might as well not be married. In fact, under the circumstances, that is very likely the best solution.' He slammed the door.

Ten minutes later he was back. Fiona stood up but he brushed past her. She heard him make a call, he then went upstairs, and ten minutes later came down carrying a large suitcase.

Fiona looked up with tears in her eyes as he came into the room. 'Simon, please don't do this; we can sort it out if you'll only talk to me. Please Simon.'

He walked to the door. 'I'm staying with Peter if you need me for anything important.'

She heard his car start up and race down the drive. Letting out a cry, which brought Sally quickly to her side, Fiona stood looking at the closed door.

'I AM SORRY darling, but you really will have to say something to him. I honestly don't think that we are helping the situation very much by letting him stay here.'

'No, perhaps you're right, but we can't turn him out. I only wish that I knew what was going on between those two. They seemed so happy.'

True to her word, Beryl had kept quiet about Fiona's problem. 'Well, I know one thing, Peter, whatever it is won't be resolved while Simon stays here.'

'No, I agree. Look, I'll take him out tonight if that's alright with you.'

Peter put the two pints on the table and sat down. He was finding it very hard-going talking at all to Simon. He had been silent and morose or irritable and short-tempered for most of the time that he had been staying with them. Tonight was no exception.

'Cheers,' Peter said as he picked up his glass, 'and here's to the good times.'

'What do you mean by that?' Simon growled as he too picked up his glass.

'Just that; here's to the good times. You must admit, they aren't too damned good at the moment.'

'Oh, so this is where I get the big brother lecture, is it?'

'Simon, for God's sake, will you act your bloody age? If you really want to know I, for one, am getting bloody fed up with your moping round the house. I've bitten my tongue several times this week when you've been short with Beryl and…'

'Oh, so she's put you up to this I—'

'Stop right there before you say something that we'll both regret. Beryl has said nothing against you but I know that she is extremely fond of both you and Fiona and is worrying herself silly about the pair of you.'

'Well thank her for me but tell her not to waste her time worrying a—'

'You are an ungrateful sod, Simon. If this is how you normally behave, then Fiona is well rid of you.' Peter pushed his chair away from the table and walked out of the pub.

Simon sat there with his hand round his glass. He knew that he had been well out of order with Peter and was now regretting it. Finishing his pint, he left the pub and walked back to Peter's house. He stood looking at the neat front garden, lit up by the light from the front door. They had both been so bloody kind to him. Frowning, he felt in his jacket pocket and found his car keys. He'd go for a quiet drive somewhere and try to calm down.

He drove along the darkened roads not looking at road signs and suddenly realised that he was nearly home. 'Blast,' he said, 'I can't keep away from her.' He slowed the car as he neared the entrance to the kennels, trying to see if there were lights on. Stopping, he saw that there was a light on in one of the kennels. Was there a bitch due to whelp soon? Was there something wrong with one of the dogs? Guilt swept over him: he had walked out and left Fiona with everything. He had so wanted to get away from the whole sorry mess that he hadn't been thinking straight. She was left with it all to do. He would just call in, just to check that she was coping and that the dogs were okay.

Putting his hand on the ignition key, he was just about to start up when the lights of a car came down the drive. He watched it turn out and drive off in the other direction. Furious, he started the car and did a U-turn screeching the tyres as he went. That bloody woman had had Paul Aston round. Up to her tricks within a week, and he had been feeling sorry for her! Well, that was that; she could rot in hell as far as he was concerned.

Beryl raised her eyebrows as the front door slammed with such force that the house seemed to shake. They heard Simon storm up to his bedroom and then slam that door as well.

Beryl looked at Peter. 'I'm sorry, love, but things can't go on like this. I know that you said that we shouldn't interfere, but I am going to see Fiona tomorrow.'

Peter nodded his head. 'Just tread carefully. After tonight's reaction, I think that there is more to this than meets the eye.'

Knowing what she did, Beryl just nodded and, getting up from her chair, went to phone Fiona.

'Oh, Beryl, I'm so pleased to see you. I'm absolutely shattered.'

'Yes, and you look it! I know that you have been up all hours with that premature litter but you really must take more care of yourself, Fiona. Can't you get someone to come in and help?'

'Ruth has come in as much as she can and, as I told you, Paul was marvellous when I phoned him about the litter. He came over straight away and was such a help with those tiny puppies. I'm sure I would have lost some of them without him.'

'Anyway, put a comb through your hair because you and I are going to the nearest pub for a decent meal, and I won't take no for an answer.'

As the hot food revived Fiona and she relaxed, Beryl decided that it was a good time to bring up the subject of Simon. 'Is there any chance of you and Simon getting back together again?'

Fiona sighed deeply and told Beryl about their last argument; how adamant Simon was about her continuing to show the dogs and how strongly she felt about not showing them because she felt that it had so changed her as a person.

'But isn't there some compromise, Fiona? Couldn't you just show a little?'

Fiona explained that it didn't work like that. If you showed a little, then you were little and you didn't count. Now that they had tasted success, nothing less would do for Simon. He wanted more champions, he wanted them to both judge Championship shows at home and abroad, and to do that you just had to be 'in' with all that that entailed. 'It's even more complicated than that. You see, I would want to judge the Championship shows fairly.'

'What's wrong with that?'

'Just about everything. We'd be finished; we certainly wouldn't win much again. Others would be too afraid of offending the powers that be to put us up any more.'

'Heavens, Fiona, it all sounds a really dirty business, so corrupt. I had no idea about all this when I watched showing on television.'

Fiona sighed. 'You do see though, Beryl, that what I want now and what Simon wants are poles apart.'

'Well, my dear girl, you and Simon can't leave things unresolved. I can tell you, he is as miserable as sin and thoroughly bad-tempered. You look on the verge of collapse. One of you must give in.'

Later that evening, Beryl told Simon that she had been to see Fiona and how very tired she looked. He shot her a thunderous glance but said nothing. She continued to say that she didn't know how Fiona was coping, especially with the premature litter as well.

'What premature litter? Which bitch was that?'

'Oh, I see, you don't care about your wife but you care about a dog! Well, if you want to know you had better phone her. I don't know which one it was.'

Simon sat there for several minutes and then got up and went out into the hall.

'Which bitch whelped prematurely?'

'Is that you, Simon?'

'Of course it bloody well is. Which bitch was it?'

'It was Speciality.'

'And...'

'And she had five pups. Three were breech and she took a long time. If it hadn't been for Paul, I think I would have lost most of them.'

'Paul... Paul Aston?'

'Yes, I rang him for some advice and he came over and looked after the pups while I saw to Speciality.'

'Why the hell didn't you ring m...' Simon stopped in mid-sentence. 'Right, I'm coming over.'

As he entered the drive he could see that the outside lights were on in the kennel blocks and, as he stopped the car, Fiona emerged from one of the kennels. He hurried up to her. 'Hello, are they all alright?'

'Yes, I was just seeing that all was well up here for the night. I've got Speciality and the pups in the kitchen so that I can keep an eye on them.'

Simon could see that she looked exhausted. He followed her down to the cottage and into the warmth of the kitchen. The whelping bed was beside the Aga. Speciality wagged her tail when she saw him and, going over to her, he knelt and looked at the five pushing, wriggling puppies as they suckled. Tears started in his eyes. My God, he'd left Fee to cope with everything. Struggling against the tears he said, 'What are they?'

'Three bitches and two dogs.'

Fiona had made some tea and they sat in silence, drinking it. Fiona was feeling very hurt that he hadn't even asked how she was. Why hadn't she seen before what an insensitive swine he could be? He really only cared about himself and the dogs. All her previous doubts about his reasons for marrying her surfaced as she sat sipping the hot tea. Well, this was still her house and she could damned well tell him to get out if she wanted to. She could make some arrangements about the kennels and get him out of her life altogether. If he thought for one minute that he could treat her like dirt yet still go on running the kennels and showing from here, he was vastly mistaken.

She opened her mouth to tell him to go when he suddenly looked up at her and said, 'Fee, I'm so bloody sorry for everything.'

Fiona just sat and looked at him as he went on. '...for leaving you with all this, all that business with bloody Alan Burgess. I'm sorry, Fee, but it bloody hurt. It still does, but I can see how it happened... all my fault. Fee, please forgive me and let's get back to where we were.'

After a long pause, while Fiona continued to sip her tea, she looked up at him. 'You forgot to mention the loss of our baby.'

'Oh God, Fee.' Simon got up, came round the table and kneeling, took Fiona into his arms. 'Oh Fee, I'm so sorry about the baby. I knew how much you wanted it and—'

Fiona interrupted him, 'And how much you didn't want it because it would have interfered with your glorious plans.'

Simon looked at her face. 'Fee, what has happened to you?'

'I've come to my senses. I can see dog showing for the under-hand, tawdry, conniving and dishonest sham that it is. I've seen what it can do to decent, pleasant people and how it can destroy them. That is what has happened to me.'

Simon got up and returned to his seat. After a long silence he said, 'Where do you want to go from here?'

'I don't know yet. I love the dogs and…'

'Well, let's do what you suggested before; you run the kennels and I'll do the showing. You could still judge, couldn't you?'

'Yes, I could, but I won't be told what I am putting up before the show.'

'No, no. Well, that's alright. We've made a start anyway, Fee.'

'Have we? Look, I'm tired and I still have some work to do, so I think that you had better go.'

'Look, let me finish everything for you and then I'll go.'

Too tired and dispirited to argue, Fiona nodded her head.

Later that evening, sitting by the Aga with Sally's head resting on her lap, Fiona was once again trying to make some sense of her life when the phone rang.

'Hello, Fiona, Paul here. Just wondered how mother and babies were doing?'

'How nice of you to ring, Paul; they are all fine and sucking away merrily at the milk bar.'

'Good, well, if you need any more help, let me know.'

'Yes, thank you. And thank you again for coming round so quickly. Paul, do you mind if I ask you a personal question?'

'Well, that all depends, but fire away.'

'Do you really enjoy showing and judging?'

'Good Lord, what a question! I suppose the answer is yes and no. It's a bit like the parson's egg really: good in parts.'

'Yes, I suppose you're right. That's it: good in parts. Goodnight, Paul.'

She had hardly replaced the receiver when the phone rang again.

'Hello, Fiona, it's Duncan. How are you?'

'Tired, but alright otherwise, thank you, Duncan. How is the puppy?'

'Thriving and keeping us very busy, but I didn't actually ring about that. I thought that you would like to know that Laura has had to go into hospital for an operation. Barbara is, of course, helping out as much as possible, but Michael is rushed off his feet and I thought that he might not have got round to telling you.'

'What's the matter with her?'

'Oh, women's problems, I believe.'

'Thank you for letting me know, Duncan, I very much appreciate it.'

Suddenly galvanised out of her depression, she phoned Michael for the details and arranged to visit Laura after she had had the operation. She then phoned Beryl, told her the news and asked her to ask Simon if he could arrange to look after the kennels on the day that she was going to visit Laura.

A week later, she was sitting at Laura's bedside. The news was not good: she had cancer and they had performed a hysterectomy. The good news was, however, that they thought that they had managed to remove all the cancer. Fiona held her hand as they chatted together. Suddenly, Laura asked about the dogs.

'You don't really want to hear about the dogs, do you?'

'Yes, I do. You know, Fiona, I've always secretly admired the way you tackled your new life. You are very brave, you know. Tell me what you have been doing lately. It will take my mind of my troubles.'

'Well, Speciality has just had a litter of five. They look most promising and I'm so hoping that there is another Sapphire there...' She stopped, appalled at what she had just said, but then continued. 'Secretive is in whelp, well, I think she is, so I'm keeping quite busy.'

'How is Simon?'

'Oh, fine.'

'And how are you, Fiona? Are you happier now? I was so worried about you. I knew what that baby meant to you.'

'Yes, I have accepted that now. I mustn't keep you talking, you must rest.'

'You will come and see me again, won't you?'

'Of course; I'll arrange it with Michael.'

She looked at the cottage as she got out of the car. I love this place, she thought. She could hear the dogs barking in the kennels and then the door opened and Simon came out, smiling, Sally by his side.

'You're in luck, I've just made a cuppa. How is Laura?'

Just for a moment or too it seemed as if the past months had never happened. She looked at him. Was there a deeper side to Simon or was he just utterly selfish?

W HEN SIMON CAME in from locking the kennels for the night, the atmosphere was charged with the unasked question. Fiona had been agonising over the answer all evening and now she said, 'Thank you, Simon, for coming today, it's been a great help. Will I see you tomorrow evening?'

He paused in the process of taking his anorak off. 'Uh, yes, if that's what you want.'

'Yes, I think that it is what I want for the moment. Don't let's rush things.'

'Okay. Fine by me. See you then.'

She breathed a sigh of relief as she heard the car disappear down the drive. She knew that she still loved him, knew that she desperately wanted him to excite the passion in her but... was it going to be enough? Could they both put the last few months behind them completely? He had to accept the business with Alan Burgess and trust her, and she must ignore her dislike of the show side of their life together and trust his motives with regard to the business.

'Well, Sally, my old friend, there's really only one way to find out. I'll give it a week like this and then we'll see.'

When Simon told Beryl and Peter that he was moving back to the kennels, they both did their level best not to look too pleased. Life had been a bit of a strain, to say the least. Beryl, especially, had found Simon difficult to live with. After her quiet, relaxed Peter, Simon seemed like a human dynamo; so ambitious, so keen to get as much as he could out of life, so impatient with the waiting.

'I can't thank you both enough for all that you've done. It'll be so good to get back to Fiona and the dogs. You must come and have a meal with us soon.'

As the car drove away, Beryl linked her arm with Peter's. 'Come on, my lovely man, you go out on the patio and I'll bring us a pot of tea.'

Peter looked at her and smiled. 'You do say the nicest things.'

Laughing, they went into the house and firmly shut the door.

Relations were a little strained for the first few days after Simon returned, but they gradually slipped into their old routine. One evening, after Fiona had showered and washed her hair, she came out of the bathroom to find Simon standing there stark naked and very aroused. She hesitated for a moment but Simon opened his arms and she went straight into them; his demanding, hot body pressed against hers instantly aroused her to a mind-numbing passion. They both climaxed within minutes and lay there so closely together that she couldn't tell where he began and she finished. Awakening from a doze, she found Simon caressing and kissing every inch of her body and her feelings became so intense that she cried out, 'Wait, wait, I want to caress you as well and I can't if you go on like that.'

That night appeared to put everything right between them and life carried on as before. It was rather convenient that they had two litters of young puppies about that time because Fiona was legitimately able to stay behind when Simon went to the shows. However, her own Championship-judging appointment was fast approaching and when the friendly phone calls started coming and a case of wine was delivered with a little card, she knew that the crunch time between them was imminent. She felt somehow that all her questions about Simon would all be answered one way or another.

Answering the phone one evening, she was delighted to hear Laura's voice. 'Hello, Fiona, I'm home and I've got the all-clear. They are pretty sure that they caught it in time.'

'Oh, Laura, I'm so pleased to hear that. As soon as you feel up to a visit, let me know. I bet Michael and the children are glad to have you home.'

'Yes, it's marvellous. Michael just keeps smiling at me and the children are all trying to be so good – it can't last!'

'Look, Laura, if you and Michael would like a short break some time I'd willingly look after the children.'

'Oh, that sounds wonderful. I'll speak to Michael and let you know.'

Two days before her big day the phone rang yet again.

'Simon, will you please answer it; I don't think I can bear to hear how wonderful someone's dog is and how well it is doing.'

Laughing, Simon went into the hall.

'Fee, it's Duncan.'

'Duncan, how nice to hear from you. Is everything alright?'

'Yes, thank you. We are all well, including Robbie the dog. Actually, I phoned to wish you well for Saturday. It is your big day, isn't it?'

'Well, yes; how did you know?'

'You told me ages ago and I made a note of it in my diary. I know how important it must be to you.'

'Oh, Duncan, that is so kind of you. Thank you very much.'


As she got out of the car and walked into the show ground she looked outwardly calm but her hands were sweaty and her stomach was tied in knots. After much deliberation, she had elected to wear a dark green suit, which she had had for a couple of years and in which she always felt happy and relaxed. Comfortable shoes and a new pale green blouse completed the outfit.

Having informed the secretary of the show of her arrival, she was offered a cup of coffee and gratefully sat down in a chair in the small tent reserved for the judges. Her legs felt like jelly and she smiled nervously at another judge at the same table. 'What breed are you judging?' she enquired.

'Oh, I'm judging Pekinese today. What about you?'

'Cumbrian Terriers.' She couldn't think of anything else to say so drank her coffee, even though it was too hot.

'Would all judges please go to their stewards? We would like judging to commence in all rings at ten o'clock, please.' The secretary's voice broke in on her chaotic mind.

Hastily swallowing the remains of her coffee and knowing,

without a shadow of a doubt, that she should have gone to the toilet first, she found her stewards and walked across the showground to ring number eight.

As she entered the ring, she caught sight of several familiar faces and smiled. To anyone watching, she looked totally composed and at ease. She knew that Simon was expecting her to 'have seen sense' and to give all the firsts and the top awards to friends, future judges or those who would show appreciation in a remunerative way. She, on the other hand, still wanted to be absolutely fair and to put up the dogs which she considered to be the soundest and the nearest to the Kennel Club standard.

As her stewards called in the first class, minor puppy dog, all doubts and uncertainties disappeared as she concentrated on assessing the dogs now standing with their owners in the ring. She was a little slow and nervous in making her choices in that first class but, as class after class came into the ring, her confidence grew and she found herself really enjoying the challenge and the mental stimulation. She also found that, like it or not, she was putting up several 'faces' with well-known dogs, but she was relieved when she was also able to put up a small proportion of people who seldom featured in the line-ups.

It seemed no time before she was awarding the dog CC to Paul Aston. She hadn't wanted to give it to him because she knew that people would say that it was because he was a friend, but she truly felt that his dog was the best there.

Breaking for lunch, she and her stewards went for an excellent meal in the judges' tent. While she was eating, she had the thought that at least Simon would be pleased with her choice of dog. Little did he know that she hadn't planned it.

She returned to ring number eight to judge the bitch classes. When she had handed out the bitch CC to an exhibitor who seldom won top honours because she wasn't in the 'winning fraternity', she was delighted. She did, however, award BOB to Paul Aston's dog.

As the clapping died down and Paul left the ring, Fiona let out a sigh of relief. She felt mentally exhausted: so many dogs to go over and assess, so many decisions to make. Smiling tiredly, she thanked her stewards and left the ring feeling satisfied that she had judged as fairly as she could. She received several black looks from various friends and acquaintances who had not featured highly, but that was inevitable. Shrugging her shoulders, she walked away. They were greedy people who expected everyone to be too intimidated to put them down.

Although he had argued, Simon had not come to the show. She had felt that it would be too distracting if she knew that he was at the ringside, possibly criticising her placings. As she walked into the kitchen at the end of the day, she sensed an atmosphere.

'There's a cuppa if you want one,' he said.

She kept thinking of things that she wanted to tell him but one look at his face stopped her.

At about nine o'clock, unable to keep silent any longer, she said, 'I gave Paul Aston the dog CC and BOB.'

'I know.'

'How?'

'Ted Roberts phoned me with the results.'

'Oh.'

'For godsakes, Fee. Why didn't you put John Campion up? He always comes to our parties and you know that he's judging shortly.'

'I gave him a second.'

'Don't be bloody funny with me, Fee. You know what I mean.'

'I told you that I was going to judge the dogs and not the owners. Some of the "big names" did have nice dogs – like Paul – and they won.'

'You do know that you've set us back now for ages. You'll be lucky to ever get another appointment and I shall have to do a hell of a lot of crawling to stay in with any sort of a chance.'

'But why? Surely they don't expect to win every time. Anyway, John's dog has already got a CC and he has a terrible fault. He shouldn't win at all. I only—'

'Bloody hell, Fee, don't talk such rot. Since when did you have to have a good dog to make it into a champion?'

Nothing more was said on the subject but it hung like a cloud over them for days.

One morning, while Simon was at work, Paul Aston appeared at the kitchen door, holding a beautiful bouquet of flowers. 'For you, Fiona, with my grateful thanks.'

'Oh, Paul, how lovely. Do come in.'

She looked at his rugged, pleasant face. He had lots of laughter lines round his eyes; he must smile a lot, she thought. I wonder how happy he is.

'Paul, do you mind if I ask you a personal question?'

'No-o. This sounds ominous.'

'What did you honestly think of my judging?'

'How can I say when you gave me the CC?'

'But I want you to say, and honestly, please.'

'Well, for what it's worth, I think that you did an honest and thorough job.'

'Yes, but did I do it correctly?'

'I'm not sure what you mean.'

'Oh, come on, Paul, I know the ropes, I know all the little arrangements, etc. You know perfectly well what I mean.'

'Ah, I see. Surely you should be asking Simon this question, not me.'

'I know what Simon thinks; I want to know what you think.'

'Fiona, you are putting me in an invidious position.'

Fiona sighed. 'I see, Paul; so you also think that I was silly to try to give everyone a fair chance. Thank you anyway.'

'Look, Fiona, you have someone who loves you. You have family and friends: a life, in fact, outside dog showing – a lot of people don't, it is their reason for their existence. If it weren't for dog showing, I would have little social life at all. Being totally honest with you, I should like to be more fair but, in order to keep my social life and all my dogs, I go along with the system. Now, I must be going. Give my regards to Simon.'

'But Paul, you're an educated man. You could pursue another hobby.'

Paul smiled sadly. 'I have thought of that but I have to admit that I just can't make the effort. Now, I really must go. Bye, Fiona, and thank you once again.'

Somebody else I've upset, she thought, as she watched him get into his car.

Later, when Simon came home and saw the flowers he scowled. 'Who are they from?'

'Paul Aston. He dropped by on his way to see a client. They are a thank you for the CC.'

'Um, and that's about all we'll get from that appointment.'

'Please don't go on, Simon. I know I shouldn't have done it. I'm sorry that I can't judge as you want me to but I promise you that, if I ever get asked to judge a champ show again, I'll go along with the system and put up those I am supposed to put up. Is that alright?'

'Bit too late now; the horse has very likely bolted.'

The normal pattern of her life resumed and, as she went about her routine, she thought over what Paul had said and realised that showing represented a lot of her and Simon's social life, too. She had lost sight lately of some of the reasons why people showed dogs, like loneliness and boredom, or no sense of their own worth. She still loved Simon, of that she was sure. She wanted to live with him and she enjoyed life, except for this worry about fairness.

The truth of what Simon had said came back vividly to her when, later the following month, John Campion did not even place either of the dogs that they showed under him.

On the way home, Simon suddenly turned to her. 'Fee, it might be a good idea if you didn't come to the champ shows for a while. You are getting a name for being honest and that will not do the business any good.'

'Why should that harm the business?'

'You know what the grapevine's like. It will be damned hard to make up champions and to get judging appointments for me if I get tarred with the same brush. I think it would be best if you lay low for a while. Judge the Open shows and show there.'

Fiona bit her lip and didn't reply, but his remarks had hurt her very much. She felt hurt, too, that she was part of something that could be so vindictive if they didn't get everything their own way.

When they arrived home, they went through their usual routine of seeing to the show dogs and checking and settling the others. As they sat having a meal later that evening, it was warm and comfortable in the kitchen and Simon was enthusing about one of their young bitches and his plans for her. He didn't seem to notice that Fiona was rather quiet and was only picking at her food.

'If I can make her up, I reckon that we could sell her for a nice figure abroad. Then perhaps I'll get a chance of judging abroad. That would be a nice holiday for us, wouldn't it?'

She wanted to reply, 'Oh, so I will be allowed to come with you, will I? As long, of course, that I don't disgrace you.' She wanted to say that very much but she merely smiled and said, 'Um, that would be nice.'

Long after he was asleep that night Fiona lay curled into a tight ball of misery beside him. Had the past few years been all for the business, after all, as she had suspected once or twice in the past? Was she now to be relegated to the position of a kennel maid in her own property? No, she was just being too sensitive and silly. They always did things together. She had just read too much into his words. Turning and cuddling into his warm back, she fell asleep.

'HANG YOUR TOWELS and cossies on the line, boys, and I'll make us all a hot drink.' Rubbing her hair by the warmth of the Aga, Fiona put the kettle on the hob. As Tom, Richard and Alec came into the room she turned and smiled at them. 'I think there might be a bit of the flapjack left in the tin.' The boys grinned and dashed to the larder.

What a week it has been, thought Fiona; only one day left before they had to go back and she had loved every minute of it. When she had answered the phone two weeks ago and had been asked by Michael if she could have the boys over for the week of half-term, to give Laura a little break, she had said yes immediately. In the following week, however, she had rushed round the cottage in a furore of cleaning and had then filled the larder with food, including plenty of home-made cake. Simon had watched this flurry of activity with amusement and had teased her about it. When she went to pick the boys up on the Saturday she was so nervous but, at the sight of Laura's pale face, she was glad that she had agreed.

In the event, it had all worked out wonderfully. Tom, now eleven, had been so interested in the dogs and had been a great help; the twins, Richard and Alec, nearly nine years old, had helped too, but would often wander off together to play a game or just chat together, as is the way of twins. They had had several outings and today's had been to the swimming baths. Most evenings had been taken up with games of Monopoly or draughts or cards, with Simon joining in as well.

As she washed up the breakfast things the next morning, she was planning the picnic for today's outing. They were going to a local society which renovated and ran steam trains. She sighed. The last day – how the week had flown and how she had enjoyed it. She felt a little guilty that she had not spent so much time with the dogs but, she shrugged her shoulders, she would make it up to them next week.

'I'm just off to see to the dogs, Tom, if you want to come and help me.'

'Okay, Aunt Fee, I'm just coming.'

Later, after Ruth had arrived, they set off for their last adventure. The boys were fascinated when they went into the workshops and saw the locomotives being repaired.

'Gosh, Aunt Fee, I didn't realise just how massive they are. Look at the size of the wheels!'

'When does the train come in that we are going on, Aunt Fee?'

'Oh, any minute now, Richard. I think that we had better start walking up to the platform.'

During the journey, they found the dining car and sat down to enjoy their picnic. All the boys had good appetites, and what had seemed a massive amount of sandwiches and cake had soon disappeared. When the train pulled into its last station on the line, they all got out and watched with interest, as the engine was shunted off and reversed, ready for the return journey. Over dinner that evening the boys were eager to tell Simon all about the wonderful day that they had had. He listened with interest, now and again casting a quick look at Fiona's laughing, animated face.

The week following the boys' visit was very difficult for Fiona. For a while she hadn't thought about anything but the boys; her own personal problems had been pushed aside but now, they all came flooding back with a vengeance. Life was a bit mundane now without the excitement of going to the Champion shows with Simon. She went to a few Open shows on her own with some of the youngsters that they were running on, but there was no adrenaline rush at these shows, no Simon to talk to. She looked around at a lot of the 'no hopers', as Simon called them, and felt infinitely sad. She had to admit that she missed going with Simon very much; missed the laughter, missed the meal together on the way home, missed the winning! Why had she been so self-righteous, so pompous? What did it matter if all these fools didn't win? It was their own fault, wasn't it? If they were too thick to see what was what, well, too bad! She banged a bucket down on the floor, startling one or two of the dogs. 'Oh, poppet, I'm not angry at you. Come on, come here and let me give you a cuddle.'

That evening when Simon came in from the kennel, having prepared two of the dogs for the Championship show the next day, Fiona looked up from the magazine that she was reading. 'Simon, I thought that I'd come with you tomorrow. We've no puppies and Ruth and Jenny can manage perfectly adequately.'

Without turning round as he washed his hands at the sink he said, 'Well, if you really want to, do by all means, but I can manage these two on my own quite easily.'

Fiona stared at his back as he continued to wash his hands. 'I see, so you don't want me to come with you?'

'Now, don't go putting words into my mouth. I didn't say that, but knowing how you feel about the show scene, perhaps it's as well that you don't come. We can't afford to have your views spread around, can we? I'm only just sorting out the mess from your judging.'

Harsh words came to Fiona's lips but she bit them back. Furious at his seemingly casual attitude to her, she got up. 'I'm going to have a bath.'

Once out of the room, hot tears stung her eyes and her throat felt blocked with anger. So she hadn't yet served her time of penance! Would she ever? This state of affairs just couldn't go on. Why should she be made to feel so guilty about doing what she considered to be right? This was no longer a partnership and she had to face that fact squarely.

Sitting in the bath with the tears running down her face, she tried to look at her relationship with Simon as it was now. His indifferent attitude towards her feelings in this had driven a wedge between them. He had not even tried to support her in her decision to judge fairly. In fact, he had constantly reminded her how much boot-licking he was having to do; how much more money he was having to spend on entertaining people just to repair the damage that she had done. They didn't make love so often now, they hardly ever went out together. It was no good creeping around feeling guilty. She had to face the fact that their old relationship was over and did she want to continue with things as they were now. She suddenly stood up and grabbed the towel. 'No, no, I bloody well don't!'

She said nothing to Simon about her decision but did phone her solicitor to make an appointment to see him. She wanted to know her position in the event of a separation. She owned the cottage and the kennel buildings and land, but what rights did that give her. Her self-esteem had taken a terrible knock. Why was she such a failure with relationships? She had tried so hard to be the sort of wife that Duncan wanted and yet, as soon as she had done something that she herself wanted, it had all gone wrong. She had thought that Simon loved and wanted her because they seemed to have so much in common. They had been so happy together but, once again, as soon as she had done something that she wanted, it had gone wrong again. Had she just been unlucky or were all men just the same – alright providing they got their own way over everything? Surely not. Could it be that she subconsciously chose men like that?

She was still in the same frame of mind after she had met her solicitor. She found out that she was quite entitled to ask him to leave the premises, but, as the business known as Simfell Kennels was in their names, unless she bought the business from him, she would not be able to continue using that name if she carried on using the kennels. She went home determined to confront Simon that evening. She phoned Beryl to tell her what she was going to do and why.

'My dear girl, I know that you must have thought this over but are you sure that this is the only way? Promise me that you'll first talk it over with Simon. Tell him how you feel. Knowing men, I don't suppose he has realised how shut out you feel.'

Fiona agreed to talk to Simon but, deep in her heart, she felt that it wouldn't resolve the issue. She'd say something tonight.

'Simon, you didn't tell me how you got on last Saturday.'

'Much as it's been the last few champ shows.'

'You mean that we're still being blacked because I didn't put certain people up?'

'Yes.'

'Well, suppose I did go along with the system.'

'I've told you, chance would be a fine thing. You've been labelled as honest. No, I've just got to sit tight and see if I can weather the storm.'

Fiona noted the 'I'. 'Does that mean that you don't want me at the shows, you don't want me to be part of the business?'

'No, of course I want you. You do a marvellous job here. You're good with the dogs and the puppies. You're good with the matings. You're—'

'So what you're saying is that you just want me as a kennel maid.'

'I'm not. All I'm saying is that perhaps it's best that you don't come to the champ shows, that's all.'

'And if I don't accept that?'

'What do you mean?'

'I mean, that we set up all this together. We did everything together, including me showing with you; me making up my champions as well as you. Now, it seems that's not to be any more and I don't like it.'

'Sorry, but I did warn you, didn't I?'

'Why don't you fight the system for me? Stand up for me.'

'Now you're really being silly.'

'Silly, am I? Right, well, in that case, I want you to leave these premises and I want a separation and possibly a divorce.'

There was total silence in the room. Sally, sensing trouble, came and put her head on Fiona's lap. Fiona automatically reached out to stroke her head. 'I understand from my solicitor that, as you only own half the business and have not contributed financially to the buildings etc., I can ask you to remove your business from my premises. This I now do.'

With a look of anger and hatred, Simon got up, flung on his anorak and went out to the kennels.

Fiona was surprised at how calm she felt. Perhaps she would now learn if he did love her or her money.

Simon stood in the kennel. He was shaking with anger. So, she'd even been to her solicitor's behind his back, had she? How long had she been planning this then? Underhand bitch. Was this why she buggered up that bloody show? She was out to ruin him.

My God, I bet this all goes back to losing that baby. She blames me for it. This is her way of getting her own back. Couldn't she see that it was for the best? She couldn't have managed the kennels and a baby, not at her age. Damn, damn, all his bloody plans up the spout. He decided to go for a drink and plan what to do to get out of this mess. Silly bitch!

Lying in bed, unable to sleep, Fiona heard him come in and bang around downstairs for a while. He did not come up to bed.

'Hello, my dear. I had to phone, I've been so worried. Have you managed to speak to Simon yet?'

'Yes, and I've asked him to leave.'

'Oh, I'm so sorry, Fiona, so very sorry. I'm sure that he loves you.'

'Yes, perhaps, but it's obvious that he loves himself more.'

'Well, I'm here if you want me. I haven't said anything to Peter yet; he will be so upset. Take care.'

With no shows that weekend, Simon was at home. 'Look, Fee, let's go out for a meal this evening. We really must talk this over.'

'Yes, I'd love to go out for a meal. It will save me cooking; but as far as I am concerned, there is nothing to discuss.'

The evening did not go as Simon had hoped it would. When they got home, he started to kiss her and fondle her breasts, but she drew away from him.

'No, thank you, Simon; I think that the time for that has passed.'

Eventually, Simon managed to get his friend Ted Roberts to have his dogs in his kennels. When he finally packed his things and left the cottage, he did so without saying one word more to Fiona than was necessary.

She had been right all along. With so much less to do, she had to tell Ruth and Jenny that they were no longer required. The parting was tearful – they had all got on so very well. After an intensive re-arranging and cleaning of the cottage and the kennels, Fiona found time hanging very heavily on her hands. Dog showing was compulsive and obsessive; it took up all your time and left time for nothing else. Had she done the right thing? Wasn't this loneliness worse with nothing else to do?

She had taken several rolls of film of Laura's boys when they had stayed with her, and had only now had them processed. She smiled as she looked at them. What fun it had all been. She could have them again. She could go and see Laura for a few hours, or Beryl. Of course, if she put her mind to it, there were loads of things that she wanted to do, like learning to paint in watercolours, making a cross-stitch cushion. She would join some classes. She'd like to go back for another steam-train ride. She had so enjoyed that day. Laughing, she got up. 'Sally, I won't be long, I'm going for a ride.'

Arriving at the station, she found that the train was about to leave. She hurried along the platform, quickly opened a carriage door and got in.

'Good heavens!' The voice came from a man sitting in the corner seat.

Peering into the gloom after the bright sunshine, Fiona saw that it was Paul Aston.

'Paul! You're the last person that I expected to see.'

'I could say the same thing. What are you doing here?'

'Oh, it's a long story, but I came today because all this fascinates me.'

'Me too – has done for some years. I think that I'm really a frustrated engine driver.'

Fiona laughed as she looked at his rugged, smiling face. 'I had no idea.'

'No, it's not something that I talk about much.'

They both settled back in their seats to enjoy the ride. 'I brought my friend's three boys here some weeks ago; they all loved it.'

'Did you? Yes, if I had had a son I would have introduced this to him at quite an early age. I'd have bought us a train set, too.'

'Did you want children then, Paul?'

'Yes, very much. It was my wife who was against it.'

F IONA TURNED OFF the television. She had been watching
the Christmas Eve carol service from King's College,
Cambridge, but it had been too painful. She had tried to
join in the singing but had broken down and cried because
it made her feel so alone and lonely. It hadn't seemed so bad until
today. She had been busy buying presents for Laura's children:
books for the boys and a doll for Amanda. She had even bought a
lovely little fire engine for Donald. She had enjoyed wrapping
them up and taking them over to the children to be placed under
the Christmas tree. Both Laura and Michael, Duncan and Barbara
had invited her to dinner on the big day, but she had declined,
saying that she couldn't leave the dogs. Actually, she didn't want
to break down and spoil their day for them.

Wiping her eyes, she poured herself a glass of wine and picked
up a magazine that had caught her eye when she had been
shopping that morning. Somehow, it didn't seem so interesting
now. Sadness overwhelmed her again. It was at times like this that
she wished that she hadn't told Simon to go. Was this silence
better than his silences? She didn't feel guilty all the time now; she
didn't feel inadequate; she was just very lonely. 'Oh, for heaven's
sake, Fiona, *do* something.'

She put the television on again and turned it to another
channel. 'That's better, Sally.' She bent down to stroke the dog.
'Sally, how about I make us a cake for tomorrow and you can have
a piece.'

She had just popped the cake into the Aga when she heard the
phone ringing. Could it be Simon? He hadn't contacted her at all,
hadn't even sent a card.

'Hello.'

'Hello, Fiona, it's Paul – Paul Aston.'

'Hello, Paul. Merry Christmas.'

'Oh yes, a Merry Christmas to you, too. Um, Fiona, I was wondering if it would be convenient to pop round with a little present. Perhaps you're too busy.'

'No, I'm not busy, do come round for a drink.'

Putting the phone down she raced upstairs to change out of her old jeans and jumper, put on a skirt and blouse, run a comb through her hair and put on a bit of eye shadow.

Hurrying downstairs again, she put on more lights and checked the cake. She heard a car draw up outside and Sally barked. She went to open the door.

'Hello, Paul. As I said before, Merry Christmas.'

He came in, carrying a large, heavy carrier bag. 'Look, Fiona, if you don't want this, say so. A client gave it to me today and I can't cope with it.' Opening the carrier bag, he pulled out a large turkey. 'I doubt that it would even go in my oven, but I thought that it might go in your Aga. Do please take it off my hands.'

Fiona laughed. 'Well, it would go in the Aga but it is far too big for me. I should have to give most of it to the dogs.'

'I don't care – give it to the dogs.'

'Well then, thank you. Now have you time to stay for a drink?'

'Oh, yes.'

While she got another bottle of wine, Paul sat down and looked at the magazine on antiques and collectables that she had bought.

'Are you interested in antiques, Paul?'

'Well, yes and no. I have always wanted to own some old wine glasses.'

'I know what you mean, the ones you see on the TV with twists in the stems.'

They got into an animated conversation about the antiques programmes on the TV until they were interrupted by the timer going in the kitchen.

'That's my Christmas cake; excuse me for a moment, Paul.'

When she came back into the room, he had finished his drink and was standing up. 'I'm sorry, Fiona, I must be keeping you from all sorts of things. I've so enjoyed our conversation.'

'Oh, must you go? I haven't got anything else to do this evening. To be honest, I'd like you to stay for a bit longer.'

They continued their conversation for a while and then Fiona made some coffee.

'What are you doing tomorrow, Paul?'

'Oh, this and that. I don't make much of Christmas. Usually take the dogs for a good walk and perhaps have a drink in the pub.'

Fiona looked at him for a moment. 'Well, in that case, as I am also on my own tomorrow, let me invite you over for dinner and we can both eat this turkey. I'll prepare it tonight and it can go in the slow oven.'

'I should like that very much indeed.'

He left soon after and as he went to get into his car he turned towards her. 'By the way, I've left a little gift for you under the tree.'

The next morning was dull and overcast, but Fiona was up early and singing as she saw to the preparations for dinner. She was constantly interrupted by the phone ringing. Laura and Michael were first, with the boys shouting, 'Happy Christmas, Aunt Fee.' Then Duncan phoned and, wishing her the season's greetings, thanked her for the fire engine.

Beryl and Peter phoned to thank her for their presents. Beryl had wanted Fiona to go there for Christmas but Peter had already invited Simon without asking her. Fiona asked how Simon was getting along but Beryl was rather non-committal on the subject. Having basted the turkey once again, Fiona suddenly remembered what Paul had said as he left last night. Running into the lounge, she picked up a little gold, wrapped box. The little card read, 'My thanks for a memorable day. Paul.' Puzzled, she opened the little box to find a pair of small, gold earrings in the shape of steam engines.

The dinner was a success and they spent a pleasant afternoon together going for a walk and watching TV. Paul left early in the evening, as he felt that he had left his dogs long enough. As she lay in bed that night she smiled as she thought how she had dreaded the thought of Christmas Day without Simon, and yet she had hardly thought of him at all.

The next few days passed swiftly and it was New Year's Eve. It seemed so strange not to be rushing around preparing for the party. She wondered what Simon was doing tonight. Was he thinking the same? He had not contacted her since he left, letting his solicitor deal with everything. Peter and Beryl had come over to collect anything that he wanted from the cottage or the kennels. She was still guilt-ridden about the whole sorry mess; hurting Duncan as she had, submerging her natural feelings and principles about dog showing in order to please Simon. She really had loved him so much, but she should have seen that he didn't love her; she shouldn't have married him. She shrugged her shoulders. It was all water under the bridge now. It would soon be a new year.

Pouring herself a small glass of whisky ready for midnight, she was a little startled to hear a car draw up and stop. Slightly apprehensive, she peered out of the kitchen window to see Paul getting out of the car. Undoing the bolts, she opened the door. 'Hello, Paul, is there something wrong?'

'No. I have been to a friend's house for a drink and was passing when I saw your lights were on. If you have friends over I wont stop but…'

'No, I'm on my own. In fact, I was just about to welcome in the New Year with a drink. Would you like to join me?'

She poured another glass of whisky and, as the chimes rang out, she raised her glass to Paul. 'Happy New Year, Paul.'

'Thank you, Fiona, and a Happy New Year to you.' He put his glass down and came forward.

Fiona panicked and moved back.

Paul stood still. 'Thank you for the drink. I must be away now.'

He had gone before she could collect her thoughts. Sitting down, flashes of Paul came to mind: Paul when he had collected that puppy from her, Paul congratulating her on her CC wins, Paul bending over her when she had fainted, Paul coming to see her in hospital, bringing her flowers; of course, why hadn't she seen it before? He must have felt awful when she moved away from him. Perhaps it was for the best. She had decided to stay on her own as she was so hopeless at marriage. She did like him, though, and he was nice to have as a friend. She might give him a call in a few weeks' time.

As Fiona sat in the dentist's waiting room on a cold day at the beginning of February she saw a dog magazine lying on the table.

Idly picking it up, she saw a picture of Simon. He had got the CC and had then won the group at Manchester. He obviously did alright without me, she thought, as she flicked through the pages. Near the back of the magazine a little paragraph caught her eye in the Cumbrian notes, to the effect that Paul Aston was now out of hospital after his skiing accident. He had told her that he was going skiing when they had Christmas dinner together. She had deliberately not phoned him because she wanted to keep the friendship light. She would phone later.

'Hello, Paul, this is Fiona. I've only just found out about your accident. How are you?'

'Hello. I'm okay. I broke my leg but I'm managing.'

'How are you coping with the dogs?'

'They're still in kennels.'

'Kennels! Why didn't you let me know? I'd have had them all here.'

'Well – it was all a bit quick – I didn't think you would want them, anyway.'

Fiona didn't reply; she knew what he meant.

She drove to Paul's house. It seemed ages before he came to the door. She looked at his drawn face. 'Paul, I've come to cook a meal for you and I won't take no for an answer.' She had made a casserole in the Aga and when she had re-heated it, she served it on a tray. He ate it with relish.

'Do you know that there is nothing in the fridge or your cupboards?'

'Well, going on holiday...'

'Quite. Well, I have decided that it would be best if you came and stayed with me until you can manage. I can collect the dogs tomorrow and they can come, too.'

'No, that's very kind of you, but no.'

She went upstairs and put some clothes and his toilet things into a bag. 'I'll lock up and we'll go.'

'Fiona, will you please listen to me. I am not coming with you.'

'Why?'

He didn't reply but shook his head and looked at the floor. The silence was heavy with unspoken words.

'Paul, Paul, this is difficult for me to say because I'm not at all sure what I want to say. I've made a mess of two marriages and I don't think that I'm too good at relationships. That is why I didn't let you kiss me at New Year. I don't want to be hurt or to hurt anyone else. I would like you to come to the cottage as a friend. Could you?'

Paul didn't reply.

'I value your friendship. I want us to be friends, good friends, and equals, so that we accept each other just as we are. No ties to make us behave differently.'

'I love you, Fiona, have done for some time now, so – I can't come.'

He tried to get up out of the chair and knocked against the TV as he stumbled.

'Paul, are you alright?' She held his arms and looked up into his face for a second or two then, putting her hands on his face, she kissed him. 'Please, Paul, please let me be your friend.'

As they entered the warm kitchen, Sally jumped up to greet them.